Unfinished

A novel by Pat Bertram

Unfinished

Print ISBN 978-1-941071-65-6
ebook ISBN 978-1-941071-66-3

Other books by Pat Bertram:

Madame ZeeZee's Nightmare
Greif: The Great Yearning
More Deaths Than One
Daughter Am I
Light Bringer
A Spark of Heavenly Fire

STAIRWAY PRESS—Apache Junction

Cover Design by Guy D. Corp, www.GrafixCorp.com

STAIRWAY PRESS

www.StairwayPress.com
1000 West Apache Trail, Suite 126
Apache Junction, AZ, USA

For Jeff

Chapter 1

CHIMES PENETRATED THE shroud of Amanda Ray's grief. She struggled to sit up, then swung her legs over the side of the bed and cradled her belly, pregnant with pain and the weight of her husband's absence. Tears spilled down her cheeks, but she didn't bother to brush them away. What was the point? Such a feeble gesture would not staunch the seemingly endless waterfall.

The doorbell chimed again. She hauled herself to her feet and lumbered to the door, still cradling her belly. A man in his twenties wearing jeans and a white shirt stood on the other side of the screen. Amanda frowned. What fool had left the front door wide open? But since the screen door was latched and she was the only one in the house, she must be the fool who had not closed and locked the door. David would have a fit.

But David wasn't here. She squeezed her eyes shut against a spasm of pain.

"Mrs. Ray?"

Resentment at the intrusion into her grief shot through Amanda, but the habit of politeness dictated an acknowledgment. "Yes?"

The young man gave her a grave smile. "I brought your husband home."

Happiness flooded Amanda in a warm rush. She scrubbed away her tears, fumbled with the latch, and threw open the screen door. "David!"

The young man stood alone.

"David?" she whispered, the awful truth settling in her belly once more.

"I'm from Adam's Funeral Services." The young man held out a brass box about six inches wide, eight inches tall, and four inches deep. "The urn with David's cremains."

Suddenly dizzy, Amanda propped a shoulder against the doorjamb to keep from falling. "I can't do this." She stared at the urn through fresh tears, but her hands reached for the box. She almost dropped the urn—she'd forgotten how heavy human ashes were. Holding the urn to her chest with one hand, she signed the delivery receipt with the other, choked out a "thank you," then stepped back into the house and shut the door.

"What am I supposed to do with you, David?" David did not answer the question. Nor had he ever answered her query. During the long last year of his life, he'd often instructed her on what to do after his death—he'd even told her to keep some of his ashes because they would bring her comfort—but he hadn't told her where to put the urn.

She set the box on the dining room table. It looked naked sitting there. A giggle rose inside her. Maybe she should cover the urn with gilded macaroni, like the jewelry box she'd made for Mother's Day when she was nine years old.

Poor David. He would so hate being a craft project. She gathered the urn into her arms, scurried to David's room—the one he'd moved into last year so he wouldn't disturb her sleep with his restlessness—wrapped a blanket around the urn, and laid it on the pillow.

She stared at the mound for a minute, unable to move, scarcely able to breathe. The pain exploded from her in a scream. "David!"

She flung herself on the bed, hugged the bundle containing her husband's ashes, and wept.

The soft afternoon light filtered through the slats of the blinds.

Exhausted by her grief but unable to nap, Amanda rose, opened the blinds, and gazed outside. The normalcy of the backyard view—the tender green leaves of the budding lilac bushes, the unmown grass, the towering poplars—seemed an affront. The world felt different with David gone, as if his absence had unbalanced the earth. She could feel the tilt—it made her queasy and a bit dizzy—so how could everything look the same?

Hoping a cup of tea would help settle her stomach, she shuffled to the kitchen, put a pot of water on the stove, then opened the cabinet and pulled out a mug.

"Did you get Dad's ashes?"

Startled by the voice, Amanda whirled. Her thirty-year-old daughter, Thalia, stood in the doorway wearing her usual outfit—a solid black tee shirt over black slacks. She looked so much like David with her sandy hair and chocolate-brown eyes that a ghostly fist seemed to squeeze Amanda's heart.

A sound like a shot reverberated through the kitchen. Amanda froze, uncomprehending, then she realized the cup had slipped out of her hand and shattered on the hard tile floor.

She dropped to her knees, fingered the white ceramic handle, and clutched the piece to her chest.

"What's wrong, Mom?"

Amanda lifted her head. Through her tears, she could see Thalia's disapproving expression, but she couldn't stop crying. She waved her daughter away, wanting to be left alone with the shards of her life.

Thalia loomed over her. "You've got blood on your hand." Impatience rather than concern colored her voice. "I'll get the broom and a bandage. Don't move."

Even if she had wanted to, Amanda couldn't have stirred—she felt as fragmented as the mug and as worthless.

Thalia returned. After leaning the broom against the counter, she crouched over Amanda, daubed at the cut with witch hazel, and wrapped a small plastic bandage around Amanda's bleeding thumb. Thalia rose gracefully and stood with hands on hips. "How are you going to cope with the rest of your life, Mom, if you can't handle an insignificant accident?"

Insignificant? True, the mug had no sentimental value—Amanda had bought it at a discount store long ago—but it was now gone from the life she'd shared with David. One by one, dishes would break, appliances would wear out, towels would become threadbare, until there would be nothing left of that life.

Amanda heard the clatter of ceramic pieces being dumped into the trash. *No*, she wanted to shout, *Let me do it*. An image flickered in her mind. Two-year-old Thalia, turning away from Amanda, her tiny hands fumbling with the buttons on her yellow blouse, screaming, "No. Me do it!"

"What is wrong with you?" the grown-up Thalia asked.

Amanda glanced up at her, the glow of nostalgia fading. "David is dead."

"I know Dad passed away." A scowl contorted Thalia's face. "Of course I know that. It's...you're such a hypocrite."

The viciousness of Thalia's tone struck Amanda like a physical blow, stopping her tears. She pushed herself upright. Face to face with her daughter, she could see the anguish in her daughter's eyes. She'd been so concerned with her own grief, she hadn't seen how much her daughter was hurting. She reached out her arms, but Thalia backed away.

"I saw you." Thalia choked out the words. "You were sitting up in bed with your laptop, and you were touching yourself."

Amanda's legs felt too weak to hold her erect. She stumbled to the table and sank into a chair. "Oh, honey. I am so sorry. But it wasn't—"

Thalia expelled a short, bitter laugh. "Don't you dare say it wasn't what I thought. You had one hand in your panties, and you were typing with the other. And you were moaning. It was exactly what I thought."

"You interrupted me before I could finish. I only meant to

say it wasn't any of your business."

"Not my business?" Thalia's voice rose to a shout. "My father—your husband—was dying, and you were carrying on a cyber affair."

"You're right, Thalia. *He* was dying. I was not." Amanda wished she could explain the need to live that had overwhelmed her and the aching arousal resulting from that need, but she did not understand why she had reacted to David's dying in such a way. Nor could she explain why her arousal had centered on that particular man—Sam—who she'd never met except online and only late at night when no one was around.

Amanda narrowed her gaze on her daughter. "Were you spying on me?"

"I couldn't sleep one night about three months ago, so I came to see Dad. Your door was open a crack. I pushed it open to tell you I was here, but..."

"I'm sorry," Amanda said. Sorry Thalia had seen what no daughter should see, sorry David was dead, sorry she had let herself find relief in Sam's virtual arms, sorry she and Thalia couldn't comfort each other in their grief, sorry she'd failed at as a mother. "So sorry."

"That's not all. I came by to see Dad about a month after that, and you said...you said..." Thalia drew in a ragged breath. "You said you wished Dad would hurry up and die."

Amanda blinked. "I said that? To you?"

"Your door was open, and you were sitting on the edge of your bed, crying. You never looked at me. You just stared at the wall, tears running down your face, and you said, 'I wish he'd hurry up and get it over with.'"

"Oh, honey." Amanda reached out a hand toward her daughter, but let her arm drop when Thalia made a pretense of sweeping the floor. "I was tired that night. So tired." Tears welled up in Amanda's eyes. "Neither of us had slept in days. David had been going through one of his bad spells. So much pain! I had to keep giving him boosters of morphine, but the stuff made him disoriented. He accused me of murdering him."

"But you did try to murder him," Thalia whispered. "He called and told me. So I came over and that's when I heard you."

"You believed him?" Hearing a hint of hysteria in her voice, Amanda modulated her tone. "You knew how Dad was at the end." But perhaps Thalia didn't know—she visited so seldom. Not that Amanda blamed her. It must have been hard for Thalia to see her beloved father deteriorating both mentally and physically.

Thalia glared at Amanda. "Dad was like that because you drugged him. He said he wasn't ready to die, and you were killing him."

Amanda propped her elbows on the table and covered her face with her hands. How had she and Thalia become so estranged that her daughter could actually believe she'd tried to kill David? Or maybe, in her pain, Thalia was striking out at the one person who would love her despite the abuse.

Thalia had gotten one thing right, though. She was a hypocrite, grieving for her husband while desiring another man.

"Are you okay, Mom?"

Amanda lifted her head and tried to smile through her tears but managed only to show her teeth. "I can't bear that David is gone."

"So you didn't kill him?"

"What do you think?"

Thalia gave the floor a final swish with the broom, then took it back to the laundry room. When she returned, she said, "I think you did the best you could," though her tone clearly said Amanda's best hadn't been good enough.

"I miss him," Amanda said.

"Do you ever think you'll marry again?" There was strange intensity in Thalia's voice that Amanda couldn't interpret. Did she want Amanda to marry again so she could be the sole heir to grief? Or did she want Amanda to become one of those widows who remained faithful to the dead?

"Oh, honey. I don't know. David's only been gone six days."

"What about the cyber guy?"

The cyber-guy. Sam Priestly. A 55-year-old professor at Ohio State University and the director of the creative writing program. "We met at an online support group for people caring for a dying spouse. His wife is hanging on. But David..."

"I can't see you with anyone else but Dad." Unexpectedly, Thalia laughed.

"What's so funny?" Amanda asked, wondering if she'd ever understand her daughter.

"Thinking about you going to singles bars. Or signing up for one of those online dating sites. Or going next door and asking that mean old Mr. Jensen out on a date." Thalia's shoulders heaved.

Amanda thought Thalia was still laughing, but a sob told her Thalia's laughter had turned to tears.

"I hate remembering Dad at the end," Thalia cried. "He was so different."

"He still loved you."

"I'm such a bad daughter. Dad called me four or five weeks ago and told me not to worry. He said, 'You're safe Thalia. I finally got the courage to do what I needed to do. The father is dead.'" Thalia brushed away her tears with her forearm. "I thought he was going to kill himself, and I didn't do anything to stop him."

"He didn't kill himself," Amanda said soothingly. "I didn't kill him. The cancer did. It's easier to handle grief if we have someone to blame, but there isn't anyone."

A final tear rolled down Thalia's cheek. "I blame me."

"Why? Because you stopped coming to visit? Dad was glad about that. He didn't want you to see him dying."

Thalia turned and ran from the kitchen. Amanda listened but

heard no footfalls, only the click of the front door closing. Thalia—a big woman, almost as big as David—somehow managed to slip through life making little noise. David had been the same way. At the beginning of their marriage, he'd appear silently, making her jump. In later years, when he knew a task absorbed her, he would stomp to warn her of his approach.

"Dammit, David," she cried out. "Why didn't you go to the doctor?" But even if he had gone to see a physician when he first noticed his weakness and weight loss, it wouldn't have made any difference. It had already been too late. When agony finally forced him to the emergency room, the doctor had intoned with barely concealed boredom, "Inoperable kidney cancer."

And now all Amanda had left of her husband were his ashes.

A scream rose to her throat, but when the sound scraped past an unshed lump of tears, it came out as a whimper.

Chapter 2

AMANDA WOKE BEFORE dawn with tears on her face. She struggled out of bed, pulled on a robe, and went to David's room to check on him, but she didn't see her husband's raddled body or hear his rasping breath.

Her heart gave a sickening jolt. David was dead. Gone. Deceased. Out of her life forever. And today, the seventh day since his death, they were holding his memorial service.

She opened the closet and stared at her husband's clothes, wondering what to do with his things. It had hurt her terribly when he had moved the garments from their shared closet to the one in the spare room, but now she felt glad at not having to endure the sight of his pants and shirts every time she got dressed.

She stroked the sleeve of a pinstriped shirt, one of his favorites. The fabric retained its new crispness. Despite being his favorite—or perhaps because of it—David seldom wore the shirt, claiming he wanted to save it for a special occasion.

The pain in Amanda's chest expanded until she thought her heart would burst out of her, leaving a bloody hole gaping between her breasts. There never would be a special occasion now, but how could she get rid of the shirt? Maybe her husband would need it sometime.

"David," she cried out. "Where are you?" Her voice fell to a more plaintive tone. "David? I can't find you. Where did you go?" Leaving the closet door open, she wandered through the house, peering in the bathrooms, the closets, the living room, the kitchen. "David? Can you hear me?"

She put a hand over the hole in her chest and was surprised to discover that under her white cotton blouse, her body remained intact. "I miss you, David," she murmured. "Dammit, I miss you."

A sudden fury swept over her. "Why did you leave me?" she screamed. She ran back to his closet, grabbed a handful of clothes, and dumped them on the floor. A muffled thud caught her attention, but it took a moment for the truth to soak into her grief-fuddled mind. Something weighty had been stashed among the clothes. She scrabbled about in the pile of garments and pulled out a threadbare terrycloth robe that seemed inordinately heavy.

For a second, Amanda considered reburying the robe in the heap of clothing. David had always been a private person, but during his last year, he had become furtive, and he would not appreciate her ferreting out his secrets. "Well, David," she said aloud. "If you didn't want me rummaging around in your life, you shouldn't have died."

Still, a feeling of dread made her hesitate. Summoning the strength of her anger, she thrust a hand into the robe's pocket. Her heart thudded when she felt the shape of the cold metal object. Gingerly, she pulled the piece out of the pocket and stared at it. It couldn't be real, could it? But the weight told her the small revolver with the two-inch barrel was genuine.

"Oh, David," Amanda whispered. "What are you doing with a gun?" Afraid of the direction of her thoughts—David had been a preacher after all, and had professed to believe in the sanctity of life—she shoved the weapon back into the robe. Hearing a faint crinkle, she dug deeper into the pocket and pulled out a scrap of paper that that had been lodged beneath the revolver. Tears sprang to her eyes at the sight of her husband's precise penmanship. She brushed away the tears, and angled the slip of paper to catch the light.

I am ending my life because in my advanced age, in my physical condition, there is no chance of ever being well again and I will not permit myself to become a helpless lingering invalid.

During the last days of his life, David had seemed much calmer, more accepting of his fate. Amanda had presumed he'd reached an accommodation with death, but perhaps the acceptance had come from knowing he could end his suffering whenever he chose.

Feeling blessedly numb, she plucked first one shirt then another from the pile until she'd neatly rehung all the garments.

Only then did it occur to her: Where did David get a gun? He hadn't been out of the house alone during the entire year of his dying.

Chapter 3

AMANDA'S FOOTSTEPS ECHOED in the empty church. She'd already checked once to make sure everything had been readied for the memorial service, but she'd come again to let the unbelievable truth sink in. David wouldn't be conducting the service. He was the service.

David had hated funerals. A minister, he'd presided at the funerals and memorial services for hundreds of people. He'd known most of those people, and many had been his friends. *"I give good funeral,"* he said, but the facetious remark hid his pain, his angst.

"So why don't you quit?" Amanda had asked him several times, and each time he'd responded with a sad little smile. Sometimes she got the feeling he needed to atone. But atone for what? He was the best man she'd ever known. The best person.

And now David was gone. He'd never have to attend another funeral, not even his own. His ashes were still wrapped in the blanket on his bed where she'd put them yesterday after the kid from Adam's Funeral Services had brought them to the house. The urn standing in pride of place on a table in front of the altar, the urn flanked by dahlias and daffodils, lilies and carnations, had come from an estate sale many years ago, one of the few impulsive gifts David ever bought her. He'd known she would love the antique, and it now seemed the perfect way to honor him. Bronze, blackened with age, an exquisitely detailed dragon entwined around the fourteen-inch body of the urn, and heavy enough that if anyone were to lift it, they would never guess it held only an empty black trash bag.

"I couldn't save you from death," Amanda whispered, "but I can save you from your funeral."

Would he have thought the empty urn a joke? Or would he have winced at her, misunderstanding her intentions as he so often did that last year?

The cancer had spread from David's kidneys to his spleen to his lungs to his shoulder bone to his brain. When the doctor showed Amanda the CAT scan, she could see nothing but cloudiness where her husband's organs should have been. The doctor said David had three to six months to live. David had survived for a year, refusing to take any medications except morphine when the pain became unbearable. Why had the poor man let himself suffer so much? Did he still feel the need to atone? But for atone for what?

Amanda sighed. She hated her circuitous thoughts, but that's all she had now—thoughts. And questions. She'd been out of it all last year, as if the "David's wife" part of her had been cryonically preserved until grief could thaw her. That state of suspended animation had been the only way she'd been able to deal with the stranger her husband had become. It had simply been too painful, not only his dying, but the way he treated her. Generally, he either shut her out or winced when she spoke as if he could barely stand her. A few times, he'd been verbally abusive, saying cruel things to her, calling her fat and stupid. Until then, she'd never understood why abused women stayed with their husbands. She'd thought they were weak; now she knew their own love drained them.

And that wasn't the worst of it.

The cancer clouding his brain seemed to have kept him from recognizing nuances. Once when David had lectured her for ten minutes without pausing on how to clean the gutters after he died, Amanda smiled and said, "I'm not totally inept, you know."

"You always misunderstand what I say," he screamed. By then she'd become used to his screaming, her gentle, soft-toned David who'd never lifted his voice to her before he got sick. "You're just like my mother."

"Don't you ever compare me to your mother!" Amanda ran to her room and slammed the door. Immediately ashamed by her uncharacteristic behavior—it had been the only time in her thirty-five-year marriage that she had fought with her husband—she went to his room to apologize, and found him pacing. Always pacing. Where did he get the energy for all that pacing? Terminal restlessness, the hospice nurse had called it.

"I'm sorry," she said. "I didn't mean to scream at you. And I didn't mean to upset you. I was being…ironic."

Her husband stared at her with those pain-shadowed eyes as if he didn't understand.

"When I told you I wasn't totally inept," she explained, "I was making sort of a joke.

"Then you should have told me it was a joke." David continued pacing.

At the memory, Amanda's heart felt as if it were breaking, but back then, she'd felt…nothing. As if he were a stranger. As if he'd always been a humorless man. David used to smile at her all the time. That's what had made her fall in love with him—the sweet smile that seemed to say he knew all her foibles but loved her anyway.

"You don't have to worry about me when you're gone," she'd said once. *"I've gotten over you."*

"I don't much like myself anymore, either," he'd responded.

Did they have that conversation the same night as their fight? She couldn't remember.

Panic raced through her. All she had left of David were her memories. What would she do if she could no longer remember him? During this past year, she'd tried to forget him—he didn't want her around, so the only way she could deal with the situation was to get on with her life. She thought she'd moved on, finished with her grief, found happiness with another man, but now, all she felt was sorrow.

"What are you doing here by yourself?" came a voice from behind her.

Amanda jerked around. Could it be time for the memorial service already? But only one old lady stood there, peering up at her in the gloom. Effie Fields, hennaed hair a cap of tight curls, eyes huge behind thick glasses.

Effie patted her arm. "Good thing I came early. This is one day you should not be alone."

"I'm okay." Amanda tried to sound upbeat, but only managed to sound wooden.

"I buried three husbands. I still cry for all of them." Effie's eyes glittered with extra moisture as if to prove her point. She glanced around the church, turning her whole body, not just her neck. "You've done a good job. David would be proud of you."

"The Women's Society sent the flowers," Amanda said. "I placed a doily on the table and set the urn on it, that's all."

"Sometimes that's enough." Effie patted her arm again. "You'll have another. You're still young."

Another? Another what? Funeral? Husband? No—never another husband. I couldn't go through this again.

A burst of laughter coming from outside caught Amanda's attention. The laughter stopped abruptly, and three pink-haired rotund women in vibrant sweat suits and running shoes tiptoed into the church.

Amanda stifled a groan. "The Merry Widows" David had called them. They weren't members of his church but still showed up for every funeral. *"Shopping for a minister,"* he'd said. *"Looking for the perfect preacher to do their funerals, but they'll outlast us all."*

Well, they had outlasted David. Her throat tightened with unshed tears, but she'd be damned if she'd cry before the bright gazes of the merry widows.

"It's so unfair," said Jackie, the tallest of the three, though she couldn't have been more than 5'2". "I'd picked Reverend David Ray to do my service. Now I have to find someone else."

"Reverend Ray gets points for being a great preacher," said Barb, shorter by an inch. "But I prefer Dr. Simpson."

"Me, too," piped the third widow, Muffie. "The Reverend Doctor Simpson did Joanie's funeral. Not a dry eye in the church. Even her no-good son shed a tear or two."

"That's because the lad was calculating the cost of the funeral," Jackie said.

The three women cackled happily.

If Amanda had any doubts about not bringing David's remains to his own memorial service, the misgivings evaporated. He belonged to her now, not to his congregation, not to the needy, not to the abused children. She'd never begrudged the time he'd spent with others. After all, that's what she loved about him—his caring—but she'd always assumed they'd have plenty of time together when he retired.

No one ever had time for me. Angrily, Amanda pushed the thought away. Today would be grueling enough without her indulging in self-pity. And anyway, it wasn't true. In their younger years, she and David would talk for hours, and later, they were together as often as his work allowed. It was only after he got sick that he had no time for her. Death beckoned and he followed, leaving her behind.

A hand touched her elbow. "Come sit down, dear," Effie said. "It's time."

Time? Amanda gave a confused look around at the full church. Where had all the people come from? When had they come? The problem with grief was that it made her lose focus. No, she corrected herself. The problem isn't with grief. It's that David is gone.

Amanda wanted to flee from the people staring at her as if she were the prize exhibit in a circus freak show. Wanted to go to back to the house and cradle what remained of David. But she strode sedately to the first pew and sat, Effie by her side.

For just a second, a smile tweaked Amanda's lips. Had Effie drawn the short straw when the Women's Society discussed who would usher Amanda through the service? At least someone was there for her. Thalia had yet to put in an appearance.

Amanda searched her for her daughter and saw her striding down the aisle. Thalia slipped into the pew beside Amanda without a glance in her mother's direction.

Amanda shifted, and her arm accidentally brushed against Thalia's. Thalia jerked away and held her arm as if it had been burned. Tears welled up in Amanda's eyes. Did Thalia really hate her that much? Would her daughter ever understand the horror of that last year? When Thalia came to visit, David had made a point of being cheerful and expansive, but as soon as she left, he'd shrivel back, depleted, into his sick body and cancer-ridden brain.

A shaft of rainbow-colored light streaming through the stained-glass window illuminated the dragon urn, and all at once Amanda saw the truth of last year. She hadn't gotten over David as she'd thought. She hadn't callously refused to feel his pain. She'd done the best she could for both of them. If she hadn't denied what her husband meant to her, what his death would mean to her, she'd never have been able to survive the year. She'd have dissolved into pain—the very pain she now felt—and what good would that have done? David felt bad enough about what his illness did to her; it would have destroyed him to see her in such agony. And how could she have survived his reclusiveness, his barbs, his winces, if she'd felt the sting of each? And Sam...

Thinking of Sam, her insight faded, and she felt as muddled

as ever. What kind of woman falls in love and carries on a cyber flirtation while her beloved husband—her soul mate—lay dying? No wonder Thalia hated her. She hated herself.

Like grief itself, the service seemed to drag on interminably, but time passed in a blink. She barely registered what people said about David but had no doubt the words were all laudatory. *"In death even the worst reprobate becomes a saint,"* David once said. *"People are afraid to speak ill of the dead."*

Would she ever tell anyone the truth of that last year? Probably not. Both she and David had made the best of an intolerable situation, but she'd never be proud of herself. How could she have ever wished that he'd hurry up and get it over with?

Well, now he was dead, and she'd give anything to have him back—not that she wanted him to suffer. She wanted him back whole, happy, healthy. She wanted their future to stretch out before them, bright and shiny and full of promise. Her future still lay ahead of her—two decades, perhaps—but the prospect seemed bleak without David's presence.

Amanda glanced at Effie, who stared intently at the preacher—the same Dr. Simpson the merry widows had rhapsodized about. How did Effie find the courage to love again, and again? If Amanda didn't already love Sam, she wouldn't be able to fall for him now. "I can't do this," she whispered. "I don't have the courage."

Effie smiled sadly at her. "Yes, you do, my dear. Women always find the courage to bury their men and go on to love again. It's who we are."

Chapter 4

THE WOMEN'S SOCIETY set up a buffet in the community room—long tables of covered dishes and white carnation centerpieces. Amanda slipped into "Preacher's Wife" mode, sort of like a Stepford wife, only perkier. She'd been to hundreds of funeral luncheons, had offered thousands of words of commiseration, but this was the first time she found herself the center of everyone's curiosity.

She stood by the door as people filed into the room, curved her lips into a semblance of a smile, and accepted the fumbling condolences, the perfunctory hugs. She wished David were by her side, helping her get through this, but if David were here, she wouldn't have to deal with the situation.

Dammit, David! I can't do this.

Thalia gave her a sidelong glance, and Amanda wondered if she'd spoken aloud, but if so, no one else seemed to have heard. The din of hundreds of people talking in hushed voices filled the room and gave Amanda a headache.

"Amanda looks like she's doing well." The youth leader spoke behind her hand to her husband, but loud enough for Amanda to hear.

The husband eyed Amanda as if inspecting livestock. Could he be thinking of offering his stud services? Some men saw widows as open terrain since they would not be poaching on another man's territory. Amanda knew a couple of widows who'd gratefully accepted such favors. The presence of death made some people seek life in any way they could, and sex was the most elemental way of embracing life.

She thought of Sam and wished he were here. Wished he'd wrap his strong, sturdy arms around her and hold her tight, then...

Amanda pulled her shoulders back. This was no time to think of Sam, especially not with Hildegarde Brumley bearing down on her. Hildegarde was a fixture in the church, a member of every committee, an attendee of every event. David felt sorry for her, claimed she was lonely and unhappy, but Amanda secretly thought the wizened old woman did everything she could to make sure she remained alone and unhappy.

Please, don't let me turn out to be like her.

"I know exactly how you feel," Hildegarde trumpeted. Her voice seemed to grow bigger every year while her body grew smaller.

Amanda gave the woman a synthetic smile and waited for the inevitable knockout punch.

"My dog died last week," Hildegarde said. "I've never felt such pain as I did when I had to put her down." She lowered her voice, though Amanda felt sure people out on the street could still hear her. "The little dear became incontinent, you know. I can't tolerate a smelly house. Got a new dog yesterday. You need to get a new man." She paused, head tilted to one side as if expecting a response.

Amanda couldn't think of a thing to say, at least not anything David would approve of. But David wasn't here.

"I had a man," she said. "A kind man. He always smelled good, and never became incontinent, not even at the end."

Hildegarde gave her a tight-lipped smile. "It was for the best, I'm sure. God has a plan for everything."

Anger heated Amanda's face and voice. "What are you

saying? That it was best David didn't become incontinent? Or best that he got sick? Or do you mean it's best that he never got to do half the things he wanted?"

Hildegarde took a step forward. "Well, he lived a long, full life."

Amanda gritted her teeth and took a step backward. "David was fifty-nine."

"Grief must be something you need to learn or else your husband wouldn't have gone first." Hildegarde threw her a triumphant look, then sailed off to find another rocky shoal to crash against.

"Way to go, Mom," Thalia whispered.

Amanda gave her daughter an apologetic smile. "I don't know what got into me. Your father's gone, and I'm bandying words with a nitwit."

I'm no good without you, David. See what happens when you leave me alone? But just for a moment she had felt alive.

"Can you believe that nasty old woman?" Thalia said. "Putting down her dog just because it was incontinent. What kind of person does that?"

Amanda stared at her daughter. Could Thalia be so insensitive to her father's death that she had more concern for a dead dog? But everyone grieved differently. And Thalia had been on her own for over a decade, so it wasn't as if she were missing the day-to-dayness of David. Missing his very presence.

Bob somebody or other, an aging bachelor with slicked-back hair that smelled of sandalwood, approached her. She cringed internally at the tee shirt proclaiming him to be a love idol, and managed to keep from pulling away when he took her hand in his sweaty palms. "It's better this way, you know. At least he's not suffering anymore. And you're strong. You'll be fine, Amanda. It's all part of God's plan."

Did you hear that, David? Everyone tells me your death and my grief are part of God's plan. Have you met the Higher Being yet? Has

He/She/It told you what the plan really is?

She slipped her hand of Bob's grip and stepped back. "Thank you for your kind words."

He winked at her, and headed toward the buffet table.

"What a jerk," Thalia whispered. "I hope you don't end up with a guy like him."

"I'm not going to end up with any guy." Tired of standing in the receiving line—if she and Thalia could be considered a line—Amanda scanned the room looking for somebody to rescue her, but didn't catch anyone's eye. "I'd better go...mingle...or something. Why don't you get something to eat?"

"I'm not hungry," Thalia said, an unaccustomed softness to her tone. "When did you eat last?"

"I don't remember. Yesterday maybe."

"Would you like me to fix you a plate?"

"No. I'll do it." Amanda started to walk away, then stopped and looked back at her daughter. "Thank you."

Thalia's thick brows, so like David's, drew together. "For what?"

For being kind to me. For forgiving me. "For taking such good care of Dad. You meant the world to him. He loves you very much."

"And I love him." Thalia's eyes overflowed with tears.

Amanda moved toward her, arms outstretched, but Thalia turned and ran. Amanda let her arms drop to her side, and watched her daughter rush down a narrow hall toward the restroom. She headed for the buffet. The knots of chatting people parted to let her pass, and stood silently in her wake.

Odd that people knew so little of grief, of how to deal with the bereft. Maybe grief etiquette should be taught in schools. Grief 101. How many times had she heard, "I'm sorry for your loss," in the week since David died? Amanda remembered all the times she had offered the very same words of condolence, and wished she had been kinder to those who'd been grieving. But really, what could one say that hadn't been said before? "God needed him more." "He's in a better place." "You have to get on with your life." "At least he's not suffering anymore." Platitudes that offered not a shred of comfort or wisdom.

Janet Finder, a lawyer who had joined the church shortly before David's diagnosis, stepped in front of Amanda. "I'm sorry for your loss."

"Thank you."

"So what have you been doing with all your free time?"

Amanda reared back. "Free time?"

"Well, you don't have to take care of David, and you don't have a job."

Amanda drew herself up to her full 5'5". "I do too have a job. I'm grieving."

Janet gave an indulgent smile, as if to a small child. "I meant you're not working."

"Grief is work. Now, if you'll excuse me..."

Effie Fields elbowed Janice aside and took Amanda's hand. "How are you holding up, my dear?"

Amanda's eyes watered at the kindness. "About how you'd expect. How did you get through this three times?"

"The grieving? You have to let yourself feel the agony as it comes. There's no way around it. Or do you mean missing David? The secret to that is maintaining a relationship with him. He still lives in your memory."

"I meant the insensitive remarks."

"Oh, that." Effie gave her hand a gentle squeeze and let go. "You never get used to it. Tell yourself that people care but don't know how to express themselves. One of the ironies of grief is that when you are at your lowest emotional ebb, when people should be looking out for you, you have to worry about their sensibilities and make allowances for their discomfort. It's not fair, but nothing about death is fair."

Amanda wiped away her tears with the back of her hand. "I

miss David."

"I know, dear. The reverend was a wonderful man and we all loved him."

"But he was my life." The words seemed to hang in the air. She'd spoken the truth, but the truth made her seem pathetic, as if she couldn't stand on her own. And maybe she couldn't. Her life had become so entwined with David's that she no longer knew who she was.

Effie smiled sadly as if she could read Amanda's thoughts. "My advice? Don't spend your life in the past. Look to the future."

"The past is all David and I have. Our future died when he did."

Effie wagged a forefinger at her. "Memories are fine, but they are not your life. You need—"

"Yes, I know. I need to get myself a man." Amanda regretted her acerbic tone, and gave Effie a wobbly smile. "At least that's what everyone keeps telling me, but I feel ancient. As if I've dried up and my desiccated body is sloughing off. Will there be any of me left?"

Effie touched the middle of her own chest. "Your heart is still there. And your spirit. Your mind will begin working again one day. The fog is normal."

Tears seeped from Amanda's eyes. "It's so damn hard," she whispered.

"I know. A new man isn't always the answer, though it is for some people. I wasn't going to say you needed a man, I wanted to say you needed to make time for yourself. To get to know yourself as a woman alone before you get married again. Remarriage doesn't always work out. My second husband thought that my loving him meant I couldn't love my first husband anymore, as if love is a finite thing that needs to be measured carefully. I'd been married to my first husband for fifty years, and it was hard to pretend that those years didn't exist.

And I had to be careful when grief flared up so my second fellow wouldn't see me crying and get hurt. I loved my second husband dearly, but there was too much we couldn't share. My third husband was different. He also had lost a spouse, so he understood. We married for companionship and grew to love each other. Now I mourn all three."

Seeing the tears in Effie's eyes, Amanda asked, "Was getting married again worth the price you've had to pay?"

"Oh, yes. Love is always worth the pain. If we don't love, who are we?"

"I'm not sure I have the courage to start over, but I think of growing old alone, and..." Amanda crossed her arms and rubbed her biceps with her hands. "It scares me."

Effie put an arm around Amanda's shoulder. "You can't let fear dictate your life." She gave Amanda's shoulder a squeeze, and let her go. "Don't forget to get something to eat. You look peaked."

Amanda made her way to the buffet table. The merry widows huddled together, poring over the selection.

"Make sure Paula brings her meatballs to my funeral lunch," Jackie said. "Katherine's lime mold is something I'd just as soon not see."

"You wouldn't see it anyway." Muffie cackled. "You'll be dead. I like a good Jell-O mold, especially with marshmallows. Put that on my list."

"Buffalo wings are my favorite," Barb said. "They're messy, so be sure to bring some of those wet wipes. Everyone will be dressed in their best, and I don't want the men remembering me by stains on their ties."

Amanda slipped away from the three long-time widows before they caught sight of her. No way could she deal with them today. Usually she saw the women as the fairy godmothers in the Disney version of Sleeping Beauty—brightly dressed, rotund, and into everyone's business—but today they struck her more like the witches in Macbeth.

Would she become like them now that David was gone, with nothing better to look forward to than her own funeral? But there was Sam…

Exhaustion washed over her. She stumbled to a chair set against the bare beige wall, and dropped heavily onto the seat. She listened to the voices wafting around her, looked at the faces of the people she once knew intimately—or as intimately as a preacher's wife ever knows anyone.

The solemn half-whispers gave way to more animated talk and gestures. This could be any party, anywhere. But these people had come for David, the last time anyone would gather in his honor. Most of these same church members had been at his silver jubilee—the twenty-fifth anniversary of his ordination. They'd helped celebrate his birthdays, his preacher-of-the-year-award, various holidays. But where had all these people been during the long, lonely months of David's dying? At first, he had many visitors, but as the weeks passed and he didn't die, his parishioners seemed to lose interest in him. Some even seemed irritated that they had wasted their time visiting a man who continued to survive, as if immediate death was the only thing for which they'd be willing to disrupt their lives.

But death takes its own time.

Amanda's shoulders sagged when she recalled that she'd been just as thoughtless as these folk, and with less reason. It had always been David. From the first moment she had laid eyes on the radiant man who would become her husband, she had no doubt they'd be together forever. How did Sam fit into the equation? Maybe he was her angel, her Cary Grant, come to help her through the roughest time of her life. If so, did that mean he'd leave her, too? It's not as if she were looking to replace David—no one could do that. And anyway, Sam was married.

Oh, God. What kind of woman was she, thinking about another man while attending her husband's memorial service?

Memorial luncheon, Amanda corrected herself. The service ended more than an hour ago, and she couldn't remember a single word.

Monica Jackson, a fortyish divorcee with three children, plopped onto the chair next to Amanda's. "Whew, it's hot!" Then, belatedly, she seemed to recognize the woman sitting next to her. The divorcee's face took on a solemn expression, and her voice dropped an octave. "I am sorry for your loss, though it's all our loss. I really liked David. I wish my ex-husband was dead."

Pain exploded in Amanda's chest. *I can't do this!* She rose and walked stiffly toward the door, afraid that if she didn't hold herself tightly, parts of her would shatter in all directions.

"Amanda!" someone called out.

Habit slowed Amanda's steps. As preacher's wife, she had always made herself available to anyone in the church. Remembering she no longer needed to play the role, she plodded on ahead.

No longer a preacher's wife. No longer married. Not much of a mother. Who am I?

Chapter 5

STILL IN HER funeral black, Amanda slumped on the edge of her bed, too tired to change, too tired to think, too tired to breathe. Her chest hurt, and even shallow inhalations and exhalations didn't seem worth the effort.

"There is no one so superfluous as the widow of a pastor." Jacqueline Baxter, who had lived in this house before Amanda, said that to her once. Jacqueline had come to the parsonage for tea before moving to Michigan to be near her grandchildren. Amanda had smiled indulgently at her, secure in the knowledge that she and David would be together forever.

And yet here she was. Fifty-seven years old. Alone. Superfluous. Living in a house that did not belong to her.

Dr. Simpson, who had taken David's place, had chosen not to live in the parsonage, so the church had allowed the Rays to continue living here during David's illness, but now Amanda would have to leave.

And she didn't know where to go. Didn't know what to do.

Superfluous.

Thalia burst into the room, the dragon urn tucked under her left arm "Where's Dad?" With her right hand, she yanked the garbage bag out of the urn with the flair of a magician pulling a rabbit out of a hat.

A wave of dizziness came over Amanda. "Why did you look?"

"I wanted some of his ashes."

"What for?"

"A friend of mine told me about this place online where I can get a Teddy bear with a pocket inside. They stuff a heart with the ashes, and put the heart in the pocket."

"What?" Amanda gripped the side of the bed to keep herself vertical. "Dad would hate that. Don't you know him at all? He's a dignified man."

"With you maybe. He always joked around with *me*."

Amanda took in a slow painful breath and let it out just as slowly. "I will not get into an argument with you about which of us David loved more. He loved you dearly, but he was my husband. He was the other half of me." She could feel tears gathering in her throat, but she swallowed them, refusing to cry in front of her daughter with Thalia in such an unpleasant mood.

Thalia had been a sunny child. In fact, that had been David's nickname for her—Sunshine. Except for rare moods, she hadn't been a sulky teen, had no reason to be. David could refuse her nothing. If Amanda ever said "no" to her, Thalia would go running to her father, and David would agree to whatever his daughter wanted.

It had been one of his few faults—that indulgence of Thalia, and more specifically, that he'd forgotten their promise to keep a united front so the youngster couldn't play them one against the other.

Amanda's heart went out to Thalia. For once, life had said no, and her sunny child couldn't handle it. She extended her arms, meaning to hug her daughter, but Thalia thrust the urn into her hands and stepped away from her.

"Where's Dad?"

"Is there anyone you can talk to?" Amanda asked. This unpleasant Thalia had shown up soon after David's diagnosis, though, to give the girl credit, Thalia saved her moods for her mother. She'd always been sweet to David.

"I don't need to see anyone," Thalia said. "I am a therapist."

"A pet therapist."

"You hate my job, don't you?"

Amanda felt like slapping her daughter. She'd lifted a hand to Thalia only once. Ten-year-old Thalia had, without permission, played with Amanda's treasured bone china tea set, a family heirloom given to her by a maiden aunt when she married David. Thalia had dropped the pot and broken it. Before Amanda's slap could connect, David had stayed her hand with a painful grip. He'd held on a second too long before letting go and stooping to help Thalia pick up the broken pieces. Later, father and daughter had gone out and returned with a teapot that bore a vague resemblance to the original pot. Amanda gave Thalia the tea set when the girl moved out of the dorm and into an apartment in her junior year, and Amanda had never seen it since.

"Mom? Mom?"

Amanda dragged her attention back to the present. "Do you still have the tea set I gave you?"

"What tea set?"

"The heirloom I gave you for a housewarming present when you moved into your first apartment."

"Oh, that. I was embarrassed to use it. The teapot didn't match the rest of the set. Heather thought it looked cool, so I gave it to her." Heather. Thalia's best friend and roommate.

"What ever happened to Heather?"

"Who cares?" Thalia stomped her foot on the carpeted floor. "Where are Dad's ashes?"

Amanda couldn't tell her the truth, that they were wrapped in a blanket and resting on his bed. Her daughter would think she'd gone nuts for sure.

She scrambled about in her mind for a lie, and in the end, she said lamely, "They didn't have the urn we ordered." Which was the truth. The urn she and Thalia spent an interminable hour choosing had turned out to be discontinued, so when the funeral home had called asking what to do, Amanda had told them to substitute something similar.

Thalia nodded. "That figures. Let me know when you get the ashes. I want some."

Overcome with nausea, Amanda set the dragon urn on the bedside table, ran to the bathroom and crouched over the toilet bowl. She heaved, but nothing came up.

"Are you okay, Mom?"

Amanda could hear the fear in her daughter's voice and realized Thalia had been trying to hide her fragility behind a façade of toughness. Amanda swished her mouth with Listerine and opened the bathroom door.

Thalia went into her arms. "I couldn't bear it if I lost you too, Mom."

"I know." Amanda patted her on the back. "I know."

Thalia pulled away. "If you don't want me to put Dad's ashes in a Teddy bear, I can get jewelry made from them. I found a place online where you can send the ashes and they compress them into fake diamonds."

"We'll see," Amanda said, while thinking, *Not in my lifetime.*

When Thalia left, Amanda started crying but angrily brushed the tears away. Enough was enough. Her cheeks felt chapped from the constant saltwater drip, and she feared the tears were chafing her soul, too.

She went into the den, turned on the television, and watched the images flickering across the twenty-inch screen.

Television had never been a big part of Amanda's life. Her parents—both academics—had seen the medium as the fall of civilization. They'd also seen universal literacy as a secondary fall, believing that universal literacy lowered the standard of writing because publishers pandered to the least common denominator, but that hadn't stopped them from reading everything they could get their hands on, from the silliest bestseller to the most obscure classic.

The only thing Amanda had inherited was her father's limp brown hair and her mother's eye-color eyes (not blue, not green, not brown, not gray, but somehow all of them together) was their love of reading.

She hadn't had any time to read during the last horrific month of David's life and she hadn't been able to get back in the habit. Reading had always been a Zen-like experience for her, focusing her conscious mind on the story while her subconscious roamed free, but now such ramblings led in only one direction—David's goneness.

Amanda picked up the remote and flipped through the channels. How many stations did they have? Hundreds, it looked like, though David had only watched a few of the offerings: sports, news, classic movies, and the history channel.

She stopped at a movie and watched for few minutes. An actress she'd seen on dozens of magazine covers at the grocery check-out stand enumerated the pluses of her life.

"I have sole possession of the remote," the actress said with what looked like a smirk curving her lips.

Amanda changed the channel. What was the big deal about a remote, anyway? Who cared? It couldn't do anything important like bring David back, healthy and happy.

Or could it?

She aimed the remote at the end of the couch where David used to sit, and clicked the remote. Waited a second for David to appear.

"I really have gone nuts," she whispered.

Amanda turned back to the television and recognized a neighbor standing on her porch, talking to a news reporter with hair so stiff the breeze couldn't ruffle it. A little girl peaked out from behind the neighbor's paisley skirt. The camera panned out to show the property—spring-green Siberian elms shading the bungalow, spots of winter-brown grass among the new growth, a string of bright tulips beneath the front window—then zoomed in on the woman's tearful face.

"Still no clues to the killing of prominent businessman Thom Taylor," an androgynous voice intoned. "It's been five weeks since Cindy Taylor heard the shots and woke to find her husband lying by the open front door, two bullets in his chest."

"Who would want to kill Thom?" the stiff-haired reporter asked Cindy.

"No one," replied a tearful Cindy. "Everyone loved him. My husband never hurt anyone."

Amanda stared at the screen in disbelief. What a liar! A couple of months ago, Cindy had come to David asking for help. Amanda hadn't meant to eavesdrop through the closed door, but she'd stayed nearby in case David needed her, and she couldn't help overhearing the distraught Cindy screeching about her no good husband. David suggested that she go to the police, but Cindy refused because she didn't want the problem made public.

Though sick and so weak he could barely stand, David had given in to Cindy's pleadings and had agreed to talk to Thom.

"Get therapy," David said when Thom came to see him, "or this will become a police matter."

And now both David and Thom were dead.

Amanda turned off the television. So much death! Thom might have deserved to die for his sins, whatever they were, but David certainly hadn't. But then, death was never about deserving or not deserving. It happened to the good and bad alike.

She paced through the house as David had done so often during those last weeks. Soon, these rooms and the furniture would be part of her past. Like the house, the furniture belonged to the church. The pieces had once been of good quality—though not to her taste—and donated by the wealthier members of the church as tax write-offs, but now the motley mix seemed like something out of a shabby genteel stage play.

She looked beyond the worn-out furniture and the shelves

overloaded with books to the home she and David had created, the home she would soon be leaving.

There, on the faded green couch in the parlor, David had cried in her arms when Joey, a boy burnt beyond recognition by his ghastly mother, had died.

There, in the hallway, the small throw rug covered the red spot where thirteen-year-old Thalia had tripped on her untied shoelaces and spilled an entire pitcher of punch. The poor girl had been mortified, not just by the spill but also by her tears. David gathered Thalia into his arms and held her until her tears turned to smiles. The two of them had done their best to clean up the mess, but the cherry-red stain remained vibrant.

There, in the bedroom, David consoled Amanda while she consoled him after her third miscarriage and the news she'd have no more children. He'd always wanted a houseful of children, and she'd felt inept at not being able to give her husband what he wanted, but David told Amanda he had everything he'd ever wished for—her, their precious daughter, fulfilling work.

And there, in the kitchen, David leaned against the wall as he told Amanda he hadn't passed his physical. He said it casually, as if all that mattered were that he'd been turned down for a life insurance policy after his original policy holder had gone out of business. Matching the casualness of her husband's tone, Amanda asked what the tests had shown. "An abnormality," David said. "The doctor is sending me to an oncologist." They'd clung to each other, dry-eyed, but later, when she was alone, she wept.

Did all of her memories involve tears? Amanda thought she'd been content, but now it seemed as if tears were all she'd ever known.

Amanda entered the dining room and frowned at the clutter spread on the table. In her grief, had she forgotten that she'd been going over some paperwork? No. That wasn't possible. She hadn't been in this room since David died.

These were David's papers. David's work.

It had been late—after midnight, perhaps—a couple of days before his death. Amanda helped David get settled into bed, then went to her own room to doze before his restlessness could overtake him.

A crash woke her. She leapt out of bed and dashed to David's room.

David stood at his desk, staring down at the drawers he'd yanked from the desk. Pen, notebooks, erasers, staples spilled across the floor. David bent over and sifted through the office supplies with one hand while keeping his left arm folded across his chest. Even with the morphine, any arm movement, no matter how slight, aggravated the metastases in his shoulder, so he kept the arm immobile.

Amanda crouched down to help. "What are you looking for, David?"

"My sesame."

"Your sesame? Like sesame seeds? You don't like sesame seeds."

"No!" David's voice grew harsh with frustration. "My sesame."

Amanda put everything back in the drawer then set the drawer on top of the desk. "This will make it easier for you to look for what you need."

David scrambled through the items in the drawer with his right hand. "Not here."

"Can I help you find it?"

"You don't know."

"Don't know what?"

"The sesame."

Amanda spoke soothingly. "Can you tell me what it is you're looking for so I can help?"

"If I knew the sesame, I wouldn't have to look." David's voice rose, and he stared venomously at Amanda. The man looking out of those deep-shadowed eyes bore no resemblance to her quiet, controlled husband. In all their years together, David had never looked at her with such loathing. And non-recognition.

"Maybe you should go back to bed." Amanda reached for her husband, but he pushed her away. "No. I need my sesame for Amanda."

"I am Amanda."

Confusion clouded David's dark eyes.

"I'm your wife. Amanda. Remember?"

David shook his head. With his chin tucked into his chest, the head movement seemed endearingly childish, but in truth, his neck muscles had become too weak to hold up his head. He grabbed his hair and used the hank like a hoist to lift his head to look at her. If it weren't so tragic, the pose would seem comical.

"Oh, David," she said. "I am so sorry. This should never have happened to you."

He stumbled away from the desk, his movements jerky and uncoordinated, and he crashed into the wall. Fearful her husband would hurt himself if he didn't lie down, Amanda went to the kitchen, filled an oral syringe with haloperidol, and ran back to David who was rummaging frantically in another drawer.

She held out the syringe. "Here. This will help."

He eyed it. "My calming down medicine?"

"Yes."

David took the syringe from her and very deliberately laid it on the desk.

"Let me help." Amanda picked up the syringe. "Open your mouth, okay?"

David clamped his lips together, took the syringe from her, and laid it on the desk once more.

"Now what?" Amanda said aloud, more to herself than to her husband.

"Work." David handed her a sheaf of white paper, a handful of pens, and a dictionary. "Come."

David led her out of his room, down the hall, and into the

dining room. One by one, he took the items from her and laid them in a row on the dining room table, then he pulled out a chair and sat down. He made a small gesture toward the chair next to his. "Sit."

Amanda sat.

David opened the dictionary and peered at the page. "I need my peepers."

"Papers?" Amanda asked.

"Peepers! Peepers. I can't see."

"Oh, your reading glasses. Just a second. I'll be right back." She scraped back her chair, hurried to his room, and checked his bedside table, his desk, and the wire basket he used for an inbox. No glasses. "I can't find them," she called out.

"They were bad peepers," he yelled back.

Bad peepers? Did he mean they needed cleaning? Amanda went to the bathroom next to his bedroom. Water had puddled on the counter and dripped to the tiled floor. The reading glasses were soaking in the sink. She fished the spectacles out of the water and dried them on an old handkerchief she found folded in a drawer next to his neatly aligned brush, comb, and razor.

She returned to the dining room. David hunched over a piece of paper, writing in a tiny, barely discernible hand. Amanda handed him his eyeglasses, and swallowed to keep from crying. If she gave in to tears every time she encountered a sign of his deterioration or his heartbreaking acceptance of his incapacity and his accommodation to it, she'd never stop weeping.

David put the glasses on upside down. Amanda rescued them before they could fall off, and gently repositioned them, being careful not to disturb his left shoulder or the oxygen tube. David yanked off the cannula that connected to him to his oxygen tank and dropped it on the floor. Gasping for breath, he hunched over his paper, filling it with his crabbed writing.

"Is there anything else I can do?" Amanda asked.

"Sit."

Amanda sat and watched David scrunch his face in concentration. Would she have so much determination to keep going if she were in his place? She wished she could do something to help. Wished he could just let go and die peacefully in his sleep. Wished he were healthy and happy. Wished...Oh, what was the point of wishing? The two of them were caught in this nightmare, and as difficult as it was for her, it must be a thousand times harder for him.

David pushed aside the paper he'd filled, seized another, wrote furiously for a few minutes, then pushed the page aside and grabbed a third. After about an hour, he dropped his pen and lifted his head by the hair.

"Thank you, Amanda," he said, his voice clear, not the mumble he usually used now. "I'm sorry to put you through this. It's worse for you, having to see me like this, than it is for me."

Amanda swallowed a lump in her throat and smiled. "I was just thinking how much harder it is for you."

"It will soon be over for me. You'll have it rough for a while, but things will come together for you. Thank you for sharing my life. Thank you for taking such good care of me."

David stood and held out his arms. Amanda went to him, laid her head on his right shoulder. They held each other for more than a minute. She was basking in the thought that he cared enough to give her this final hug, when she heard a small snore.

"David," she whispered.

He jerked away from her and swayed, off balance. She tightened her arms around him to keep him upright.

He frowned at her. "Where's Amanda?"

"Amanda's right here."

"She's my wife, you know."

"I know." Amanda picked up the cannula and handed it to David.

He put his arms behind his back. "What's that?"

"Your oxygen."

"Do I need it?"

"Yes. It helps you breathe."

"Oh, okay."

She put the prongs to his nostrils and slipped the head loops behind his ears.

He held a length of the oxygen tubing between his hands and peered at it. "What does it say?"

"Nothing."

His voice grew harsh and insistent. "What does it say?"

Amanda studied the tubing and saw a shadow along the length of the clear plastic that seemed to move like a scrawl at the bottom of a television show.

"It's a shadow." She held the tubing up toward the light of the chandelier. "See? It's clear." When he seemed satisfied, she took his right hand. "Are you ready for bed?"

"Yes. I did my work."

Amanda walked with David to his room. "Do you need to go to the bathroom?"

"Yes."

She started to go into the bathroom with him, but he dropped her hand.

"I can do it myself."

She waited outside the open door, drooping against the jamb. He flushed the toilet, washed his hands, and shuffled into the hall, leaving the water running.

"Stay right here." Amanda took a few steps into the bathroom, shut off the water, and turned to David, but he wasn't where she left him. She hesitated. How could he have moved so quickly? She glanced in his room, but didn't see him.

"David?"

A crash came from the kitchen.

Amanda ran. David lay sprawled on the floor, but seemed unhurt. He got to his knees, yanked open the bottom drawer, the one where she kept such things as plastic bags and wax paper, and started throwing everything on the floor.

"A knife," he cried. "I need a knife."

Amanda hunkered down and put her arms around him. "Why do you need a knife?"

David jerked out of her arms and pushed her away with a strength she didn't know he could summon. He grabbed the oxygen tube hanging down the front of his chest. "This snake! It's killing me. Get me a knife."

"Hold still a minute," Amanda said as if to a recalcitrant child. To her surprise, David obeyed her command. She lifted the cannula off his face and showed it to him. "See? No snake."

"No snake," David mumbled into his chest.

Amanda had been afraid to leave him alone after that, and until now, she had no reason to enter the dining room.

The tiny scratching on the papers, so different from David's normally neat writing, tugged at her heart, and tears rolled down her cheeks.

She wanted to be glad David no longer had to endure such suffering, but dammit! He shouldn't have had to suffer in the first place.

Amanda gathered the papers and clutched them to her chest. She should throw them away—David would hate her having this remembrance of his deterioration—but they represented his determination to be useful, to live no matter what horrors befell him.

What had been so important to him at the end? A final sermon? Amanda tried to decipher his words, but between her tear-blurred vision and his crabbed writing, she could only make out what looked like Thalia's name written over and over again.

Perhaps she should give the papers to Thalia, proof that David loved their daughter to the end. Amanda placed the papers in a manila folder and slipped it into the bottom drawer of his desk. Thalia hadn't visited much during David's last weeks because she couldn't face his deterioration. She would hate having this evidence of what her father had become, and David would hate her seeing it.

But David had wanted Amanda with him that night. He'd trusted her enough that he shared his final work with her. He'd told her one last time he loved her. He'd hugged her.

That was worth remembering.

Chapter 6

FEELING ABANDONED IN the too-quiet house, Amanda made herself a cup of tea, set the cup next to her laptop on the breakfast bar, perched on a stool, and opened the computer to see if Sam had sent a message. He knew about David's memorial service today, and she expected him to send her words of comfort, but though emails filled her inbox—advertisements from local businesses, chain letters and articles interminably forwarded by churchwomen, a note from the church office reminding her she had to vacate the premises by April thirtieth—none of the messages came from Sam.

Hoping to feel close to her cyber lover, Amanda opened the folder with the transcripts of the Instant Messenger conversations with Sam, and clicked on the first one.

In the beginning, Sam had been just one of the many people Amanda had met through the online support group for people whose mates were dying of cancer, but over the months, she learned how smart he was, how kind, how empathetic, and she found herself looking forward to seeing his user name.

Apparently, he'd felt the same way. One evening, it had been just the two of them in the group. They'd talked about the loneliness that overwhelmed them, their feelings of sadness and rejection. They'd talked about the way their mates—his wife, her husband—were dealing with the knowledge that their deaths were approaching. They talked about the state of suspended animation the imminent deaths of their spouses created in them—unable to make plans about the future because they didn't know how long they'd have with their mates, trying not to wait for the end but unable to enjoy these last moments since both his wife and her husband had become reclusive as their ends drew near.

When others had come online and entered into the discussion that night, Sam suggested they switch to Instant Messenger.

Amanda felt shy at first, as if they'd become strangers once more. Sam must have felt the same way because he acted as if they'd just met.

At the time, the conversation had seemed vibrant and exciting—and painfully arousing—as if they were two heroic people on the verge of a new life, but now the exchange seemed to be nothing more than an ordinary dialogue between two ordinary people.

SAM: Let me introduce myself. My name is Sam Priestly. Samuel Lane Priestly.
AMANDA: How odd. My husband is a preacher. A minister in a liturgical church. The closest one can get to being a priest without being one.
SAM: I'm a priest in name only. I'm a professor at Ohio State University.
AMANDA: Amanda Louis Ray. And I'm nothing. Just a preacher's wife. Or at least I was a preacher's wife. Now I don't do anything but take care of David.
SAM: What does a preacher's wife do?
AMANDA: She goes to all the church functions. She's a member of the Women's Society. She fills in for the secretary, youth leader, or janitor if they call in sick. Accompanies her husband to church meetings. Acts as chaperon on youth group excursions.

SAM: Doesn't sound like nothing to me.

AMANDA: When I wasn't needed as a fill-in at the church, I worked at the safe house for abused children David started. He always felt that was his main ministry—children, especially abused children. Once when he heard about an abused girl, he went to her house and just took her.

SAM: How brave of him.

AMANDA: The father, who was twice my husband's size, came charging after him, but David stood his ground. Stared at the man. I don't know what the guy saw in David's eyes—hell, maybe—but he never made a move to get the girl back.

SAM: What happened to the girl?

AMANDA: Her body healed, though she's still scarred from all the cigarette burns on her breasts and between her legs. Luckily, she suffered no permanent damage. She has a little girl of her own now, and seems happy. Well, as happy as anyone can be after such trauma followed by years of therapy.

SAM: Does she visit David?

AMANDA: No. None of the children do. He wanted them to stand on their own and not use him as a crutch. It broke his heart when he had to return a child to an abusive situation.

SAM: Why would he have to?

AMANDA: The courts. David's ways were not always legal, but he didn't care about that. Only the children.

SAM: You're telling me about David. I want to hear about Amanda.

AMANDA: I am talking about Amanda.

SAM: You're fulfilling David's dreams. Was there never anyone with whom you were intimate in such a way that all the dreams you had seemed possible, that all the yearnings you had were fulfilled?

AMANDA: No. Never. Do you know what's funny? I didn't want to be one of those people who reach middle-age with absolutely no idea of who they are, so I got to know myself very

well. Yet here I am with no idea who I've become. No idea what I want. No dreams of my own to fulfill. I was fine until David got sick. Now, I don't know anything.
SAM: You're beautiful!
AMANDA: I wish I really were beautiful. For you.
SAM: You seem so alone. Do you have children?
AMANDA: One daughter. Thalia. She's grown now and on her own.
SAM: Pretty name.
AMANDA: David named her. Never even considered another name.
SAM: I have four grown children. Two boys. Two girls. Exactly what my wife wanted. And we have six grandkids with a seventh on the way.
AMANDA: Your wife is the type who always gets what she wants?
SAM: Always. The doctors told her she had three to six months to live, but she's survived for almost a year so far.
AMANDA: David was given the same prognosis, and it's been three months now. I wonder if he'll hang on like your wife is doing. It must be wonderful to still have her with you.
SAM: Yes…it is…
AMANDA: But?
SAM: But it puts me in an awkward position. She'd filed for divorce before she got sick. She met another guy, fell in love with him, wanted to start a new life, but he dumped her when he found out she had pancreatic cancer. Didn't want to have to deal with a sick woman. Not that I blame him. She is NOT a good patient.
AMANDA: So you stayed?
SAM: I'd already moved out. She asked me to move back home. I don't love her anymore, but we have a history together, and she is the mother of my children. They might be grown with children of their own, but the thought of losing their mother has been

hard for them. I didn't expect to still be taking care of her.
AMANDA: What are you going to do now?
SAM: What I've been doing all along—waiting to see what happens.
AMANDA: I feel guilty at times because I get tired of waiting. I feel as if I'm in limbo, and I want something to happen. Anything. Then I feel guilty because David has little enough time, and it's not fair for me to wish it away. What kind of woman wishes her husband would die and get it over with?
SAM: A woman like any other. Well, you're not like any other. I've never met anyone like you. Well here's a question. You know I've sort of been flirting with you?
AMANDA: Yep.
SAM: Will this destroy our friendship?
AMANDA: No. It's been nice.
SAM: Do you think that we'll have this moment and then lose it and remember it with longing? Or do you think that the situation can grow and get better?
AMANDA: I'm afraid it will be the first. I hope it will be the second. You are definitely the most fascinating man I've met in a very long time.
SAM: What makes you think we'll lose the moment?
AMANDA: Experience says so. Entropy guarantees it.
SAM: I've been hoping we could get closer. I'm not trying to intrude or come between you and anybody. I only thought that you were someone intriguing and really worth knowing.
AMANDA: You're not intruding. You're not coming between. I love the idea that someone thinks I'm worth knowing. Do you know how seductive that is?
SAM: Seductive? Am I not the safest person in the world to talk with like this? I'm 1000 miles away. I'm totally respectful. Curious to know all about you and willing to accept what you're willing to reveal on your terms....
AMANDA: You've rendered me speechless.

SAM: All your life people have been letting the air out of your self-esteem so you won't know your own strength, worth, and beauty.
AMANDA: I like seeing myself through your eyes. Strong, worthy, and beautiful.
SAM: There are so many things I don't know about you that I want to know.
AMANDA: You can ask me anything.
SAM: Did you ever hear the joke about the teacher who comes to the middle school class and gives a lecture on sex education. She asks at the end, "Are there any more questions?" A little voice replies, "Are there any more answers?" Tell me, what else should I ask tonight while you are granting me this wonderful gift?
AMANDA: What happens when you learn all there is to know about me, and discover that there's nothing more?
SAM: First of all, until I know everything that's happened to you to bring you to this place in your life and until I've gotten to know you much, much better, there is absolutely no danger that I will have discovered everything I want to know about you.
AMANDA: Well, you didn't ask the one question I thought you would. But I'm going to be a tease and not tell you which one that is.
SAM: I'll ask it if you give me a hint.
AMANDA: Actually, I'm mostly trying to figure out if I should just come out and say it, but it might be way too inappropriate.
SAM: Please, my dear Amanda, just come out with it.
AMANDA: I halfway expected you to ask me how long since I've had sex. See? Inappropriate.
SAM: No. Actually I was going to come right out and ask you if you haven't taken a lover. Only I consider that to be too inappropriate and none of my business
AMANDA: That question I can answer. No.
SAM: Is David your one and only, always?
AMANDA: Only two men in my entire life have ever shown any

interest in me of any kind.

SAM: You know, Amanda, I find you a very appealing person.

AMANDA: I know you do. You are the second person. Pretty pathetic life I've led.

SAM: You mean, I'm one of the two you were talking about?

AMANDA: Yes.

SAM: As we've been conversing, especially about the personal things, especially when you told me I could ask you anything, I've been aroused.

AMANDA: Well, I've got to admit: me too.

SAM: You too what?

AMANDA: Aroused.

SAM: So good to hear you say that! So, the question we both agreed was too inappropriate for me to ask: how long since you've made love?

AMANDA: Years. I don't even remember any more.

SAM: Okay. Wow. My mind is spinning with things I want to say. I want it all to come out right.

AMANDA: We've come this far, might as well continue.

SAM: About making love, would you consider yourself a liberated person or an inhibited person (recognizing this is all on a continuum and nobody is completely at one end or the other)?

AMANDA: I have no way of answering that.

SAM: Did I step over the line?

AMANDA: No. I simply don't know. And we've stepped over so many lines tonight, I don't think there are any left.

SAM: Okay, well, if I can ask, with your lover would you be a person who would initiate making love or wait on him?

AMANDA: Depends on how safe I felt, I imagine.

SAM: You are intriguing beyond words. You know, you're taking longer and longer between answers. I'm wondering if you're really uncomfortable with this conversation.

AMANDA: Longer because I'm thinking.

SAM: Thinking and not offended?

AMANDA: Not offended.

SAM: Is it okay if I use, maybe, terms of affection for you; like, 'sweetheart"? Would you find that offensive?

AMANDA: I would love to be called sweetheart. No one's ever called me sweetheart.

SAM: Have you ever had this kind of conversation before, sweetheart?

AMANDA: No. Have you?

SAM: Not in a long, long time--since I was dating. And never like this. Am I perverse for not being bothered by this conversation?

AMANDA: Am I?

SAM: You know what I miss? Pillow talk. I miss making love and then lying beside them and talking to them. That's real intimacy if you ask me.

AMANDA: That's what this seems like. Pillow talk. Weird.

SAM: It does, doesn't it? Darling, I'm so sorry. I don't mean to complicate your life.

AMANDA: You're not complicating it.

AMANDA: You're...

SAM: Really!

AMANDA: My life is so damn complicated, it can't get any more complicated.

SAM: So, would you finish that: You're . . .

AMANDA: Augmenting it? Adding spice? It's nice having someone take an interest in me.

SAM: Now that we each know this, what shall we do about it?

AMANDA: I have absolutely no idea. Maybe it's a good thing we live 1000 miles apart.

SAM: I can't picture us going a long time without talking. There is so much I still want to know about you, Amanda.

AMANDA: Okay, so we'll just ride it out. See where it takes us. I hope I don't end up offending you.

SAM: Why would you offend me?

AMANDA: Sometimes people misunderstand me. Things I say come across as negative when I am simply being truthful.
SAM: So you're bluntly truthful even if it hurts?
AMANDA: Not really. I try not to hurt people. Ever. But I don't like lies. I need the security of truth. I hope we can always be honest and open with each other.
SAM: Honesty is a real turn-on.
AMANDA: Except for David and now maybe you, no one ever wanted the whole truth of me. The people I was closest to always prided themselves on "getting" me, when all they did was discover part of the truth. And I let myself be tethered by their partial truths because I was tired of outgrowing people, and I didn't want to be floating in the cosmos alone.
SAM: You are truly an amazing and beautiful person, sweetheart. Perhaps this is the right place to leave things.
AMANDA: I suppose so.
SAM: I'm grateful for our chat tonight. It was such a surprise and a delight. I hope that we can keep the closeness we have tonight.
AMANDA: Me, too. It's been wonderful. Made me feel alive.
SAM: I hope you don't feel guilty tomorrow.
AMANDA: I won't. Thinking of our chat will give me something to hold on to as my life falls apart.
SAM: I'm sorry.
AMANDA: It helps that you understand. I have to go check on David. He is in such agony but refuses to take the morphine except at night because he wants his mind as clear as is possible.
SAM: I think the end will be harder for you than you expect.
AMANDA: I've done my grieving. Went through all the stages—anger, bargaining, the whole bit.
SAM: I hope you're right. I can't bear the thought of you in pain.

Is that why Sam hadn't contacted since David died? He couldn't bear the thought of her in pain? Amanda wrapped her arms around her middle, and wondered how anyone ever got through this.

But not everyone did get through it. Her father, a late-life parent, had died of a heart attack soon after Amanda graduated from college, and her mother had killed herself several months later. Amanda had spent many years hating her mother, but now that she'd experienced the true nature of grief and its awesome power—like an alien beast had taken up residence within her body and mind, controlling both physical and mental functions—she could understand how her mother had felt.

"I'm sorry, Mom," she whispered. "I didn't know."

The IM window popped up on her computer screen, and for a second she had the wild thought that her mother was trying to contact her, but then she saw Sam's name.

SAM: How was the memorial service, love?

A thrill went through Amanda at seeing the endearment on her computer screen. David had not been an endearment sort of person. He'd been too grounded, too down to earth to pay attention to romantic gestures, and she thought she'd been the same. Or maybe it was Sam himself who made her feel like a giddy schoolgirl.

AMANDA: Hard. I'd seen or talked to a lot of the people in the first days after David died, so it wasn't as much of a shock as I expected, but still, I found it difficult being around people.
SAM: I wish I could have been there for you.
AMANDA: Me, too. I feel so lost. Don't know why all this happened.
SAM: Maybe David's God needed him more than you did.
AMANDA: Do you really believe that? It sounds like something you'd tell a child.
SAM: I'll have to remember not to mention this idea again.
AMANDA: Why? Because I disagreed?

SAM: I don't like conflict.
AMANDA: Neither do I, but conflict seems to be a constant in my life. Thalia knows about us.

Amanda looked at the words she'd typed onto the open instant messenger screen on her computer, and waited for Sam's response. She could feel his concern, but she couldn't tell if the concern centered on him or on her.

SAM: Are you okay?
AMANDA: I'm fine. No. I'm not. She called me a hypocrite, and she's right.
SAM: I know a lot of hypocrites, and you're not one of them.
AMANDA: Grieving one man while lusting after another isn't hypocritical?
SAM: You loved David very much. Your grief is real.

At the sight of her husband's name, Amanda's chest constricted, forcing her to gasp for breath. *Dammit, David. Why did you have to die?*

SAM: You still there?
AMANDA: Still here. Thinking about David. I miss him. But I miss you, too. I feel as if I'm grieving two men.
SAM: I'm not going anywhere.
AMANDA: But you live a thousand miles away.

And, though he claimed the divorce papers had been signed but not filed, Amanda had to face the truth that Sam was still married. What had she expected, that she would go from one man to the other, that Sam would take David's place? That her life would remain the same? Or better yet, that she would finally get the heart-and-flowers romance that David had withheld from her?

SAM: I love you very much.

Tears blurred the words, but Amanda didn't need to see them clearly to feel their truth. Sam couldn't take David's place, but perhaps he could take her somewhere David couldn't.

AMANDA: And I love you.
SAM: How did Thalia find out about us?
AMANDA: She doesn't know about you, just that there's someone. She saw me touching myself once.
SAM: I'm sorry.
AMANDA: Me, too. It complicates things.
SAM: You're a complicated woman.
AMANDA: Not complicated. I'm very simple and basic. It's my life that's complicated.
SAM: Do you believe in fate?
AMANDA: It always comes down to that, doesn't it? You must have asked me a dozen times.
SAM: If our meeting and falling in love is fate, does that make the situation more complicated or less?
AMANDA: It's complicated either way. And it makes no sense. How could we have found each other? How could we have come to mean so much to each other when we've never met? And how could I have fallen in love with you while David was dying? I don't like what it says about me.
SAM: Your heart is big enough to hold the love of two men.
AMANDA: I thought I'd finished grieving for him. I told you that in our first chat. You and I met after I came to an acceptance of his dying. That was the only time I was emotionally available. Before that, I was too focused on David's presence, and now I'm too focused on his absence.
SAM: See? Fate. We're meant to love each other.
AMANDA: The thing is, I went through all the stages of grief except one—grief itself. I didn't understand what grief meant

until after David died.

SAM: I wish I could be there for you.

AMANDA: Everyone hugs me, even strangers. But it's only your arms I want to feel holding me.

SAM: Are you eating?

AMANDA: Not much. People brought me a lot of food, but I took it all to the church for the buffet.

SAM: Are you sleeping?

AMANDA: Some. I want to sleep so I can dream of David. I miss him more than I thought I would. This past year was so hard. I'm still ashamed that I refused to face his pain and weakness.

SAM: But he didn't want you to face it. He kept to himself most of the time. Shut you out.

AMANDA: I know, but still, what kind of wife carries on a flirtation while her husband is dying?

SAM: The kind who does what she needs to do to protect herself, love. The kind who finds strength any way she can to keep going in an untenable situation.

AMANDA: Our bond was so strong, I always thought I'd die when he did. I didn't think I could live without him, but about a year ago, I hugged him, and he shoved me away. It was painful for him to be touched. Deep inside me, a voice said, "He might be dying, but I have to live." It's like I split apart. One part of me continued to live, as if he were already dead, and the other part of me—the grieving part—went into some kind of suspended animation.

SAM: And after his death, the grieving part woke up. No wonder you're grieving so deeply. You have all those feelings stored up from the past year.

AMANDA: That year wasn't at all what I expected. When we got the diagnosis, he told me he wanted us to be close, that maybe he could finally open up and be the man I deserved. But after that day when he pushed me away, he closed himself off from me.

SAM: He had his own journey to take, love.
AMANDA: His pushing me away seemed to be more than that. David acted as if he were intent on a task he needed to accomplish, and he needed all the resources he had left to complete it.
SAM: What kind of task?
AMANDA: I don't know. Something he had to come to terms with? A decision he had to make? Something he had to do? He lived so much longer than the doctors expected. A year instead of three months. He seemed to be fixated on living until he finished that final task.
SAM: Maybe he didn't want to leave you.
AMANDA: Could be, but I don't think so. He was ready to go, to be done with the horror of his life. He was always in pain and he felt so cold, he said once that he welcomed hell.
SAM: So whatever he wanted to do would send him to hell?

Amanda paused, her fingertips on the keyboard. She'd taken David's comment to be a bit of facetiousness to lighten the gloom of his dying, but now she saw how out of place the comment had been. One of the side effects of the tumors in his brain and the drugs he had taken was a complete lack of humor. Irony or facetiousness or any other subtlety passed him by. And although David had never been a fire and brimstone preacher, he believed wholeheartedly in the devil and fires of hell.

SAM: Are you still there, love?
AMANDA: Thinking. You could be right that whatever he wanted to do could have sent him to hell.

The image of the gun in David's bathrobe pocket popped into her mind. She gasped. How could she have forgotten the weapon and the suicide note? But he hadn't killed himself. So why the thoughts of hell? Did he think God would punish him just because he considered suicide? *Oh, David, what terrible conflicts you must have had to deal with. And I didn't know.*

SAM: Are you still beating yourself up over last year?
AMANDA: How could you tell?
SAM: I can feel what you're thinking when we're IMing. The human mind is an electronic medium, just like a computer. Somehow IMing seems to link us on a fundamental level.
AMANDA: Medium? Like a channeling devise?
SAM: I meant medium as the singular of media, like radio. But the computer does seem to be a channeling device. How else could we have found each other? How else could we have fallen in love with someone we've never met?
AMANDA: You're so real to me, I forget we've never been together in real life. Do you think we ever will be?
SAM: I believe we will, love. I have to be honest, though. I'll never marry again. I love you, but I don't believe in marriage any more. I'm not sure I believe in God, either, after seeing Vivian suffer. How could anyone be so cruel as to put someone through that? And I sure as hell don't believe in the state, so basically there's no one to marry us. Would you mind living in sin, my darling?

Amanda started crying, though she had no idea why. Perhaps the thought that they had a future together? Or maybe that David's death had set her free to pursue other ways of living? Tears splashed on her fingers. It always came down to that simple fact: David was gone. Would she ever be happy again, knowing he was dead? Could she ever be happy? She wiped away the tears so she could see Sam's new message.

SAM: I think you're going to be entering the happiest time of your life.
AMANDA: If you're right, what does that say about my life with

David?
SAM: It doesn't say anything about your life with David. Maybe when you were with him, other things were more important to you than happiness.
AMANDA: It was important that we were together. The work he—we—did was important. I thought we were happy.
SAM: But you were doing his work. What about your own needs? Wasn't there something you always wanted but couldn't get?
AMANDA: Not really. It would be nice to have sex once more, though. David didn't much like sex. It's not so much he thought sex was for procreation, it was more that he lost heart. We seldom made love after Thalia was born. He said we were complete as we were.
SAM: I'll give you an orgasm at the first possible opportunity, but isn't there something you'd like to do that you had to put on hold when you married David?
AMANDA: When I was young, I wanted to write a novel about a love that transcended time and space, a story of truth and beauty, told with wisdom and understanding.
SAM: Do it.
AMANDA: I tried once. Right after I met David. He seemed so special that his being in the world made the world seem a special too. I felt I could do anything.
SAM: What happened?
AMANDA: Nothing. I sat down to write, put pen to paper, and no words came. I thought that's all I had to do—sit down and let the words flow. Turns out I had no talent for that sort of writing. No wisdom, either.
SAM: You've lived a lifetime since then. Writing isn't just about words. It's about having something to say. And you are very wise.
AMANDA: Perhaps, but there is still the small matter of talent.
SAM: There are two types of genius. The innate kind, where one

is born with a certain talent, such as musical or literary prodigies. Then there are the late bloomers. These people aren't born with a full-grown talent. They learn to be creative, and so can you. I can help you with the writing process.
AMANDA: So you think I'm a genius?
SAM: Yes.

Amanda stared at the stark word unembellished by any qualifiers. She'd meant her question facetiously. She was no genius, just a woman who tried to do the right thing, yet Sam seemed to have taken the question seriously. Then hearing an echo of her thoughts, she laughed at herself. A woman who tried to do the right thing? There was nothing right about falling in love with another man while your husband lay dying.

And yet, if she looked at the conundrum from the position that she did try to do the right thing, then perhaps falling in love with Sam had been the right thing for her to do.

AMANDA: I just had a strange thought. What if David's task was to get you and me together? Not a conscious task, but a subconscious one.
SAM: I've often thought that. From what you've said, it seems as if he could have been worried about leaving you alone. The life he foisted on you pretty much cut you off from intimacy, and I think he didn't want you to be by yourself.
AMANDA: David didn't foist this life on me. I chose it when I chose him.
SAM: But did you choose? Or did the universe choose him for you?
AMANDA: So the universe gives and the universe takes away?
SAM: I think so.
AMANDA: You give a lot of credence to the universe.
SAM: Well, we are all a part of it, and it is a part of us.
AMANDA: I don't trust your universe. It seems to me the

creative force of the universe is that of a child at play. Sometimes a cruel child, but still a child. I bet the universe is laughing its fool head off. Or if not the universe, then the trickster gods.
SAM: Old man coyote. Loki.
AMANDA: The universe brought us together and then kept us apart. Such a joke.
SAM: Not much longer and we'll get to be together.
AMANDA: It would be nice, though I'm not counting on it.
SAM: You seem down tonight. I mean about us.
AMANDA: It's hard for me to believe in a happy outcome. Still, if we can tap into the playfulness of the universe, we can do anything.
SAM: Can hardly wait to do "anything" with you, love.
AMANDA: And me with you. We've spent all evening talking about me. How are you? How's Vivian?
SAM: I hate to leave you, but I better to go check on my wife. Will you be okay?
AMANDA: I'll be fine. Don't worry about me.
SAM: Know that I am holding you in my thoughts until I can hold you in my arms. I love you, Amanda.
AMANDA: I love you, Sam.
SAM: Goodnight.
AMANDA: Goodnight.
SAM: I love you.
AMANDA: I love you.

Amanda could see that he felt as reluctant to disconnect as she did, but no more words appeared on the screen. She studied his final message, searing it into her brain, then she folded her arms over the keyboard, rested her head on her crossed wrists, and wept.

Chapter 7

IT'S BEEN EIGHT days since David died. You can do this.

The laden shelves of the grocery store loomed over Amanda as she pushed the grocery cart through the aisles. She felt as if she were running a gantlet, with memories of her husband flaying her on every side. She tried to find items that didn't remind her of David, but every time she reached for a can, bottle, or box, her stomach lurched. Finally she spied the yogurt section. Neither of them ate yogurt—David had dismissed the flavored brands as candy because of all the sugar, and he didn't like it plain. When she had been pregnant with Thalia, she used to buy plain yogurt and add a bit of jam for flavoring. Back then, it had been one of the few foods she could eat, and maybe it still would be.

She put three quarts of plain yogurt in the basket and wheeled the cart around, almost running into an improbable blond about her own age. The woman's look of annoyance changed to one of commiseration.

"Amanda, my dear. I heard about David. I am so sorry for your loss."

Amanda blinked back tears and scrambled in her mind for the blonde's identity, but she hadn't a clue. Perhaps an occasional member of her husband's church.

She mustered a semblance of civility. "Thank you."

"David was such a good man. The world is a poorer place

without him."

Amanda ducked her head, not wanting the woman to see the tears she could not keep from falling. The woman pushed the carts out of the way and put her arms around Amanda.

Amanda stiffened. Not since her pregnancy thirty years previously had strangers felt so entitled to touch her. She endured the embrace for a couple of seconds before gently pushing herself away.

The woman stepped back to her cart. "Let me know if you need anything." She started to roll the cart away, then stopped. "David was such a health nut. Took all those vitamins, ate right, exercised. How did he allow himself to get sick like that?"

Amanda glared at her. "*Allow* himself to get sick? Is that what you think? Sometimes people get sick for no reason. Sometimes it's out of their control."

The woman shrugged. "Whatever."

Amanda watched her walk away. The woman's jeans were so tight and her heels so high that she minced rather than walked. Amanda felt a faint ping of recognition. She had seen that same walk before, maybe strutting down the aisle in David's church, but she didn't care to trace the memory. It didn't matter. Nothing mattered now that David was gone.

She placed a jar of apricot preserves in the cart, threw in a package of raw sunflower seeds, a pound of butter, and a loaf of French bread—all foods David disliked—and proceeded to the check-out stand.

The twenty-something clerk with a nose ring and tattoos peaking above her shirt scanned the items without looking at Amanda. "Twenty dollars and ten cents." She bagged the few groceries, then glanced up. "Oh. Hi, Mrs. Ray. How is David?"

Amanda handed her the money, hoping the woman would drop the conversation, but the clerk continued to talk.

"I used to go to the youth group at his church, but now that I'm married, I go to my husband's church. I miss David." The clerk's brows drew together. "It's okay if I still call him David, isn't it? That's what he told us to call him."

David is dead. Amanda marveled that such anguish could be contained in three little words, words that refused to escape her lips.

The clerk prattled on about David driving the church bus to a retreat at Estes Park. Amanda slid her debit card through the machine and stared blankly at the message that appeared on the small screen: *refused.*

The clerk laughed.

Amanda felt her face grow hot, but when she glanced at the woman, she saw that the clerk wasn't laughing at her, wasn't even looking at her.

"We didn't think that old bus would make it up the mountain," the clerk said, still laughing. "But David told us God would get us there."

Amanda reached out to swipe her card again and noticed she'd been trying to pay with her driver's license. She pulled out her debit card and this time the transaction went through.

"Tell David hi from Heather, will you, Mrs. Ray? Have a nice day now."

Amanda grabbed the bag of groceries and fled the store. She reached the middle of the parking lot and paused to search for her car. Where had she parked? A beige sedan in the midst of all the black, sliver, and white vehicles should have been immediately apparent, but she couldn't see it. She had driven to the store, hadn't she?

She walked forward a few paces. Oh, there it was. A massive SUV had parked next to it, blocking her view. Juggling the bag of groceries, she fumbled in her purse for the keys. Good thing David couldn't see her. He always told her to be prepared, to have keys in hand when she left the store. *Well, David, I can do what I want now.*

A voice said, with low-toned menace, "Give me your purse

or I will kill you."

Amanda jerked her head up. Standing between her and her Corolla were two men who looked barely old enough to shave. One jiggled from foot to foot like a child who needed to go to the bathroom, but the other stood firm, hands steady on a gun.

The scene didn't seem quite real. Perhaps she'd wandered onto a movie set? Amanda looked around. No cameras. Just the two men standing before her in broad daylight.

Was there such a thing as narrow daylight? She giggled at the thought. Then stopped abruptly. *I really am going crazy.*

"What's with you, bitch?" screamed the man with the gun. "Gimme your purse or I'll kill you."

"Promise?" Amanda clasped her purse and her groceries to her chest.

The jiggling man lifted his hands and pointed a finger at her like a gun. "Yeah, we'll kill you, bitch."

"Okay." Amanda stared at them, hope blossoming in her chest. God provides, David had been fond of saying. Maybe God was providing a way out of her grief.

The hand with the gun began to waver.

"Do it, man," the jiggler yelled.

"Yes, do it," Amanda said softly.

"I'm out of here." The gunman took off running.

The jiggler danced in place. "Where are you going?"

"She's crazy. Or a cop." The words floated back to them from between a pick-up and a mini-van.

The jiggler looked longingly at Amanda's purse, then trotted after his companion.

Come back here, Amanda wanted to cry out, but she kept her mouth shut. She could almost see David's wince and feel his disapproval, though she couldn't tell what he disapproved of—her sassing the muggers or her wanting her life to be over with.

"But I'm alive," she told him. "For whatever that's worth."

She stowed the groceries in the trunk, and when she climbed

into the driver's seat, she collapsed into tears. Carefully, half blinded by tears, legs unsteady on the gas pedal, arms almost too shaky to steer, she drove home. No, not home. To the parsonage. She had no home. No house of her own. No husband. Homeless. Alone.

"I can't do this," she screamed when she stopped for a red light. A woman in a bronze Lexus in the next lane stared at her. Amanda shouted through her closed window, "What? You want a piece of me, too?" The light turned green. The Lexus peeled off, leaving Amanda sitting at the intersection. Honking horns finally penetrated Amanda's emotional storm. She drove slowly and congratulated herself on making it back to the parsonage. But back for what? Nothing had changed. David was still gone.

She put away the groceries, moving as if she'd aged a hundred years in the past few hours. No one had ever mentioned how debilitating grief could be, like a bone-eating disease that took everything and left nothing in reserve.

Finally, her few groceries stowed, Amanda fell onto her bed and lay there, too exhausted to move.

Light seeped between the slats of the closed blinds. *Time to get up and fix David's breakfast.* Amanda lay still and listened for any sound that might indicate he had risen. Hearing only the hum of the refrigerator and the drone of distant traffic, she burrowed deeper into the comforter and tried to enjoy a few minutes of freedom, but the stillness in the house felt unnatural. Maybe she should go check on David. She struggled to sit up.

The awful truth slammed into Amanda, knocking her back onto the pillow. David was dead. Yesterday they'd held his memorial service, this morning she'd gone to the grocery store, and now she needed to find a way to get through the rest of her life without him.

Amanda glanced at the time. 1:40 pm. David had died exactly eight days ago to the minute. She hadn't been keeping track of time, at least not consciously, but apparently, his death and her birth into the world of grief had reset her internal clock, and now 1:40 had become etched on her soul.

She wrapped her arms around her midsection, and curled into a ball. Tears spilled from her eyes.

"Dammit, David," she whispered. "How can you be dead? Why did you have to leave me?"

When David didn't respond, she sat up and cried, "David, where are you? Can you hear me?"

She knew, even as she called out to him that she was being foolish, but she could not stop the cry of pain. "Please? Where are you?"

Amanda felt a moment of panic, as if the world suddenly stopped rotating, and her stomach heaved. She staggered to the bathroom. She crouched over the toilet bowl, gagging and sobbing. After a few minutes, the nausea subsided, but dizziness remained. She splashed cold water on her face.

As she patted her face dry, she could feel the tears well up again. She took several deep shuddering breaths, trying to hold back the storm. *I'm so tired of crying, David. If you'd come back, I wouldn't have to cry any more.*

An image lodged in her mind. David sitting up in bed, hunched over his crossed legs because the pain in his cancer-ridden left shoulder bone wouldn't allow him to lie back.

How did you ever survive that torture? And how thoughtless of me to want you back. For what? So you can suffer more?

Amanda thought of the gun in the pocket of her husband's robe, and it amazed her that David hadn't used the weapon. What had kept him from taking that quicker way out? Had he been unable to make the leap from plan to action? Or had the mere possession of the gun given him courage to survive another minute, another day?

She tried to picture herself in his situation—pain too deep for morphine to eradicate, wanting to end it so as not to linger as a helpless invalid. Then she pictured herself raising the gun to her temple.

Like a bud on a flesh-eating plant, understanding blossomed. She could be with David. Right now. She didn't have to wait for the lucky accident of another mugger, one who would pull the trigger. She could do it herself.

Feeling free for the first time in months, Amanda darted to David's closet, pushed aside the garments on the rack so she could get to the robe, then stopped when she saw the box on the floor of the closet. During one of David's last coherent spells, he told her about the box and asked her to burn the contents, though he hadn't said how. They had no fireplace and no incinerator. Still, she had promised to dispose of his "effects" as he called them.

Amanda's shoulders bowed. *I can't do this.* She tugged the box out of David's closet and spread open the flaps of the box—a carton from a long-defunct 12" television—and stared at the mass of papers, files, and old envelopes. Perhaps she could burn them in the hibachi grill, but it would take days.

"Dammit, David," Amanda said aloud. Her voice sounded mild without its now customary anger, though she detected an edge to it. Despair, maybe, or perhaps desolation. Hell, what difference did the name of the emotion make? It was all part of grief—the hundreds of emotions that raged through her body every day.

Amanda picked up an empty envelope that had once held a gas bill, and gazed at the notation on the back in his neat hand. *To wish for a different life is to waste the life we have.* Could this have been a note for a sermon? Or a quote he wanted to remember?

She dropped the envelope back in the box. "Dammit, David!" This time she did hear anger in her voice, and felt comforted by the rage. At least anger gave the illusion of strength. Amanda wished she could tape the flaps of the box and pack it away, or better yet, empty it into the recyclables bin, but the habit of acceding to David's wishes remained too strong for even anger to overcome.

Amanda kicked the box and enjoyed the stab of pain in her big toe. The pain had a real physical cause, unlike the amorphous pain of grief that made her chest feel as if it would explode. She kicked the box again, and tears spurted from her eyes.

She sank beside the box and cradled it. "I'm sorry, David," she whispered, though she didn't know why she felt the need to apologize. Maybe because she still lived? But she'd just as soon be with her husband, wherever that might be.

When the tears subsided, Amanda pushed the box back beneath the slacks where David had stored it. "I'll take care of it, I promise," she said, repeating the words she had used when he made his last request.

"I'd planned on getting rid of the papers myself," David had said, grimacing against the pain the morphine no longer masked. "But I've run out of time."

"What do you want me to do with the papers?" Amanda asked.

"Burn them. Burn everything. No need to go through the box. Just burn it." The desperate look in his sunken eyes, the intensity of the gaze that locked onto hers had scared her almost as much as the coughing fit that followed.

"I'll take care of it, I promise," Amanda said when David gained control of himself.

David nodded, relaxing back against the pillow. He'd fallen asleep, and when he awoke hours later, he mumbled. "Remember everything I said."

Those were the last words David ever spoke. He went to sleep and never woke again.

And so Amanda had committed herself to burning the papers, she who had never managed to start a fire in her entire life.

Amanda shut the closet and leaned her forehead against the

cool wood. "I'll do it," she said. "Just not today."

She could almost feel David's wince of disapproval—he'd never liked her penchant for procrastination. Amanda straightened her shoulders and stepped away from the door. "If you don't like how I'm doing things, you shouldn't have died."

It took Amanda almost a week to burn the papers in the small grill in the backyard, one handful at a time. When the last paper had been tossed on the dying blaze, she peered into the box to make sure nothing remained. David had always double-checked everything, and though his thoroughness had irritated her, she felt it appropriate to follow his example while disposing of his effects.

A penny poked out from beneath a bottom flap. She lifted the flap to retrieve the coin and found a black and white photo of a little girl. A word had been written on the back in David's precise penmanship. The pencil notation had faded, but she could make out a name: *Thalia.*

Curious, she studied the photo. The toddler did look like Thalia, but Amanda couldn't remember her daughter owning that particular coat and beret. Nor did she remember David ever taking black and white pictures. Maybe he had Photoshopped the image to give it an old-fashioned look. But that didn't seem like something David would do. Her husband had been strictly a point and shoot photographer, and not much of that.

"David," she called out. "Do you remember taking a black and white photo of Thalia?"

She listened for a response from inside the house, but did not hear David's voice. Then the truth slammed into her…again. *Dammit. I can't do this.*

She ran into the house and screamed, "David, where are you? Why did you have to go? I need you." Her voice broke. "I'll give up Sam if you come back. Please?"

She cocked her head and held her breath, hoping to hear

David's footfall, but if David still paced the house, his steps were as silent as they had always been.

"I'm going to turn into a crazy old lady, talking to myself, and it's your fault, David."

But David did not respond.

Chapter 8

THALIA STOPPED BY to see Amanda as she had been doing most afternoons since David's death two weeks ago, though Amanda never knew why her daughter came. Perhaps Thalia needed to feel connected to her beloved father by visiting the place where he had lived and died, and Amanda just happened to be there. Or perhaps Thalia needed to feel connected to her mother, wanting to be assured she hadn't been orphaned, but their conversations were stilted, little more than blasts of sound from Thalia and faint echoes from Amanda. She had no idea what to say to bridge the gap between them.

Amanda couldn't say she was sorry for flirting with Sam, because she wasn't sorry. She couldn't say she'd never meet him online again, because she wanted him to be part of her life.

In desperation, needing to say something to her daughter besides responding to questions about Amanda's state of mind and when she was going to get on with her life, and deflecting requests for some of David's ashes (which now resided, still wrapped in the blanket, on Amanda's bed), Amanda went to David's room, scooped the photo of Thalia off the desk, and turned, almost bumping into her daughter.

"This doesn't look at all like my room," Thalia said. "There's not a trace of me here. You could hardly wait to get rid of me."

Amanda opened her mouth to reply, and for a few seconds

no words came out. She'd forgotten that when they moved to this house, thirteen-year-old Thalia had been in a rare sulky mood. Trying to put a smile on her daughter's face, she'd promised Thalia she could decorate the room any way she wished. Amanda hadn't expected pink paint and ruffles, but still she'd been appalled by the red curtains that gave the impression of dripping blood and the black walls decorated with posters of movie vampires and rock stars who looked as if they'd crawled out of a crypt.

When Thalia went to college, David claimed the room for a den, but it had been Amanda who had been cajoled into redecorating the room to David's taste. "*Shouldn't we at least wait until Thalia's out of college?*" Amanda pleaded. But for once, David had not been thinking of his daughter. "*I need a place to be by myself to work*," he said. "*We'll put in a sofa bed. Thalia can stay there during the summer*." But Thalia had never come back, and it had been David himself who used the sofa bed when he moved out of their shared bedroom.

"I wish this house had more than two bedrooms," Amanda said. "Then we could have kept your room."

"I'm glad he had a place to get away from you."

Amanda flinched at her daughter's words, but didn't bother to correct her. When David had moved out of their room, it had been to spare her his relentless pacing and allow her to sleep, not to get away from her. Or so he said. Could Thalia be right and he wanted to get away from her? Could he have said something to his daughter that he wouldn't say to his wife?

Realizing she was crushing the black and white photo, Amanda loosened her fingers and showed it to Thalia. "I found this in a box of Dad's papers this morning. Do you remember when he took the picture?"

Thalia gave the image a cursory glance and shrugged her shoulders. "That's the other Thalia when she was little."

"What other Thalia?"

"I don't know. Dad showed me the picture once and said he named me after her. He said she was a special girl, and that I was special too."

"You are special, Thalia," Amanda murmured, though her thoughts were spinning. *Who was the other Thalia? And why had David never mentioned her?*

"Yeah, so special you painted my room the minute I moved out." Tears rolled down Thalia's cheeks. "Is that why you're going through Dad's things? Getting rid of all traces of him like you did me?"

She stumbled from the room, sobbing.

Amanda felt like crying, too, but for once, no tears came.

Chapter 9

THE OTHER THALIA.

The words echoed in Amanda's mind, momentarily driving out her pain. Then the agony came rushing back, doubling her over with renewed grief.

Amanda pulled herself upright, threw back her head, and howled, "How could you do this to me, David?" She collapsed into a heap on the floor of her husband's room. "How could you?"

Although Amanda believed David had no secrets from her, she'd always known her husband hadn't shared every detail of his life before they met, but still, something as major as their daughter's namesake should have been mentioned at least once in thirty-five years of marriage.

It had been mentioned once—to Thalia. "But I was your *wife*!" The words began as a whimper and ended as a screech.

I'm going crazy.

Amanda once pasted a sticker on the bumper of their car that said, "I'm having a nervous breakdown. I earned it and I owe it to myself." She'd found it amusing then, but now, teetering on the edge of grief, it didn't seem so funny.

The thing is, if I don't know who David is, how do I know who I am? My life is so wrapped up in his that I don't know where his life ends and mine begins. But David's life had ended. Her life—her life as a woman alone—was just beginning.

Tears filled Amanda's eyes. *I can't do this. I'm too old to have an identity crisis.*

She put her hands on the floor and pushed herself upright, feeling ungainly and heavy despite all the weight she had lost since David died. When had she eaten last? The thought of food turned her stomach, so Amanda shunted the thought to the back of her mind with all the other things she couldn't bear to think about. Like David's death. Like her continued life. Like the gun. Like her daughter Thalia. Like the other Thalia.

Amanda stood in the middle of her husband's room and pivoted slowly, trying to find something mindless to do, but she had already given the room a thorough cleaning. The sofa where David had spent his last months looked like a sofa again, not a death bed.

She could picture him lying there so still, his face gaunt, mouth open, Adam's apple bobbing once. Then…nothing. No more breaths. No smell of death. No leaking from bladder or colon. David would have liked that—his simple, dignified death.

Amanda had waited a few minutes to make sure his ordeal had ended, then she called hospice to tell them of his passing. Until the nurse came, she sat calmly in a chair by her husband's side. The nurse checked for a heartbeat with a stethoscope and told Amanda what she already knew. "He's gone."

The nurse cleaned David and wrapped him in a white blanket—his shroud. A woman from Adam's Funeral Services came a half an hour later. The woman and the nurse gently lifted David's body onto a gurney and covered him with a red plush blanket. No body bag. Just his barely discernible shape beneath the blanket as they rolled him out to the plain black SUV.

Amanda watched the vehicle until it drove out of sight, then walked back inside to David's room. The nurse bustled around, gathering up medications, dumping them into a Ziploc bag filled with kitty litter, and stashing the mess in her carry-all to be disposed of later. The woman paused by the front door. "Is there anything I can do for you?"

Amanda smiled. "Can you bring David back?"

The nurse laughed ruefully. "No."

Amanda nodded sadly, acknowledging the truth of the woman's word. "Then there's nothing you can do."

"Will you be all right by yourself? We can get someone to stay with you if you want."

"I'm okay. It's not as if I haven't been expecting this."

The nurse raised one eyebrow and tilted her head in a way that clearly indicated her doubt. "You shouldn't be alone."

"Truly," Amanda said. "I am okay."

The nurse hugged her. "I notified the oxygen company. They'll come for the tank in a few days. Call if you need anything. Anything at all. We're here for the family as well as the patient." She stood at the door a few seconds longer, as if waiting for Amanda to say a few final words, but what was there to say? David's death had been so hard won she'd been glad he finally had been able to let go.

She lost the next few hours in a flurry of calls and people. First Thalia came, then ladies from the church bearing covered dishes, unwelcome hugs, and awkward words of condolence.

At nightfall, Amanda found herself alone. She trudged to David's room. "I did fine, David. You'd be proud of me."

She heard no response, no moan, no breath.

"David?" Amanda moved to his bed and stared uncomprehendingly at the emptiness. And then it hit her. David was dead. Gone forever from her life. Gone from this earth.

Like a wrecking ball, pain slammed into Amanda, knocking her off her feet and onto the bed. She felt as if she'd been torn apart, as if half of her had been amputated and all that remained was the bloody stump of her psyche. Tears gushed from her eyes, a cataract that brought no relief. She clutched the sheets to her, and screamed, "David, where are you?"

The only answer was a surge of agony greater than anything

Amanda could have ever imagined. The force of the grief stunned her. The *fact* of grief stunned her even more. She'd assumed she accepted David's fate, assumed she'd gone through grief, assumed she'd moved on, and she felt totally unprepared to deal with the reality. *How does anyone survive this?*

Two weeks later, Amanda still didn't know how to deal with grief. But somehow, she'd managed to muddle through fourteen days. Days that David had never seen.

Days that seemed to get harder instead of easier.

Standing in the middle of her husband's room, Amanda howled. She felt as if a giant hand were squeezing the life from her and all that remained were the two vivid images in her mind—how David looked when he died and how he looked when they first met, so radiantly healthy, strong, full of laughter.

I can't do this. But she had to do something.

Frenzied with grief-induced adrenaline, Amanda dashed to the kitchen for a trash bag then hurried back to David's room. She yanked open the door to David's closet, pulled out the drawers of the built in dresser, and shoved his underwear into the large black bag. Since David had never liked to shop, he had few clothes besides his suits and church robes, but he had so many boxer shorts they filled the entire bag. Amanda twist-tied the bag closed and hauled it outside. She blinked in the sunlight, surprised by the brightness. It didn't seem right that the sun should shine so merrily when David was dead. Glowering skies or rain would be more fitting.

Amanda stuffed the bag into the trash bin and dragged herself back to his room. She still couldn't bear to get rid of the rest of his clothes, but she needed to do something to keep from dissolving into tears once more. She'd cried enough to last her a lifetime, yet tears continued to damn up, ready to spill when she let her guard down.

On the shelf above the clothes rack in his closet, Amanda found a stack of shoeboxes. *David won't need his shoes. I can get rid of them*. Proud of her resolution, Amanda pulled down one of the boxes and opened it, expecting to see a pair of black dress shoes. Instead, she found a stash of Thalia's drawings and stories that had once graced the refrigerator.

Amanda went through her daughter's drawings one at a time, seeing the stick figures gradually take shape into recognizable images of David and Thalia, with Amanda looming large behind them. Had her daughter seen her as a guardian or as a menace? Since Thalia had drawn herself and David as being approximately the same size, perhaps she considered David a friend and Amanda the parent of them both. Whatever Thalia had tried to depict in these family pictures, it helped explain the rift between her and her daughter, and why Thalia felt so betrayed. If Thalia identified with her father, then her mother's betrayal of him became personal.

But my relationship with Sam has nothing to do with you, she told her daughter's photo, one of the many photographs at the bottom of the box. David had kept all of Thalia's school pictures, and Amanda could see at a glance how her daughter had grown from a pixyish little girl to the beautiful woman she'd become.

Amanda had forgotten how beautiful Thalia was—the glower her daughter so often wore now made her seem unattractive and unapproachable. *But she's my daughter. There should be a way to bridge the gap, to reconnect.*

As Amanda carefully placed the items back in the box, an essay entitled "My Dog" in a childish hand caught her eye. "My mommy won't let me have a dog. She doesn't like dogs. When I grow up, I'm going to have lots and lots and lots of dogs."

Amanda felt a moment of shame. Why couldn't she have let Thalia have a dog? Amanda had never had a pet as child and didn't feel comfortable around animals, but it would have meant so much to the little girl Thalia had been if they'd gotten her a puppy. Just one more regret to add to the growing list of lamentations.

She put the box back on the shelf, picked up another. Inside, Amanda found a small doll with mismatched arms and legs and a sneer painted on the muslin face—her one attempt at making a doll for the annual Christmas Bazaar. She'd thrown it away, embarrassed by her failure, but apparently David had dug it out of the trash and kept it all these years.

Tears stung Amanda's eyes. *Oh, David, how can you be gone? You were such an appreciator—you appreciated everyone and every good they did. The world is smaller without you in it.*

Holding her breath, wondering what else David had kept, Amanda sifted through the box. A few pennies. A flyer for a book sale she'd held at his first church. A couple of indeterminate designs she vaguely remembered doodling on a phone pad. A stack of notes in her own handwriting. "I'm at the Woman's Club dinner tonight, David. There's stroganoff and a salad in the refrigerator for you and Thalia. Don't forget to heat the stroganoff." "Taking Thalia to the doctor. Just a small cut, but she might need a stitch or two. Back soon."

All her notes were the same. Stark messages with no endearments, no words of love. Amanda wished she'd told David more often how much he meant to her. They'd never been a romantic couple, and David had been uncomfortable with professions of love, but still, she should have told her husband frequently that she loved him. And now she'd never have the chance. *Too damn much left unfinished.*

During the final moments of her life, would she be like David, hanging on through pain and disorientation, dwelling on all the unfinished business of life?

She set the box aside, and reached for a third. Heavier than she expected, it slipped from her fingers and crashed to the floor. Out tumbled a black-stained shop rag enclosed in a Ziploc bag, and a can of gun oil.

Chapter 10

AMANDA SAT ON the edge of her bed and typed a text message to Sam, asking him to call or message her, then paced the room and waited for him to respond. She desperately needed to talk to someone about the gun, the gun oil, the rag and what it might mean, and Sam would help her make sense of it all.

The longer she waited for a response, the more Amanda wished she could recall the message. Sam had been responding to a few of her messages, but hadn't been contacting her first, which made her feel like a stalker. Sam often told her how much he enjoyed hearing from her, so why couldn't he make the mental leap and realize how much she enjoyed hearing from him? Maybe he didn't love her anymore. Or maybe he'd been playing games with her. Sometimes Amanda got the impression she was a fantasy of Sam's, a love he could put on the shelf like an old doll and take out when he needed comfort or a reminder that he hadn't always been the husband of a dying woman.

A repugnant thought struck Amanda. Could Sam have lied about his dying wife and had trolled the support group for an easy mark? In the end, what did she know about him?

Only what he said.

Only what she felt.

The phone rang. Amanda ran the two steps to the bedside table and snatched the phone.

Not Sam. Mary Lynn McCormick, once a close friend, now a stranger. The last time the two women had talked, ten months ago, Mary Lynn had claimed she couldn't bear Amanda's pain. "I'm a problem solver," she said. "And there's no way I can solve your problems, so it's best if I stay away." Best for whom, Amanda had wondered, though it had turned out okay. She got involved with Sam shortly after that and would have had a hard time keeping the secret from Mary Lynn.

Amanda punched the button to accept the call. "Hello, Mary Lynn."

"Hi, darlin'. How are you?" The sweet southern voice evoked a simpler time. A time before David. A time before the seeds of grief had been sown.

"I'm fine. How are you?" Amanda could hear an echo of tears in her voice, and she hoped the sound escaped her friend's notice. Mary Lynn had no use for crying—or so she claimed, but it seemed impossible that a woman who had divorced two different men for cheating on her could be immune to sadness.

An awkward silence strummed between the two women. Amanda tried to gather the strength to tell Mary Lynn that David had died, but the words refused to be spoken.

"Thalia called and told me about David," Mary Lynn finally said. "I'm sorry for your loss."

"Thank you," Amanda responded automatically, while inside she screamed, *Is that the best you can do? Thirty-seven years of friendship and all I get is "I'm sorry for your loss"?* As suddenly as it came, her anger died. At least Mary Lynn had called. In Mary Lynn's world, such an effort loomed large.

"Thalia's worried about you. She says you've changed."

"Of course I've changed. Everything has changed." The tears Amanda could no longer hold back rolled down her cheeks.

"She thinks you need to get on with your life."

"I am getting on with my life. Grief is how I'm doing it."

"Ah, darlin'. Tears never did anyone any good. Makes your

skin red and blotchy."

Amanda could not tell if Mary Lynn meant that as a joke or if her erstwhile friend believed blotchy skin should be considered when one's husband had died. "Crying is good for you," Amanda said. "Studies have shown that tears help release the hormones that build up during the stress of grief." The words came out sounding stiff and formal. She felt no connection to the woman on the other end of the call, none of the easy camaraderie that had characterized their friendship.

"You need a man," Mary Lynn said. "Sex is the best way to relieve stress."

"I have a man." Amanda immediately regretted her snappy response. No way could she talk about Sam, and especially not to Mary Lynn. Her friend would think her foolish for getting involved with someone who lived so far way. Someone, moreover, she'd never seen. Luckily, Mary Lynn misunderstood.

"I know, darlin'. But David's gone. You need someone who's alive. Unless you're into necrophilia, and that doesn't seem like you."

"Do you have someone?"

"Jackson. He's small but he has big…feet." Mary Lynn giggled. "He's married, of course. All the good men are."

"Doesn't it bother you that he has a wife?"

"I had two husbands. Both of them had a wife. Me. Yet it didn't stop them from cheating. It's so much better to be on the other side of the mattress. I have all the perks of the relationship without any of the responsibility."

Amanda felt a lightening of her spirits. Maybe it would work out with Sam.

Mary Lynn sighed. "That's not true. It's what I tell myself so I don't have to deal with the reality of the situation. The truth is, we never get to spend holidays together. I can never relax with him. I can't dress in old raggy clothes or let my gray roots show. Not that I want to, but his wife, bless her heart, let herself go, which is one reason why he needs me. I can never tell him what I really think because we might have an argument. He gets that at home, and I'm the one he comes to see to get away from conflict. It's hard always trying to be at my best."

"You make it sound so dreary."

Mary Lynn gave a lady-like snort. "Not so dreary as being married to a cheater. Not so dreary as having a guy leave his wife for me. Beauregard, my last boyfriend, did that. What a nightmare! My place seemed to be crawling with his grandbabies. His children were always in one sort of financial trouble or other, and Beau kept calling his wife so they could straighten things out. I sent him back to her."

"Does an affair ever work out?" Amanda asked in a small voice.

"Does any relationship ever work out? Look at you and David. You were so full of joy before you met him. We were finished with college and it seemed as if you thought the whole world was a banquet spread out for your delight and you could hardly wait to start grabbing the goodies with both hands."

Amanda tried to imagine herself as the woman Mary Lynn described, but only remembered how inept and gauche she had felt. How lost. "Are you sure you're talking about me?"

"Of course I'm talking about you, darlin'. I hated watching all that promise fade over the years. David took everything from you and gave nothing in return."

Amanda felt her mouth open and close, but no sound came out. Is that truly how Mary Lynn had seen her? Maybe she and David hadn't always been happy, but they'd been together. Connected. Suddenly Amanda saw herself the way she'd been before David. Not joyful. Not ready to feast. She'd worried about the meaning of life—life generally and her life specifically. She'd drifted through the college syllabus, taking classes in archaeology, astronomy, psychology, philosophy, history, trying to make sense of life. By graduation, she still hadn't found enlightenment. Then David came along, and if he didn't give her life meaning, he gave it focus. When David was alive, Amanda's life made sense. And now he'd set her adrift again. Was she clutching at Sam—or at least the idea of him—in an attempt to regain focus? But she did love him, didn't she?

Amanda forced herself to concentrate on the conversation with her friend, and picked up the tail end of Mary Lynn's discourse.

"...a trip! Come visit me."

"I can't." Just the thought of making reservations, let alone actually getting on a plane and flying across the country to Georgia, sapped Amanda's strength. Besides, she had too much to do in Denver, packing up and clearing out of the parsonage.

"Well, you have to go somewhere," Mary Lynn said. "You might as well come stay with me. I bought a fabulous ten-bedroom house a few months ago. The real estate market has been good to me, and I was top agent two years in a row. I had to do something with all that lovely money."

Ten rooms? And soon I won't have even one. "So you know about my having to leave the parsonage?"

"Thalia told me. It's one of the reasons she's worried about you."

"That daughter of mine sure got chatty with you. What else did say?" Amanda held her breath, wondering if Thalia had mentioned the cyber affair.

"Nothing really. She thinks you need to see someone. A therapist."

"I don't need a therapist." Amanda's voice broke. "I need David. I need my life back."

"I know, darlin'. I wish I could take away your grief."

For a second, the thought of having her pain disappear brought relief, then Amanda understood that grief was all she had left connecting her to David. She started to explain she needed her grief but the other woman hadn't paused to let her speak.

"…told me the only way out is through, and you'll come through this."

Amanda sighed at hearing that same old phrase. "That's what people keep telling me. But I'll never be who I was. That woman died with David."

"You must have loved David very much to be grieving so deeply now."

"I'll always love him." The need to talk of her confusion about loving Sam while loving and grieving for David burned in Amanda's throat. Maybe Mary Lynn, with all her wisdom in the ways of men, could help make sense of the situation. "I need to talk to you, Mary Lynn. I need your advice."

"When you come to visit, we'll talk all you want," Mary Lynn said. "We have so much to catch up on, but I don't have time now. Jackson is on his way over, and I don't want to make him wait. He hates that. His wife can never be ready on time. Let me know when you can come, okay? Oops! Look at the time. Gotta go. Love you, darlin'. Hang in there."

Hang in there? Was that supposed to be a comfort? If so, the reassurance didn't work because the phrase conjured up the image of a noose.

Realizing she was still listening to the dial tone, the loneliest sound in the world, Amanda set the phone in the cradle and wished Sam would call. Now that their circumstances had changed—her husband gone and his wife improving—Sam didn't contact her as much, and that left her feeling isolated.

I wish you were here, David.

The tears that had dried when she'd talked to Mary Lynn started again, but Amanda didn't know for whom she cried. David? Sam? Herself? Did it matter? The tears seemed to have an agenda of their own, deluging her at every opportunity.

Amanda envisioned herself as a white-haired old woman, brown-spotted arthritic hands brushing away the endless tears that had gouged scaly ruts in her cheeks. She didn't want to be that woman, but had no idea how to become the woman she did want to be—strong, brave, wise, bold.

She tried to picture Sam by her side, but couldn't see the two of them together. She threw herself on the bed. *It wasn't supposed to be like this, David. We were supposed to grow old together.* They used to laugh about their old age, and how they'd walk, leaning against each other for support, like conjoined twins.

She wiped her face on one of David's soft old handkerchiefs and thought about Sam. Why did his presence in her life make her feel even lonelier?

Because he wasn't in her life. He was in Ohio. Their sporadic chats, texts, calls didn't add up to much of a relationship. Most of the time, he resided in her memory, like David. Is that all life came down to—memory? She could look forward to seeing Sam, though that option no longer held true for David—at least not here on Earth. Perhaps looking forward was but a memory of the future.

All Amanda had besides memory was this moment, and in the moment, she was alone. She'd spent many moments alone in her life—her parents hadn't doted on her, had ignored her if the truth be told. David left her alone as he went about his work. And Thalia had escaped the house as often as she could when she lived there because although she'd loved her father dearly, she'd hated being "the preacher's kid." So why did being alone now make Amanda feel especially lonely and bereft?

"Oh, shut up," Amanda told herself. "You're not the first person who lost her spouse. Get over it."

Ignoring the tears trickling down her face, Amanda went to David's room and sorted his clothes—one pile to be thrown away, one to be donated to the church's rummage sale, one for Thalia to go through to pick what she wanted. The pinstriped shirt she kept for herself.

When Amanda cleared off the clothes rack, she yanked open the dresser drawers. She'd already thrown away his underwear and socks. Only his collection of sweaters remained. She scooped them out of the drawer by the armload and dumped them on the pile for the rummage sale, and went back for the rest. In the bottom drawer, along with a penny, she found his old celery green and gray sweater, the one he'd been wearing when they met.

Amanda hugged the soft garment to her cheeks, soaking it with her tears, and remembered the strong, vital, radiant man she'd fallen in love with.

The Gilded Canary, a cartoon version of a British pub, was a popular hangout on lower Colfax Avenue for rebellious young adults and buttoned-down government workers, a strange mix for the times, but since each group kept to itself and pretended those unlike them didn't exist, no clashes developed, at least none Amanda heard about. But then, she didn't often go to bars. She didn't like being around people who drank—even a little alcohol seemed to make people less able to connect on a personal level—but Mary Lynn, her roommate, had met a guy there the night before and didn't want to seem too easy by going alone, so she begged Amanda to go with her. Amanda thought a relationship begun in a bar doomed to failure, but Mary Lynn insisted Cooper was her soul mate. Amanda, still young enough or naïve enough to believe in the power of true love, put aside her misgivings and agreed to go. Although Amanda didn't like to dress up, she did as Mary Lynn asked and slipped a pretty top over the dark slacks she always wore, and added a bit of blush to her cheeks. Mary Lynn, of course, looked gorgeous in a deceptively simple dark red challis dress. In her high heels, she towered over Amanda, but Amanda refused to wear anything but flats.

They opened the double stained-glass door of the pub and walked into a wall of noise. Amanda recoiled. Mary Lynn grabbed her arm and propelled her toward a freckle-faced boy with a shock of red hair who looked too young to be in a bar.

"Hi, Cooper," Mary Lynn said, feigning nonchalance.

The redhead stared at Mary Lynn's chest. "Do I know you?"

Amanda thought he was playing Mary Lynn's game of disinterest, but the hurt look on her friend's face told her the truth. Cooper didn't remember her.

A blonde with huge breasts slid into the booth next to Cooper and leaned toward him so her breasts caressed his arm. "I probably caught a disease from the toilet seat."

Cooper laughed as if the remark were the wittiest utterance he had ever heard.

Mary Lynn stood immobile for a moment, then swung her rich auburn hair like a girl in a shampoo commercial, and stalked to a small table in the middle of the pub. She sank daintily onto a chair as if she were a debutante at a cotillion.

"Did you see that girl? If she were an inch taller, she'd be round, bless her heart."

"She's nowhere near as pretty as you." Amanda eyed the sticky spills on the table. "Are you sure you want to stay?"

"I don't want to give him the satisfaction of knowing he hurt me."

Amanda refrained from pointing out the obvious—that Cooper didn't care—and said, "He doesn't deserve you."

Mary Lynn jutted out her chin. "You got that right, darlin'. I gave him the best three hours of my life, and if he doesn't appreciate that, he hasn't got the sense God gave a goose."

A burst of laughter from the next table caught Amanda's attention. She turned her head to glance at the source of the sound, and froze. Flanked by five other young folk—three male and two female—sat the most radiant man she'd ever seen. He seemed bathed in light, his smile wide enough to warm the entire room. He wasn't handsome, but his chocolate-brown eyes sparkled and his neatly combed sandy hair shone like old gold. Even the celery-green and gray sweater he wore seemed to reflect the light.

A voice inside her wailed, *"But I don't even like men with beady brown eyes and blond hair."*

"What do you see?" Mary Lynn turned to look, and shrugged. "Oh. Them."

"Who are they?"

"Seminary students."

Amanda sneaked another look at the group. "Seminarians? Really?" They didn't look like seminary students, but then, she didn't have any idea what an incipient preacher would look like. "Who's the guy in the middle?" Amanda tried to sound indifferent, but she could hear the breathiness of her words.

"Don't know, darlin'. Haven't seen him here before. I got a mind to go tell that snake in the grass a thing or two."

"What? I thought you said you didn't know him?" Amanda followed her friend's gaze and realized Mary Lynn's last sentence referred to Cooper. "Let him go. Truly, he's not worth your time."

Amanda turned to look at the radiant seminary student again and found him staring at her. He rose. As if pulled by a magnet, Amanda stood, too. They met in the small space between the two tables. Amanda couldn't think of a thing to say, and apparently, neither could he. For a few eternal moments, they stared into each other's eyes.

"Say something," Mary Lynn hissed.

Amanda couldn't summon a single word.

"Oh, for pity's sake." Mary Lynn raised her voice. "Her name is Amanda. Amanda Nordstrom."

"His name is David Ray," one of the women from the other table called out.

"Hi, Amanda." David's voice sounded reedy from emotion.

"Hi, David." The words barely scraped past the lump in her throat.

Mary Lynn stood up. "I'm leaving. You can have my chair,

David."

"You sure?" David asked, his gaze still locked with Amanda's.

"Positive."

Amanda heard the click-clack of her friend's high heels as she walked away. She thought she should accompany her friend back to their apartment, but she couldn't move.

One of the seminarians picked up the beer mug from where David had been sitting, stepped between Amanda and David, and put the mug on Amanda's table. The spell broken, or mostly broken, Amanda stumbled to her chair on legs that seemed too weak to hold her upright.

"What are you celebrating?" Amanda asked.

"Graduation. My first church. My new life."

"New life?"

"For the first time in my life, I'm happy. There's so much to accomplish. So much good I can do in the world, but all I've been doing is going to school. Now I'm through, at least for a while. I want to go back eventually and get a doctorate in theology, but I'm anxious to get started on my real work."

"Converting people?" Amanda's feeble attempt at a light-hearted remark didn't garner the smile she'd hoped for.

"People can't be converted," David said. "Not really."

"So, what is your real work?"

"You'll laugh."

Amanda drew a cross over her heart with her right forefinger. "I promise I won't laugh."

"I want to spread the word of happiness. There is so much misery in the world, and it doesn't have to be that way. I don't believe God created us to suffer. What good does our pain do him? He wants us to be happy, to join him in the joy of creation."

"People don't choose to be miserable." Amanda hated to disagree with the radiant man, but she also didn't want to start their relationship on the wrong foot by pretending to be someone she wasn't. She held her breath and waited for his response.

David nodded, and Amanda found herself relaxing into love.

"Most people don't choose to be miserable, that's true, but they let everyday life get in the way. Some people have misery thrust on them by other humans, not by God. Like abused children. God doesn't harm the little ones. People do." David's radiance dimmed. "I want to help those children find the happiness that was stolen from them."

Amanda smiled. "Sounds wonderful."

"You're laughing at me."

"Never. I think you're amazing. It must be lovely having such a clear mission. I never knew what I wanted."

David tilted his head as he regarded her. "No dreams?"

"Just the night kind."

He laughed as she hoped he would, a throaty sound that made something jump deep in her groin. "What about the day kind of dream?"

"None. When I was a kid, I wanted to be an author, but I don't seem to have much talent for writing. And anyway, it's not a burning desire. I don't know of anything that would make me as incandescent as you."

"You think I'm incandescent?"

The intensity of David's gaze made Amanda's legs tremble. "God, yes!" She clapped her hands over her mouth. "Oops. Sorry."

"Don't be. If you apologize every time you inadvertently use the name of God, you'll spend the rest of our lives apologizing and not rejoicing."

Feeling giddy and a bit daring, Amanda said, "The rest of our lives?"

"Don't you feel it?"

Remembering Mary Lynn's feigned nonchalance when saying hi to Cooper, Amanda wondered if she should act coy, too, but looking at David, at the guileless light in his eyes, she couldn't play the game.

"Yes," Amanda admitted shyly. "I feel it, too."

David nodded once. "Good."

They were married three months later. All his friends officiated at the wedding. Mary Lynn stood as her maid of honor.

Church politics dimmed David's incandescence, the accumulated sorrow over the plight of abused children diminished his radiance more, and death destroyed his light completely.

Amanda cuddled David's sweater to her chest. Falling *in love and falling in grief—the bookends of my life. But now what? Where do I go from here?*

The need to look at David seized her. She searched in her closet for the box containing her memorabilia—the wedding album, Thalia's baby book, Thalia's baby bracelet and her first pair of booties and the few pictures she had of David. The framed professional photo taken on his silver jubilee was the most recent photo she had. Why didn't they take more pictures? How could she not have considered a time when images would be her only link to him?

Amanda found the framed picture and held it to her chest as she took the few strides to her dresser. She set the photo upright, stepped back to look at David, and let out a cry.

No!

When Amanda had first seen the studio photo, she'd been impressed with the way the photographer had captured David perfectly—his kind, intelligent eyes, his erect yet relaxed posture, his sweet smile. But now…She stared at the image, appalled that it didn't look at all like the man she carried in her mind. It looked like a young stranger, someone who bore scant resemblance to her David.

Hand over her mouth, Amanda backed away from the photo. If this wasn't David, where was he?

"David," she screamed. "Where are you? Can you hear me?" She paused to listen.

No response.

Amanda climbed into bed, huddled on her side of the mattress—still her side though he hadn't shared the bed with her in a year—and hoped that when she woke she wouldn't remember this waking nightmare. The nightmare where David died and left behind a photo of a different man.

Chapter 11

AMANDA DRAGGED HERSELF out of bed on the fifteenth morning after David's death and went into the bathroom to take a shower. She started to remove her nightgown—the frilled blue one David had given her for her birthday two years ago—then pulled it back into place. She didn't have the energy to lift her arms above her head, didn't have the energy to do anything, actually, and getting ready to face a new day didn't seem worth the effort. It wouldn't make her feel better, and besides, who would see her?

She crawled back into bed and curled her body around the bundle containing David's ashes. The smell of her husband on the robe made her feel broken—not just heartbroken, but soul broken.

Strains of music filtered through the shuttered window. Her neighbor, Bill Jensen, a retired and retiring man whose only passions seemed to be the Beatles and his motor trike, must have returned from one of his frequent cross-country trips. Did he know about David? The two men had visited over their back fences when both happened to be doing outside chores, and he came to see David a few times after David got sick, but Bill had seldom spoken to Amanda.

A new song began, and the music grew louder. Amanda listened to the words of "Let It Be," and something inside of her perked up. Could that be the answer to her pain? To let it be? Forget that David was gone. Forget her grief. Forget her confusion over loving Sam while grieving her husband.

Let it be.

The idea sank back into the recesses of her mind as she grappled with the truth. The whole purpose of going through the grieving process, of embracing the pain, the craziness, the hole inside her, was so that eventually she'd be able to embrace life in its entirety again. She didn't want to let it be. She wanted to feel, to become strong enough so she didn't have to simply accept life's vagaries but could be an active participant.

Amanda jumped out of bed, removed her nightgown, and took a shower. When she turned off the water, she could still hear, "Let It Be." Maybe it was a broken record, playing that same song over and over again. Or maybe Bill needed the reminder to let things be.

The music stopped. A few minutes later, after she'd pulled on navy slacks and a bright flowered top, the door bell rang.

She opened the door. Bill Jensen shifted from foot to foot. The deep lines in his face that looked as if they'd been carved with a jagged knife made him appear mean. His fingers moved spasmodically, twisting an invisible cap.

"Hi. I heard about David." Bill gestured toward his house.

Despite the vagueness of the motion, she understood that one of the neighbors had given him the news.

"I'm sorry," he said. "I know how you feel."

Amanda felt herself bristling. How could he know? How could anyone?

Bill Jensen shifted his weight again. "I don't know how you feel, of course, no one can, but I've been there and I know the pain."

Tears came to Amanda's eyes. "I'm sorry. I didn't know."

"It was decades ago." He twisted his invisible cap. "But sometimes it feels like last week."

Amanda stood aside. "Won't you come in?"

Bill entered the house, took a step toward a chair in the parlor, and stopped.

Amanda held out a hand. "Please. Have a seat. Would you like a cup of coffee or tea? Or perhaps something stronger?"

"Coffee or tea will be fine. I don't drink. At least, not anymore. After my wife died..."

Amanda nodded in sympathy. If alcohol did anything but make her sick, she'd probably also have turned to drink in an effort to dull the pain. She left Bill perched on an overstuffed chair, and went into the kitchen. While the water boiled, she fixed a tray with sugar, lemon, a small basket containing a variety of individually wrapped herb teas, and a small plate of cookies one of the church ladies had left. She reached into a cabinet for two cups and saucers—her wedding china—but her hand settled instead on a couple of mugs that held no emotional connotations.

Amanda took the tray into the parlor, set it on a coffee table, and offered the basket of tea to Bill so he could choose. For a second, while she poured the hot water over the teabags—orange spice for him, mint for her—everything felt normal, as if David were working at the church and she were entertaining a church member.

Her fingers trembled as the truth hit her again.

David was dead.

Quickly, she set the teapot on the tray and clasped her hands together in her lap. Bill settled back in his chair, but she continued to sit upright on the edge of the couch.

"It's hard," Bill said. "But you'll get through it. Somehow."

Amanda heard the pain in his voice. She raised her head to meet his gaze. A shadow of grief clouded his gray eyes, and a line between his brows deepened.

"What happened to your wife?" Amanda asked in a small voice.

Bill sipped his tea, then set the mug on the table and

straightened his shoulders. "We met at the University of Colorado in Boulder. East coast city kids away from home for the first time. We fell in love with each other and the mountains, and vowed to spend our lives together away from the things of man. We worked for a few years after college to get a grub stake, then we opened a business in Estes Park taking people on wilderness treks. We were naïve, overestimating our skills, but we learned and became experts in the business of trekking and of life. I never knew it was possible for two people to be so happy—both my parents and hers were miserable. We grew up in families where the normal tone of voice was a shout or a scream. Grace and I never raised our voices to each other."

He blew out a short laugh. "If we had kids, it might have been different, but we figured there were enough people in the world, so we decided to remain childfree. A way of killing off our families, so to speak. We teased each other about being dead ends in the gene pool. Ironic, considering that she drowned."

Amanda held still, not wanting to interrupt the flow of his story, but her heart went out to him. How did anyone survive this pain? How did anyone find the will to go on alone?

"We wanted to do something different for our fifteenth anniversary, so we decided to go canoeing in Canada. The river, winding through a forest with a lake on either end, was as enchanting as we'd expected until the freak blizzard. We'd checked the weather, and the most we were supposed to get was a few showers. We didn't think anything of it. I mean, it was July, for cripes sake."

Bill's voice broke. He gulped the rest of his tea, poured more water over his teabag, and sat with his face in his hands. When he raised his head, his eyes seemed to have sunk deep into their sockets.

"High winds. Swirling snow. Zero visibility. Grace took everything in stride. All part of the adventure, she said. Then the snow turned to rain, and with the rain came lightning."

Amanda held her breath. Bill had already told her the tale's unhappy ending, but his raspy voice kept her spellbound.

"Lightning struck a tree a little way ahead. We could see it falling, but we could do nothing about it. The river was in control and the whitewaters took us directly under the tree. It fell on Grace and capsized the canoe. I tried to swim, tried to find her, but the river carried me for miles before I could finally drag myself up the bank. I started to walk back to where I'd lost Grace. I met a couple of guys on four wheelers. I always hated those things. They've done more damage to the environment in a few years then the logging did in a century. But I sure was glad to see those fellows. I thought they could take me to Grace, but I passed out after I told them my story, and woke up in the hospital. The cops told me they found Grace. Said the tree had killed her instantly and kept her trapped so she wasn't swept away. I couldn't handle her being gone. Took to drink. Sold the business. Moved here. Didn't want to have anything to do with the wilderness that killed my beloved Grace. Now I'm sober, but that doesn't help much."

Bill lifted the mug to his lips then set it down again without drinking. "I'm sorry. I don't know what got into me. That's not what I came to tell you." He fell silent again.

"I'm listening," Amanda said. "What did you want to say?"

He gave a start as if he'd forgotten she sat across from him. "Grace told me once she wanted her ashes scattered in the mountains, in all the special wilderness places we'd discovered together. Took me five years to get to where I could part with what remained of her. I found peace in the mountains on that two hundred mile trek. It was like a final gift from her to me, that peace. But I wish I'd kept her ashes, or at least some of them. Even though I did what she wanted, I feel as if I threw her away."

Bill stood abruptly and held out a hand. "Do what you have to do to get through this. Scream. Cry. Hit things. Don't look beyond each day or each hour or each minute, whatever increment you can handle. Time will pass even if it feels like it's standing still. You will find a way to live again, though part of you will always miss her. I mean him."

Amanda clutched his hand, feeling the calluses on his leathery palm. His fingers slipped from hers, and he marched to the door. Stopped. Turned around.

"Thank you for the tea," Bill said formally, his eyes hooded like that of a stranger.

Amanda watched him cross her lawn and enter his house. As she shut the door, she caught the first faint strains of "Let It Be."

Something Bill had said echoed in her mind, and as she cleaned up the tea things, she replayed the conversation trying to pick out the words that had struck a chord.

"I feel as if I threw her away," Bill had said. And then Amanda made the connection.

It had happened about a month before David died. Amanda put him to bed, gave him his morphine, and made him promise to ring the bell if he needed anything. She showed him the bell, an electronic door bell that rang in her room when he pushed the button. He'd played with it a minute, smiling when he heard the distant ring, then he settled back on the pillows.

"Adios, compadre," David said in a perky childlike voice.

"Good night, David. Go to sleep."

"Okeydoke."

Amanda turned off the light in his room but left the light on in the hall. She sank onto her bed fully clothed, meaning to rest but a few minutes.

The sound of something falling woke Amanda. She jumped out of bed, flipped on the light switch and dashed to David's room. His light was on, but she didn't see him.

With visions of him knocked out, having hit his head on the porcelain sink, she charged to the bathroom, and tried to open the door, but it only budged a few inches.

Amanda peeked through the opening. David lay on the floor, his feet wedged against the door. She reached into the room and gently bent his knees so she could move his bare feet out of the way, then opened the door enough to slip through.

David looked up at her and flinched, as if he thought she would hit him.

"It's okay, David," Amanda said in a soothing voice, the one she'd once used for a colicky Thalia. "I'm here. What happened?"

"Fell."

When Amanda had tucked her husband into bed much earlier, David had been wearing a sweat suit, a heavy gray cotton thing left over from high school, but now he wore dress slacks, a tan shirt, and over that a sleeveless undershirt.

"How come you got dressed?"

"I had to do my paper route," David said impatiently, looking up at her through sunken eyes as if he didn't recognize her.

"Do you know who I am?"

David nodded.

"Do you know who you are?"

His lower lip trembled. "No."

"You're David Ray. A minister. My husband. Thalia's father. You have kidney cancer."

"I do?" He paused, apparently digesting the news. "Am I going to die?"

"Yes."

"Oh." David lifted his arms. Amanda took hold of him, surprised that his grip was still so strong, and tugged him upright. She helped him out of his clothes and into his sweat suit, and tucked him into bed.

"I'm scared," he said in a little boy's voice.

"I know you are, honey. I'll stay here until you fall asleep. Let's get your oxygen on first."

"Okeydoke." David took the cannula from her and tried to slip the tubing over his head."

"Here. Like this. Put the loop over one ear first and then the other." The same instruction she gave him a dozen times a day.

A deep furrow creased between his brows. "I never can remember how to do it."

"I know. It's hard."

Amanda pulled the cranberry and forest green comforter over her husband, then slipped under the bedclothes and wrapped her arms around him. There wasn't much else she could do except drug him into a coma, and that she wouldn't do even though the hospice nurse claimed it would be better for both of them if she gave him the drugs.

"Have the hospice people told you yet how to end me?" David asked, his voice barely audible.

"They don't end you. They just try to keep you comfortable." Amanda pulled him closer, feeling his bony body beneath the sweatshirt. *Nothing but skin and bone.* She'd always thought the expression a cliché, but truly, there seemed to be nothing left of him but a skeleton with a bit of skin holding the bones together.

"Do you know who you are now?" she asked.

"David." He pulled away from her.

She loosened her hug. "Do you want me to leave so you can go to sleep?"

"No. I want to walk." He crawled out of bed, stood on wobbly legs, and held out a hand. "Come with me."

Amanda held David's hand, but he broke free and yanked off the oxygen tube. She tried to stop him, but he dropped his chin to his chest and shook his head.

"No oxygen," he said, voice strong.

Amanda smiled at him. "Okay. No oxygen."

He took her hand again. They walked slowly out of the room and down the hall. He talked, but he spoke so softly, his chin tucked onto his chest, that she couldn't make out the mumbled words.

Hand in hand, they paced the living room. Amanda kept her attention focused on the feel of his frail hand to keep from thinking that the smartest person she ever knew, the kindest and gentlest man, had been reduced to this childlike condition. Even worse, he seemed to know what was happening to him. He had times of lucidity where he acted like himself, and then he'd slip into this alternate state, and be lost.

The hospice nurse vowed the drugs weren't the problem, but Amanda knew they were a major cause of his disorientation. David had been fine—well, except for the pain in his cancer-ridden body—until he starting taking morphine on a regular basis. The tranquilizers were even worse. Worst of all had been the sleeping pills. The drug hadn't put him to sleep but gave him waking nightmares of shadow men who told him he deserved his pain, so Amanda had stopped giving him the pills.

"We got along well, didn't we?" David's voice came out strong enough that she could understand his words without straining to hear.

"Yes, David. We got along very well."

"We had a good life, didn't we?"

Amanda's eyes burned. "Yes."

"I'm not ready for you to throw me away."

Amanda swallowed past the lump in her throat. "I'm not throwing you away. I want nothing more than to spend the rest of my life with you."

"Oh, right. It's the cancer. I forgot." David clutched at his shoulder where the tumors had invaded the bone.

"Do you want some liquid morphine?"

"Is it time?"

"You can have the liquid whenever you want it."

He shook his head, his chin skimming across his chest. "I don't want to go to Hollywood and be an actor."

An actor? Amanda scrambled about in her mind, trying to decode his words. His diseased brain seemed to take convoluted paths when simpler words wouldn't come. Then she remembered a television special they'd seen a couple of months ago about all the celebrities with addictions.

"You won't become a drug addict, I promise." Amanda left the second part of the thought unspoken. *You won't live long enough to become addicted.*

Poor David. He'd endured so much pain, hating to give in to the fuzziness and disorientation the morphine brought. He'd hated even more the heavy duty tranquilizers that had been prescribed to subdue his terminal restlessness.

No one had been able to explain to her why some people were afflicted with the need to be constantly on the move as death neared. Were they running from death? Adrenalized from all the changes taking place in their bodies? Thinking of tasks unfinished and the people they were leaving behind?

During the last couple of days of his life, David lost the ability to swallow. And still he paced. He couldn't keep his balance, so Amanda walked with him, holding his hand as if they were courting each other, not courting death. And still he paced.

Amanda thought of Bill's wife and her almost instant death. Would it have been better if David had died in such a manner—alive then not alive with no pain, no disorientation, no lingering health issues?

Would it have been better for her?

In the end, what difference did it make? The dead were dead either way, and the survivors were left to deal with life the best they knew how.

Chapter 12

A WEEK AFTER Amanda texted Sam asking him to contact her, he finally replied to her message, saying he could meet her online. She opened a message window.

AMANDA: I'm here.
SAM: Good to talk to you, love. How are you doing?
AMANDA: Doing okay. That is if you consider crying all the time doing okay.
SAM: How long has it been since David died?
AMANDA: Three weeks today.
SAM: It's been hard, huh?
AMANDA: You can't imagine. I always thought I was stoic. I figured I'd cry a few days and then just get on with life, but it doesn't work that way. So much is not in my control. Grief takes over. A few times when I've found a bit of respite from grief, I felt my body crying. I think it realized it's going to die, and it's panicking.
SAM: Could be. Our brains were built on an older brain, the lizard brain, and it's possible the lizard brain has some sort of consciousness separate from the consciousness we are aware of.
AMANDA: I want David back. Even the way he was when he got caught up in his work and forgot me. Even the way he was at the end, like a little boy. I want him back.

SAM: What about if he were in pain?
AMANDA: No, of course not. I still can't bear to think of all he suffered. He was ready to go. I thought I was ready to let him go, but I can't. I miss him. I miss you.
SAM: I wish I could be there for you. I wanted to fly out when he died, but I couldn't think of an excuse.
AMANDA: How about that your paramour lost her husband and you needed to be with her?
SAM: Oh, sure. Vivian wouldn't have had a problem with that.
AMANDA: What would your kids think if I came to her funeral?
SAM: Nothing. They're still at an age where they don't notice old folks except as potential babysitters.
AMANDA: So now I'm "old folks"?

Amanda wrote the comment meaning to be funny, but by the time the words appeared in the window, they lost their tinge of humor and seemed plaintive. She was older than Sam by a couple of years, but she liked that. Maybe he'd outlive her. Then she wouldn't have to go through grief a second time.

SAM: Not to me. To me you're eternally young and beautiful.
AMANDA: I worry that you will be disappointed when we meet. I mean, aren't you supposed to go for a much younger woman the second time around?
SAM: Only if you were the younger woman. But I'm glad you're not younger. What would we talk about? Look at us, the way we IM. Full words, no abbreviations, or at least not many.
AMANDA: I know. I hate LOL. Why not just L for laughing? Or...I don't know. Something other than LOL.
SAM: LOL
AMANDA: Cute. Real cute. But seriously...
SAM: Yes?
AMANDA: I changed my mind. I don't want to be serious. Seems as if I've been serious my whole life. Shouldn't I be

celebrating David's life, not mourning his death? But right now, I don't feel like celebrating. Every good thought I have of him leads inexorably to his death.

SAM: I love you!!

AMANDA: I'm glad, but what brought that on?

SAM: Inexorably. I've never known anyone who used that word in conversation. You're wonderful.

AMANDA: Which brings me back to my earlier point. What if you're disappointed in me when we meet?

SAM: I won't be.

AMANDA: How can you be so sure?

SAM: Because I love you. All of you. I'm not a teenager who's only into looks. I like what I've seen of you in your pictures. I love your smile. Your eyes. But more than that, I love who you are.

AMANDA: I'm changing. I'm not the same as I was when we met.

SAM: I love that you're changing. It's part of who you are—an incredible woman who adapts to whatever life throws her way.

AMANDA: I wish I were half the woman you think I am.

SAM: Trust me. You're everything I think you are. I probably know you as well as anyone, and better than most, which is to say that I probably know you as much as you can be known.

AMANDA: You make me sound mysterious.

SAM: You are mysterious. You have depths you probably aren't aware of. Being part of your life these past months, I have watched you go through many difficulties. You're like a great impressionist painting. Stand back and you see this beautiful flower blossoming in intricate loveliness right before your eyes.

AMANDA: And up close I'm just a bunch of paint blobs?

SAM: I haven't seen you up close. Can hardly wait. Hard being the operative word.

AMANDA: All we've been doing is talking about me. How have you been doing?

SAM: Busy. Always busy. Now that Vivian doesn't require as much physical care, she seems to be more emotionally needy. We're babysitting the grandkids a lot. Vivian wants the little ones around, but she can't take care of them, so I have to be there. And I have a heavy teaching load this semester in addition to my administrative duties. I wish I had more time for you.
AMANDA: Me too.
SAM: What's happening in your world besides grief?
AMANDA: Did I tell you I found a gun in David's bathrobe pocket? I thought he got it to help when the pain grew too bad, but I started cleaning out David's closet a few days ago and found gun-cleaning stuff. If David got a gun to kill himself, why would he need to clean it?
SAM: Maybe he practiced with it to get the feel of it and to make sure he could do it right.
AMANDA: But when could he have practiced? He's barely been out of the house the last year.
SAM: Was the gun new?
AMANDA: I don't know. Didn't look at it. Afraid of what I might do with it.
SAM: Not an option, love.
AMANDA: I know. It's just that I get so overwhelmed with pain that I want to stop it.
SAM: Remember what they told us at the support group? The only way out is through.
AMANDA: My mother killed herself almost a year after my father died of a heart attack. She never got over her grief. What if I never get over mine?
SAM: You're strong, love. Stronger than you give yourself credit for.
AMANDA: I wish I believed that.
SAM: So do I. You're such a amazing woman. Giving. Kind. Strong. Smart. Yet you esteem yourself so lightly.
AMANDA: You say such sweet things about me.

SAM: Someday you will see yourself through my eyes and realize how beautiful you are.
AMANDA: I never thought curiosity was much of an emotion or much of a reason for doing anything, but I'm finding out that curiosity keeps me going. I'm curious how our story will develop. Curious to see what my life without David will be like. And now I'm curious about the damn gun. Damn, I say damn a lot now. I never used to.
SAM: You're turning into a wild woman.
AMANDA: And there's something else. I found a photo of Thalia, or at least that's the name on the back of the picture, but when I compared it to other photos of Thalia at the same age, I could see that it wasn't her.
SAM: So who is it?
AMANDA: Don't know. I asked Thalia about it. She told me it was the Thalia we named her after. Actually, David named her. Odd that he never told me why he chose that name. Never mentioned another Thalia.
SAM: Seems there's a lot he didn't tell you.
AMANDA: I thought we had no secrets from each other. I told him everything. Who knows, if he hadn't been sick and uncommunicative, I might have even told him about you. But if he hadn't been sick, and if he hadn't been so reclusive, you and I would never have gotten to know each other, so there wouldn't have been anything to tell.
SAM: I'm glad we met. You bring such joy to my life.

Amanda studied the words on the screen. How could she bring joy to his life when he only brought more sorrow to hers? He lived so far away and had so little time for her...But he was here with her now. No sense in crying about him until later, when she went to her lonely bed. She waited to see what Sam would say next, but no words appeared in the chat window.

AMANDA: Are you still there?
SAM: Sorry. Vivian's calling for me. She's restless tonight and says she aches. Be right back.

Amanda's heart constricted at the words. What was she thinking, falling in love with a married man? It hadn't felt wrong when both their mates had been dying, but now that David was dead and Vivian getting better, the gulf between them yawned wide. Perhaps the low self-esteem Sam mentioned made her accept the situation. Would a woman who saw her own importance accept so little?

She'd never understood those women who chucked everything—husband, family, home—to be with the one they loved, yet she found herself in the same situation. *Not quite,* she reminded herself. She didn't plan to throw her life away on Sam, nor he her. So what was the point? Maybe love was the point. Love in whatever guise it came.

SAM: I'm back. She's okay. Probably just wanted some attention.
AMANDA: Do you think she knows about me?
SAM: I don't see how she could.
AMANDA: I didn't see how Thalia could have found out about you and me, but she did. Well, not you specifically. Mostly she jumped to conclusions. For all she knew, I could have been looking at porn.
SAM: I wish I could make love to you right now. I wish I could taste your kisses. Wish I could touch my tongue to your lips, both sets.

Amanda stared at the words. They didn't arouse her the way they had during the months preceding David's death. Had her libido died, too? Then all at once she felt such a yearning to be in Sam's arms, to feel cherished, to feel his skin against hers, that she cried out. She took a deep breath, and resumed typing.

AMANDA: I hate this. I hate that David's dead. I hate that you're so far away. I thought I'd gotten used to skin hunger, but now that torments me, too, and I hate it.
SAM: Skin hunger?
AMANDA: When David first stopped having sex with me, my skin seemed to call out for his. It wasn't like an itch, though it made me antsy. It was like hunger or thirst. I thought I got over it, but apparently you've awakened that hunger.
SAM: Sorry.
AMANDA: Don't be. I just wish I could touch you.
SAM: Our day will come. And then we'll come.

Amanda covered her eyes with her hands. Maybe her mother had the right idea opting out of life, but what if Sam was right and things could work out for them? Things would never work out if she were dead. Would Sam mourn her, or would he find someone else? *How did this happen, David? You were always the one. You were my soul mate. My split-apart. Well, you've split apart from me for real. And now there's Sam.*

SAM: I love you, darling.

Tears welled up in Amanda's eyes. *God, I'm so sick of crying!* Angrily, she brushed them away, and sent her response.

AMANDA: I needed to see that. Thank you.
SAM: I have to get some sleep. Early classes tomorrow. I'd much rather be with you. You know that, don't you?
AMANDA: I love you, Sam.
SAM: Goodnight.
AMANDA: Goodnight.

By the time Amanda's "Goodnight" appeared on the screen, Sam had already signed out. The thing she'd always loved about their chats was that she could feel his longing and how it matched hers, but tonight his departure had been so abrupt, she should feel nothing—just emptiness.

How had she gotten herself into such a predicament? Grieving one man, loving another. But if she didn't have Sam, she'd have nothing—no hopes, no dreams of love, no future.

During the last terrible month of David's illness, she'd often thought of what she'd do when he died. She thought she'd feel light and free when the burden of his pain lifted from her shoulders. She'd seen herself driving to Ohio to be with Sam. How naïve she had been! She now had the burden of her grief, and Sam had little time for her.

"What am I supposed to do, David?" Amanda said aloud. But, as always, she heard no response.

Chapter 13

A COUPLE OF weeks before David died, the ravens had appeared. The birds gathered in the neighborhood, one small group at a time. Amanda lost count after a dozen birds, and still they came. Their raucous cries and the whoosh of their wings filled the air with an oppressive sense of doom. Suddenly, at one-forty on the afternoon of March 7th, the very moment of David's death, the ravens let out one last haunting cry and disappeared, leaving behind a funereal silence and a feeling of suffocation, as if all the air had been sucked from the atmosphere.

David's absence created that same sort of vacuum. Odd that such a shrunken body could leave behind such a vast hole. Wasn't a bullet like that? A small entry wound and a huge and shattering exit wound?

Amanda pushed the thought of guns out of her head and wandered around the house. She picked up first one object then another, though she had no clear sense of what these relics of her life with David were for. Without him, they had no meaning, no shape, no substance.

She patted herself, needing the reassurance that she still existed. Where was the determination to live that had descended on her a year ago after the diagnosis, after David had shoved her away, after that silent cry: *He might be dying, but I have to live?*

The words had shocked her as much as his rejection, and she

felt as if their bond had been severed. Like a divorce, but more final than any legal decree.

Until David got so sick he needed constant care, Amanda never again touched her husband. She lived her own life, talking long walks, reading, playing solitaire on the computer, hanging out with the caregiver's support group. And after she met Sam, she spent as much time with her cyber lover as she could.

But somehow, David's dying had reconnected Amanda to her husband even as death tore them apart forever.

"I'm such a terrible person, David," Amanda said aloud. "How could I have done that to you, leave you to die alone while I went on with my life?" She added silently, not wanting to voice the rebellious truth, *But how could you have left me to live alone while you went on with your dying?*

Why did grief have to be so hard? Why couldn't it be the way she had imagined—a few tears, bittersweet memories, some loneliness and sadness, but with a strong determination to get on with her life?

Determination took energy, though, and during the past week, she hadn't done anything to get ready for the move, hadn't seen anyone except Thalia. All her energy had been depleted by a blizzard of pain and tears. How did anyone survive this? Maybe they didn't. Maybe they became someone different.

Yet here she was—plain old Amanda Ray.

She stopped pacing. Was she still Amanda Ray? She'd vowed to love David, to cherish him, to live as one until death parted them. And death had come. So who was she now?

Amanda went into her bathroom and stared at the reflection in the mirror. The woman looked familiar, as if she had known her intimately a long time ago. Who was she? Wife? Mother? Daughter? Was she still all of those things or none of them?

Her husband had died, been cremated, and what remained of him had been stuffed into a brass box that bore no resemblance to her idea of "husband." Without a husband, could she still consider herself a wife?

She remained a mother, but her daughter no longer needed her and in fact acted as if the she were the mother and Amanda her half-wit daughter.

She had once been a daughter for real, but her parents were dead, dead within a year of each other. When one lost a spouse, the risk of dying from all causes, including self-inflicted wounds, increased by 27%, and that's what happened to her mother.

Amanda leaned forward and peered more closely at her reflection. Was that a death's head she saw beneath her skin? Could that shadow behind her be the grim reaper? She placed her hands on either side of the sink and bowed her head. Did she care if death rode on her shoulders? If death came for her, she wouldn't have the power to resist him. Or her. She didn't have David's strength. But what good had all his strength, all his resistance done? He still fell beneath the reaper's scythe.

"Why did you do this to me, David?" Amanda whispered. "You always stood back so I could go first into the house, into the store, into the car, into the church. Why couldn't you let me go first this time, too?"

But then David would be the one who would have to feel this pain, this horror called grief. Did she want that? Yes!

No. She couldn't bear the thought of David having to shoulder this burden along with all the others he had borne with such determination.

Amanda heard the sound of water dripping into the sink and realized she was crying. She tried to raise a hand to wipe her face, but her arm felt heavy, immovable.

What would David think of all her tears? He believed in keeping one's emotions on an even keel. *"If the pendulum swings too far in one direction, it must swing equally far in the other direction,"* he often counseled, though the idea of an even temperament seemed at odds with his belief in the divinity of happiness.

Would David have been able to keep his emotions in check if

their positions were reversed? *Doesn't matter. He'll never have to feel grief at having lost his life mate.*

Amanda's head jerked up and she stared wide-eyed at her image in the mirror. Who said the dead didn't feel grief? Maybe David missed her as much as she missed him. Maybe he felt as amputated as she did, and as bewildered. And maybe he still loved her as much as she loved him. But how can you love someone who is absent?

Sam was absent, too, and she loved him.

As if the thought of his name conjured him up, her phone pinged with a text from Sam. *Can you meet me online in fifteen minutes?*

She shot back a response. *Yes!*

SAM: I have a few minutes and wanted to talk.
AMANDA: About anything in particular?
SAM: I miss you.
AMANDA: I miss you, too.
SAM: How are you doing?
AMADA: I don't seem to be handling things well. Everything makes me cry. Or scream.
SAM: For what it's worth, I think you're handling things very well. I know how hard it is to deal with David's death. I know how hard it is for you to deal with my lack of time for you.
AMANDA: It is hard. I wish
SAM: What do you wish, love?
AMANDA: I meant to delete that but hit enter instead. I spend too much time wishing for impossible things.
SAM: Nothing is impossible.
AMANDA: That's not true and you know it.
SAM: Oh, you are so contrary.
AMANDA: I am not contrary.
SAM: You always disagree with me.
AMANDA: That doesn't make me contrary. Contrary means

disagreeing for the sake of disagreeing. We just see things differently is all.
SAM: If you were an intentionally convoluted person and someone called you on it, wouldn't you say you weren't contrary?
AMANDA: You're right. An intentionally convoluted person would say they weren't contrary, unless of course it would make them seem doubly convoluted by agreeing that they were contrary. But I wasn't being contrary.
SAM: If you say so.
AMANDA: Why are we arguing? The truth is, all things are not possible. It is not possible for David not to have died because he did. It's not possible for him to come back so I can do those last few months over again, and do them better.
SAM: I didn't mean to bury you in platitudes. I'm sure you get plenty of those. I wish I could help.
AMANDA: You are helping. You let me talk about David and my grief for him. You don't expect me to ignore his place in my life.
SAM: He was your major focus for many years.
AMANDA: Thirty-five years. Grief has really turned me inside out. I don't remember who I was before I met him. I don't remember who I was when I was with him. So who am I?
SAM: A beautiful woman on her way to becoming the magnificent person she was always meant to be.
AMANDA: But who am I meant to be? And who do I be that person for?
SAM: You're meant to be yourself. For yourself. And for the universe.
AMANDA: That's no answer.
SAM: It's the only one I have. I'm not like David. I don't pretend to have all the answers.

Amanda clenched her hands and set her jaw. How dare he talk about David like that! David never pretended to have all the answers. He preached what he believed. Even though she hadn't believed in what he preached—except for his message of happiness, perhaps—she had always loved that he believed. When Amanda had finally gathered to courage to tell David she didn't believe, he'd smiled at her and said, "I have enough belief for both of us." Where had that belief gone now that he was no longer here to act on it?

SAM: Are you still there?
AMANDA: Yes.
SAM: I'm sorry. I didn't mean to disparage David. I know he was a wonderful man—you couldn't have loved him if he wasn't.
AMANDA: Which means you're a wonderful man, too.
SAM: I wouldn't say that, but thank you, love.
AMANDA: I miss him. Until the diagnosis, David was always so…tender. Even if he didn't agree with me about something, he never raised his voice. He just walked away. So I'd get in a huff and walk away, too. I'd think over what he said, and often would come to realize he was right. I'd go looking for him to tell him so, and usually he'd be on his way to tell me I was right.
SAM: I envy him.
AMANDA: Why? He's dead. You have no rival.
SAM: But he had you for all those years. He was with you when you grew from a girl to a woman. He was with you when you found your first gray hair. I can't understand why he didn't love you. You're very loveable.
AMANDA: He did love me. It's just that sex wasn't that important to him. His work was so emotionally taxing that he'd fall asleep early. For several years we had sex once a week, then twice a month, then…I don't know. It was like we forgot to make time for touching, and the years passed. Until I met you, I didn't realize how much I missed sex.
SAM: You *never* missed it?
AMANDA: Well, there was that time shortly after we stopped

having sex that I cried myself to sleep every night. It wasn't the sex I missed but skin against skin. I told you about my skin hunger.

SAM: I'm looking forward to skin time.

AMANDA: Me too. But now I have all these unfulfilled parts of my life with David, and I don't know what to do about them. I'm grieving for him, for the loss of our sex life, for the babies we couldn't have, for the shared future that will never come.

SAM: You'll create a new future.

AMANDA: But it won't be his and my future.

SAM: It might be our future.

AMANDA: How will you explain me to your wife?

SAM: I don't think about that.

AMANDA: Well, I do. Your being married didn't bother me when David was alive, but now I can't stop thinking that I'm the other woman.

SAM: You're the only woman I want to make love to.

AMANDA: We keep coming back to that—making love. It would be divine, wouldn't it? But we don't even have cybersex anymore.

SAM: I figured it was too soon.

AMANDA: Maybe it was.

SAM: At the first opportunity, I plan to make you come with such ecstasy that your brains liquefy and run out of your ears.

AMANDA: Sounds great. The ecstasy, I mean. Not my brains running out of my ears. I need my brain so I can figure out what to do with the rest of my life.

SAM: My wife is getting better, and then my life will be mine again. Maybe someday we can be together. Live together.

AMANDA: I'd like that.

Amanda studied her words and wondered if she really would like to live with Sam. She couldn't see herself washing his underwear, fixing his meals, sharing a checking account, meeting his children. Nor could she see him doing the same for her. But they couldn't spend the rest of their lives in bed, either. Maybe Sam accepted the illusion better than she did. Is that why she'd accepted the strictures of her life with David? Because a meaningful life was more important to her than love's illusions?

SAM: Are you still there, love?
AMANDA: Yes. Thinking.
SAM: About?
AMANDA: Life. Love. Meaning. You.
SAM: What did you figure out?
AMANDA: That I think too much.
SAM: Grief does that—makes you rethink your life, your values. I hope I will still be a part of your life when you get it all figured out.
AMANDA: It might not be up to me. You might break it off.
SAM: No. Never. I love you. I want you in my life however I can.
AMANDA: You mean however you can fit me in.
SAM: I'm sure I can fit in you just fine.
AMANDA: Huh? Oh…But you know what I'm talking about.
SAM: I wish I could stay and make mad passionate love to you, but I have an early class tomorrow. I'll try to call.
AMANDA: That would be nice. I love you.
SAM: Kiss me, love.
AMANDA: Big kisses.
SAM: Tell me you forgive me for abandoning you yet again
AMANDA: I forgive you. Someday you won't abandon me.
SAM: True. One last kiss.
AMANDA: Sweet dreams.
SAM: I love you. Good night.

Amanda reread the transcript of their chat. For all Sam's talk of sex, when it came down to it, he seemed to prefer a good night's sleep, just like David. Maybe the problem was with her. After a while, she hadn't missed sex with David, and now she didn't miss cybersex with Sam. As exhilarating as it had been to explore her erotic side, cybersex—which was nothing more than sex talk, after all—had made her uncomfortable. And uncomfortably aroused.

Where had that arousal gone? Amanda touched herself and felt nothing. Sometimes she had felt that Sam was leading her on, but what if she'd inadvertently been the one teasing him, promising sexual delights she could never perform? What if sex wasn't like riding a bicycle, and she couldn't do it? Heck, maybe she couldn't even ride a bicycle anymore.

I hate this, David. Why didn't you love me enough to put me first? And why doesn't Sam love me enough to put me first?

If she were smart, she'd end it with Sam

But then her future would be even bleaker.

Why did life have to be so complicated?

Amanda opened the Spider Solitaire game on her computer and played the same hand over and over again until she finally the won the game, but the successful conclusion brought her no satisfaction.

She dragged herself to bed, and she must have slept through the night because the ringing phone woke her in the bright light of morning.

"Hi, love." Sam's voice, rich and mellifluous, like melted chocolate.

"Sam! It's so good to hear from you."

"Are you doing okay?"

"Doing good so far today. I'm talking to you!"

"I wish I could be with you."

"Me too."

"We need to work something out. Find a way to meet."

Her heart swelled with feelings that wanted to spill over, and her mind filled with all she wanted to say, but she heard voices in the background and felt his distraction, so she answered simply, "I'd like that."

"We'll talk. I have to go now, class is ready to start, but I wanted to hear your voice. I love you, darling."

"I love—" The phone went dead before she could finish the sentence.

Amanda dropped the receiver into the cradle, tears running down her face. What was the point of love if it brought such sorrow?

"I hate this, David." Her shoulders heaved, and the spoken words disintegrated into sobs. *Two great loves in my life and here I am...alone. Is this the way it's always going to be? Waiting for my real life to begin?*

But she'd had a life, a real life. It didn't matter that the dreams she'd followed had been David's instead of her own. Nothing—except her love for David—had ever consumed her the way David's ministry, especially his need to save the children, had consumed him.

A thought struck Amanda, stealing her breath. Did this need to save the children have something to do with the other Thalia? He claimed to be an only child, so the girl could be a cousin. Or a sister—a dead sister.

David's mother would know. Crap. She'd forgotten about David's mother, and no wonder—she'd only met her once, and the woman had been creepy beyond words. Cruella de Ville without the dogs. Still, the woman should be told that her son had died.

Amanda turned on David's computer. She'd shut it down after he died, thinking the machine had no reason to go on living if it's controller was gone, and it took a few minutes to boot up.

She opened his mail folder, clicked on "contacts," and searched for Barbara Ray. An address in Colorado Springs. No phone number.

How long would it take to drive to Colorado Springs from

Denver? A couple of hours? Considering traffic, it would be closer to three hours, and full dark would arrive before she got there. Amanda felt relieved at finding an excuse to put off her double mission—telling David's mother about his death and asking about Thalia—because it seemed as if she were betraying her husband. *But David is not here to betray any more. Besides, he never told me not to talk to his mother.*

Amanda clicked on David's calendar, wanting to feel a connection to his days, even if those days had passed without him, and the date startled her. April second. Twenty-six days since David died. Five more days until the first month anniversary.

Through tear-blurred eyes, Amanda read the note David had appended for the day: *TAXES!* Sheesh. She'd forgotten about income tax. David always prepared the tax forms himself, and she hadn't a clue what to do. He'd tried to tell her what needed to be done several months ago before the cancer and the morphine clouded his brain, but she'd closed her ears, thinking he was making too much of a small thing and that he'd be around to do the taxes as always.

Amanda sighed. More denial. How could she not have clung to his every word? How could she have come to take his dying for granted, as if that's the way their life would always be, he dying, she struggling to live? Looking back, the year of his dying seemed to have evaporated within minutes, but at the time it had seemed endless. And now her empty future stretched in front of her just as endlessly.

I'm spending too much time alone. Too introspective. I have to do something.

Amanda searched through David's folders looking for "taxes." She found and opened the file. A sticker note said, *"Amanda, I finished the taxes and filed them electronically, so that's one thing you won't have to deal with when I'm gone."*

Unchecked, the tears fell from Amanda's eyes and spattered

on the keyboard. Even as David grappled with death, he'd thought of her. She closed the tax file and glanced through his other folders. Notes for a book he wanted to write about abused children. Sermons. Church Newsletters. Fund Raisers. Personal Letters.

Amanda opened the letters folder. There was a single document. A letter to her. Her heart beat faster. What did David have to say to her that he couldn't have said in person? With shaking fingers, she clicked the mouse to open the document. According to the date, he'd finished writing it a month before he died.

Dear Amanda,

There is much I want to say to you, and time is running out. I have so few moments of lucidity now, between the tumors in my brain and the drugs. I say no to the drugs too often. I accept the pain as my punishment for all the wrong I have done, but the pain is getting surreal and unbearable.

I hope I can finish this letter before I lose the ability to think. I am writing it in bits and pieces, deleting more than I keep because I don't want you to remember what I was like at the end.

We've spent a lifetime together, and you deserve to know the truth of me. I should have told you sooner, but I am a coward. I've always been a coward, and that cowardice cost the life of someone I loved dearly. My naiveté, my youthful high spirits died with her, and you got cheated out of knowing that man, that boy. I wrote it all out—what happened when I was young, and how I found the courage to atone as an adult. I'm not sorry for what I did, and since contrition comes before God's forgiveness, we might not meet in heaven. I could be spending eternity in hell, though nothing could be worse than the hell of my own making.

The story is in the computer, in a file called "Journal." I

password protected it because I don't want you to open it accidentally while I am alive. I don't have the courage to face you once you know the truth.

I'll leave you the password. It's something simple, something I thought I'd never forget, though for some reason it's slipped my mind right now.

I don't mind dying. I don't mind being ill, but I hate that I can't hold anything in my head. I hate that I can't remember the good times, and we did have good times, didn't we? We had a good life together, didn't we?

I'll be gone soon.

I have never told you how much you meant to me, how much I care for you, and I see now how wrong that was. You were so beautiful when we met, so generous and spontaneous. You're still beautiful, of course, but with the beauty of maturity and wisdom and strength. I've never met anyone with such generosity of spirit. The way you accepted my life and embraced my dreams was way beyond your call of duty as my wife. But living with me all these years cost you your spontaneity, your spirit of adventure, and for that, I'm sorry.

You tried to make me happy, and I know it pained you that you couldn't, but it wasn't your fault. I'm not a happy man. I would have liked to be happy, but I didn't know how. I believe happiness is a gift God wants to give us if we don't let our own agendas get in the way. You were my gift, and I squandered it on my agenda. I squandered you. I squandered your dreams.

You always said you had no dreams so you were pleased to share mine, and I took that as a sign of your love, but I gave no sign in return. I should have encouraged you to look for dreams, to look for your own gifts, but I was selfish. I loved having you work with me. I love you. I always have. I'm sorry I told you that so seldom.

There's an old adage when a door closes a window opens, but I don't believe that's true, and especially I don't believe it's true for you. When this door closes—the door to our shared life—the whole world will open to you. You may not see it at first—your grief will be overwhelming. I wish I could take that pain with me when I go and leave you nothing but the joy of that open world, but grief is my final gift to you. Embrace it, and it will take you where you need to go.

I love you, sweetheart.

Amanda reread the last line. *I love you, sweetheart.* David had never called her anything but "Amanda." How odd that when her husband finally used an endearment, he adopted the very one Sam always used. Or rather the one that Sam had started out using. Though she loved the endearment, Sam never called her sweetheart anymore. When had he stopped?

A month before David died.

She tried to hold back her grief so she could ponder the bizarre coincidence, but all thoughts of Sam washed away in a flood of tears. She could think only of David, of the man he wanted to be and the man he became instead.

When the tears finally stopped, Amanda read the letter again, and yet again. The third time she read it, a word caught her attention. *Journal.* When had he started keeping a journal?

Amanda looked through his folders and found the file. She tried to open the journal, but found it password-protected as he'd said it would be. She typed in "ThaliaRay," the password he used for his email, but the file didn't open. She tried Thalia's birthday, date of graduation, phone number. None of them opened the file. She tried everything else she could think of—their anniversary, her name and important dates, David's important dates. She reversed all the names and dates and tried again. The file remained closed.

Fear washed over her. What did David have to say that was so terrible he needed to hide it from her? "Oh, David," she whispered. "What happened to us?"

Chapter 14

THE HOUSE WHERE David grew up looked smaller and dingier than when Amanda had last seen it, more than three decades ago. The neighborhood had changed. Most of the small bungalows had been torn down and replaced with enormous houses that were too large for the small lots, leaving only a few feet between abodes.

Barbara Ray's house sat like a toad among the newer houses, the peeling paint resembling warts.

Amanda pulled up to the curb, wondering why the old woman didn't sell. Maybe the house contained precious memories. But Barbara hadn't seemed like a sentimental woman, and anyway, Amanda wasn't there to speculate on why Mrs. Ray remained incarcerated in this rotting residence.

The woman who answered the door wasn't the unkempt slattern Amanda had met, but an elegant woman with pure white hair carefully coiffed and a dark blue rayon dress draped over her fragile-looking figure.

Amanda was all set to apologize for disturbing the stranger and then scuttling away, when the woman spoke.

"Waddaya want?"

The grating voice, her mother-in-law's voice, hadn't changed at all.

"I'm Amanda Ray. David's wife."

"So he's finally dead, is he?"

Amanda recoiled as if she'd been slapped.

The woman's laugh sounded like the cackle of a cartoon witch. "It doesn't take a rocket scientist to figure that out. Why else would you come except to gloat?"

"Gloat?" The word was so far from what Amanda felt that for a second she couldn't grasp the meaning.

"You proved me wrong," Mrs. Ray said. "I told you when you married my son that he'd break your heart. David has no love in him."

No love? Amanda stared at the woman, unable to find a response. David may not have been able to express his love aloud, but he had more love in him that anyone else she'd ever met.

"You stuck with him, I'll give you that," Mrs. Ray opened the door. It screeched on rusty hinges, making Amanda wince. She hesitated, then stepped inside.

The heavy drapes had been pulled over the windows, shutting out all but a thin stream of light where they didn't quite close. The house smelled of garbage, unwashed toilets, and Bengay.

Mrs. Ray moved through the murky light to a dark hulk the size of a couch, but Amanda remained still, waiting for her eyes to adjust.

When the furniture took shape, Amanda picked her way through stacks of glossy magazines with long-dead celebrities on the covers. She perched on the edge of a chair with tufts of stuffing poking out of the worn upholstery.

Mrs. Ray waved a delicate, long-boned hand, the gesture almost regal as it swept through the air to indicate the shabby furniture. "If I had known you were coming—" She laughed her Cruella de Ville laugh and finished, "I wouldn't have done anything different."

Amanda didn't respond. Her years of training as a preacher's wife in how to put others at ease, how to find the perfect comment for every situation, failed her.

"Well?" Mrs. Ray demanded. "What do you have to say for yourself? You must have come for some reason. To tell me my no-good son died in terrible agony, I hope." She licked her lips as if savoring the thought of his pain like a fine wine.

Finally, Amanda's training kicked in. She straightened her spine and curved her lips into the sweetest smile she could summon. "David went quickly and easily." And that was no lie. The end, the very end, had come quickly and easily. No way would she tell this harridan about the long months of agony David had endured.

"I'm sorry to hear that. I hope he rots in hell for what he did."

"What did he do?"

"Didn't he tell you?" The faded blue eyes glittered.

"He told me everything," Amanda said.

"Did he tell you he killed his fifteen-year-old sister?"

"Thalia?"

A disappointed look crossed the woman's face. "So he did tell you."

Amanda's thoughts skittered in a thousand directions, but one shred of comprehension remained. No way had David, her David, been a killer.

"I gave that kid everything. Spoiled him rotten. But when I asked him to do one simple thing, did he do it? Noooo."

"He didn't think it was simple," Amanda said, though she hadn't a clue what they were talking about.

"He deserved to be killed for what he did to my baby."

"David?"

"No, no. His father." The eyes narrowed into slits. "You're lying to me. He never told you any of this."

The truth mushroomed in Amanda's mind like a noxious cloud. "Your husband abused Thalia, and you stood by and let it happen." No wonder David had been so obsessed with helping abused children. No wonder his love for his daughter seemed overdone at times. He never had a model to follow for raising a child. But his love for Thalia had been pure and simple. Amanda had never doubted that.

Another revelation crashed over her. David had found it easier to love Thalia than his wife because Thalia hadn't expected anything of him other than to be loved. Amanda, with her hopes of being so close to David that they were as one, would have made her harder to love. But her husband had loved her. She'd staked her life on that belief.

"Is that what David said? That what happened to Thalia was my fault? Then he's a liar as well as a coward. I did what I could. I gave him the gun—"

"*You* gave him the gun?

"Of course. You didn't think he was smart enough to get one for himself, did you?"

The words stung on David's behalf. "He was smart. The smartest man I ever knew."

"It never did me any good. The son of a bitch never pulled the trigger."

"Then how—"

"But he didn't mind leaving the gun for Thalia to find. Oh, no. That he could do."

"And she shot herself."

"Yes." The woman seemed to collapse into herself, like a puffer toad that lost its air. "I never forgave him."

"Your husband?"

"No. David." Anger ballooned in the toad woman again. "After Thalia died, John left me. He *divorced* me."

"And that wasn't a good thing?"

"No, of course not. We're Catholic."

Amanda gaped at her, unable to believe what she had just heard. "So divorce is against your religion, but murder isn't?

"It wasn't murder. More like killing a cockroach. And anyway, it wouldn't have been me who did it. That was David's responsibility."

"But David was just a kid!"

"Sixteen and full grown. If he was old enough to leave the Catholic Church, he was old enough to—"

"Commit murder," Amanda whispered. *Oh, David! Why didn't you ever tell me? How could you have carried this burden with you all those years?* And then she saw the truth: David, like his mother, believed he had killed his sister. Amanda wished she could put her arms around her husband and protect him from all he'd suffered, but he had gone beyond her reach. Beyond his mother's, too. How could he have grown up to be such a good man coming from this bitch?

"What happened to the gun?" Amanda asked, though she'd figured out the answer.

"He kept it. I asked for it back, but he wouldn't give it to me. Maybe he thought I'd kill him with it. And I might have."

"I thought you didn't believe in murder?"

"I don't, but it wouldn't have been murder. It would have been self-defense. He stole everything from me that I ever loved."

Unable to cope with the woman's insanity a moment longer, Amanda stood and headed for the door.

Mrs. Ray followed her, whining plaintively. "Don't go. Stay for tea. You're the only family I have left."

So David had never told his mother about their daughter. Good for him. "I have to get back to Denver before it gets dark."

"Then go on. Go. Be glad you never had kids. Sharper than a serpent's tooth is an ungrateful child."

Amanda climbed into her beige Toyota Corolla and peeled away from the curb, almost running into an oncoming truck in her haste. She took a deep breath and let it out slowly, trying to still her trembling legs. Unable to find the strength to drive, she parked the car a block from the wretched house where David had grown up, and wept for the boy who'd suffered such mental abuse and for the man who'd carried the burden alone.

Chapter 15

THE SUN HAD long set by the time Amanda got back to Denver. She dreaded the thought of going into the dark house, but when she turned down the tree-lined street she saw the parsonage ablaze with lights.

Her heart beat with anticipation. David! He'd come home.

Amanda pulled up to curb and hopped out of the car. The trees swayed in the breeze and painted shadows on the sidewalk. For just a second, she forgot her grief, forgot her ghastly mother-in-law, forgot the conundrum of David's life, and threw her arms wide to embrace the beauty of the night.

She ran up the stairs. The front door burst open, and Thalia came charging out. A man followed her and stood in the doorway. The fellow was as tall as David had been before illness diminished him, as wide in the shoulders. And as old. But he wasn't David.

Grief came crashing down on her again. Why couldn't she get it in her head once and for all that David had died? That she would never see him again in this world? Why did she have to go through this same hideous disappointment over and over again?

Thalia's happy expression seemed to slip, and Amanda held out her arms. "I'm so sorry, Thalia. I'm glad to see you. It's just..."

Thalia moved into her embrace. "I know, Mom," she

whispered. "You hoped to see Dad. I understand."

When Amanda felt Thalia pull away, she immediately dropped her arms, not wanting to seem clingy.

"There's someone I want you to meet." Thalia grabbed the man by the hand, and beamed at her mother. "This is Josh Nolan. My new boyfriend. We met last week at Sandra's party."

Sandra? Amanda scrabbled around in her memory, but the name didn't compute. A few synapses later, Thalia's words hit her. "Your new boyfriend? But he's—" *Old.*

"A wonderful man." Thalia finished.

Amanda couldn't help smiling at her daughter's triumphant expression. Thalia had worn that same look on her eight-year-old face the day she'd brought home a filthy mutt almost as big as she was. Luckily, they'd found the owner a couple of hours later.

"Josh used to be married to Sandra's first cousin's best friend," Thalia continued, "but they've been divorced for three years."

Amanda shook his out-held hand, and her skin crawled. "Pleased to meet you, Josh." She didn't care if he heard the lie in her voice. What was he doing with a woman half his age? And Thalia. Did she really like this guy? She must care for him at least somewhat—it had been years since she'd brought a boyfriend home to meet her parents.

"You have a wonderful daughter." Josh looked away from Amanda, as if he weren't any happier about meeting her than she was at meeting him. He took Thalia's hand, tucked it beneath his arm, and gave it a pat. "You must be very proud of Thalia."

"We are." Hearing her response that automatically included David, Amanda wondered if her daughter was trying to deny her grief by finding a new father figure. She thought Thalia was smarter than that, but grief wasn't about intelligence. It was about emotions, about stress hormones, about brain chemistry. About pain. And Thalia had never been able to tolerate pain of any kind.

Amanda wanted to cry the tears her daughter couldn't seem to manage, but swallowed them instead. She felt as if she'd been losing her daughter, but now it seemed as if Thalia wanted to reconnect. Through Josh.

"Can I offer you something to drink?" Amanda asked. "We have soda, filtered water, ice tea. Or I could make coffee."

Thalia rested her head on Josh's shoulder. "We're going out for dinner, but Josh insisted we stop in and say hello."

"I'm sorry for your loss," Josh said without looking at Amanda. He smiled at Thalia. "You ready to go?"

"Sure. See you, Mom."

Amanda watched them walk down the sidewalk to his BMW convertible, he heavy on his feet, she dancing lightly by his side.

David, you always understood Thalia much better than I ever did. What do I do now?

When no answer came, she trudged into the house and wandered into her husband's bedroom. She sat at his computer and played with passwords. The file remained locked, but opening the document no longer seemed to matter. She'd learned David's story, the story he meant to tell her, and seeing the truth of his childhood in his own words would only make her sadder.

Amanda shut down the computer and went to her bedroom to use her laptop. She checked her email. A message from Sam. Short and unsatisfying. *I'm babysitting my grandkids. Just wanted to tell you I'm thinking of you.*

She sent a return message. *Hope you're having fun. I love you, Sam.*

Should she tell him she missed being called sweetheart? But maybe he didn't consider her his sweetheart anymore.

The ringing phone startled her.

"Isn't it wonderful about Thalia and Josh?" Mary Lynn's voice bubbled with enthusiasm. "Josh seems like a great guy, and rich! He's an executive at IBM. Made use of all the stock options that were offered to him."

"How can you say it's wonderful?" Amanda's tone felt heavy and cumbersome in comparison to Mary Lynn's giddiness. "I just met him."

"I know. Thalia texted me a minute ago and said she'd introduced Josh to you. She seems so happy. I'm glad she's moving on. It does no one any good to mourn."

Amanda struggled to decode her friend's message, none of which made sense. Thalia happy? Moving on? Not good to mourn? Once she would have argued with Mary Lynn, enjoying their volatile discussions, but now she couldn't find a way to explain how wrong Mary Lynn was, and even if she could explain, she didn't have the energy.

"It's too soon to talk about Thalia moving on. She and Josh are brand new."

Mary Lynn laughed. "Three months is plenty of time to discover you're in love."

Amanda's shoulders sagged. "She's known him three months? And she's in love?"

"Oh." A long silence. "I forgot you didn't know."

"Why didn't she tell me? Why did she lie about how long she's known Josh?"

"She thought you'd be mad at her."

"For what?" Amanda wondered if she'd strayed into a weird world where nothing made sense. Maybe her grief had finally pushed her over the edge into madness.

"She couldn't handle seeing her father deteriorate," Mary Lynn said. "So she stayed away."

"I know. I never blamed her for that. Neither did David. He wanted her to remember him the way he was, not as a living skeleton with half his mind gone."

"See? This is why I hardly ever call you and why I try not to mention David. I always make you cry."

Amanda touched her face and felt the wetness on her cheeks.

She'd become so used to her tears, she hadn't realized she'd been crying. "You're not making me cry. And I need to talk about David. He might be gone, but he's still a part of my life."

"Thalia worries about you, darlin'. She says you still cry all the time and it's been a month. Maybe you're not grieving right."

"Not grieving right? What does that mean?"

"It means it's time you moved on. Got back in the dating game. Men love widows because they come without baggage."

"David has *not* been gone a month. It's only been twenty-seven days. That's not too much time to grieve. People used to honor grief. They set aside a year for mourning, but now people expect us to continue on with our lives as if nothing has happened. For thirty-five years, David was in my mind. His well being was as important to me as my own. You don't get over that in a month or a year. Maybe you never do."

"You'll get over it eventually, darlin'. Time heals."

"Time does not heal!" The spurt of anger surprised Amanda, but she could not stop the outburst. "People don't want us to grieve because it makes them uncomfortable, but the truth is, time does not heal. Grief heals. The only way to get to the point where you can find a renewed interest in life is to embrace the pain. If you try not to grieve, you end up concentrating on holding in the grief, like holding in your stomach for the rest of your life. It can be done, but then grief defines you. I want to be able to embrace life, and to do that I need to embrace grief, to find a way to make it part of me."

Mary Lynn laughed. "You make grief sound like a gift."

"It is a gift. My last gift from David. If I accept it, it will take me where I need to go."

"But that doesn't mean Thalia needs to grieve."

"Thalia does need to grieve, and in her own way, she is. She's angry, she's denying what David's death means to her, and she feels guilty for not being there for David at the end. She is also simultaneously clinging to me and pushing me away. She resents me because I am still here and her beloved father isn't. She's also trying to find a way to process David's death. Those are all stages of grief, though truly, there are no stages. It's a never ending spiral of conflicting emotions."

"Are you angry?"

"Not at Thalia. She's a grown woman and has to find her own way, but I am disappointed my daughter felt she had to lie to me about when she met Josh. She said she met him last week."

"She was afraid you'd be mad at her for going to that party and having fun while you took care of David by yourself."

"I'm glad she had fun. Her being miserable wouldn't have helped the situation at all. I worry that Josh is so much older. I'm afraid she's trying to replace David. Does Thalia really love him, or is she clinging to him as a new father figure?"

Mary Lynn chuckled. "I knew those psychology classes you took weren't a good idea. Don't you ever live without trying to analyze everything?"

"Don't you ever analyze anything before trying to live?" The words came out by rote. They'd teased each other this way for as long as they'd known each other, but Amanda didn't feel the affection behind the bickering. She hadn't been angry at Thalia for her defection, but she had been angry at Mary Lynn. Mary Lynn didn't have to confront David's deterioration as Thalia had to, and yet Mary Lynn hadn't been there for her best friend. Amanda had always known Mary Lynn possessed a pathological need for happiness, but she'd never understood that her friend's need would always take precedence over Amanda's. Mary Lynn seemed to think they could pick up where they left off, but their friendship would never be the same because Amanda would never be the same. Would Mary Lynn be able to accept that? Would she even notice a difference?

Amanda listened to Mary Lynn rattle on about whether to stick with Jackson or move on to Willard, the most divine man on Earth.

Without a pause to indicate a change of topic, Mary Lynn said, "I have to go, darlin'. Willard will be here soon. Be glad for Thalia. Josh will be good to her."

Amanda hung up the phone. Even if she couldn't be glad about Josh, she could be glad that Mary Lynn, Thalia's godmother, had been there for Thalia during the months of David's dying, and that meant a lot because she, Thalia's mother, had been concentrating on David. And Sam.

I'm a terrible mother. And a terrible wife. And a terrible lover. And a terrible friend. Can't seem to give anyone what they want.

Amanda gathered the bundle of David's ashes from his side of the bed, cradled him to her aching heart, and wished she were someone else.

Wished she were somewhere else.

But why couldn't she be somewhere else? Why couldn't she go see Sam? She still had much work to do to clear out the house, but taking off for a few days shouldn't hurt.

Amanda set David on the bed, grabbed her cell phone and texted Sam.

Hi, Sam. I need to talk to you. Can you call?

He responded: *Sorry, love, can't call. Will probably be able to meet you online tomorrow night. Will that be okay?*

What time?

Nine o'clock?

See you then.

Amanda scurried to her walk-in closet, opened the door, and took inventory. Most of her clothes were old, frumpy, though once they had been acceptable if not fashionable. David had never imposed a dress code on her, but she had chosen clothes that would not bring her to the attention of gossipy church members.

Except for a dark purple velour warm-up suit, a couple of pairs of slacks and three or four recently purchased tops, none of her clothes were suitable for her new role as no one's wife. Amanda swept the fusty suits and boring dresses into her arms and dropped them on the bedroom floor, then went back to the closet for her church lady hats and uncomfortable mid-heel shoes, and tossed those on the pile, too.

A plastic storage box that had been pushed to the back of the closet floor and hidden by all the garments caught her attention. Amanda had forgotten about the box—presents from David the Christmas before last. His diagnosis a month later had made a mockery of the Yule festivities, and she'd packed the gifts away, unable to bear the sight of them.

Amanda sat on the floor of the closet, pulled the box toward her, and set the lid aside. These were the last gifts David had ever given her and were precious because of that if for no other reason. She lifted out a sheer, ivory silk nightgown with a large open-work butterfly across the bust. She'd worn the gown to bed that Christmas night, thinking it an invitation to resume their sex life, but David hadn't seemed to notice.

Sam would notice. The thought flickering through Amanda's mind brought a smile to her lips. Odd that he'd found the erotic woman inside her when she hadn't been aware that part of her existed any longer. She pictured herself wearing the lovely gown for Sam. Suddenly hot, Amanda fanned herself with her hands, and then, for no reason she could fathom, she was crying.

Amanda clutched her husband's gift to her chest. Once the tears stopped falling, she folded the gown neatly, set it aside, and reached for the rest of the items. A book about awakening one's creative soul. A journal. A large road atlas of the United States. A compass. And finally, a digital camera.

When she'd received these presents, Amanda had been vaguely disappointed, wondering how her husband could have known her so little. But now, looking at the splendid gifts spread out around her, and imagining her new self using them, she wondered if David had known her too well. Had he sensed he was sick? Seen her future without him? Seen what she would become? Somewhere deep in his subconscious, could he have somehow arranged for her and Sam to meet? Or at least known it would happen?

David, I miss you. I hope you're happy and filled with the joy of creation you used to preach about. But couldn't our new lives have waited a little longer to begin? I'm not ready.

Chapter 16

SAM: JUST STOPPED by for a kiss before I go night-night.
AMANDA: Blowing you a kiss.
SAM: Your kisses are so nice, my love
AMANDA: Wishing we were kissing for real.
SAM: :x
AMANDA: What's that?
SAM: Kiss emoticon.
AMANDA: You seem so at ease with that kiss emoticon. Makes me wonder how many people you've sent it too.
SAM: Personally, I'm looking for the erection emoticon.
AMANDA: Sounds like you.
SAM: In answer to your question, I haven't sent any kind of emoticon to anybody, love.
AMANDA: Good. I want you to save your emoticons, especially the erection one, for me.
SAM: Riddle: why is sex like snow fall?
AMANDA: Don't know.
SAM: You never know how many inches you'll get or how long it will last.
AMANDA: Laughing.
SAM: Saving all my inches for you.
AMANDA: Do you still believe the universe brought us together?
SAM: Yes.

AMANDA: It doesn't make sense to me. Why would the universe bring us together only to keep us apart?
SAM: That's a good question to ask the universe.
AMANDA: The universe doesn't speak to me.
SAM: It doesn't talk to me much, either.
AMANDA: You told me once you weren't a religious man, but it seems to me as if you often substitute "the universe" for "God."
SAM: Ever since Vivian got sick, I've had a hard time believing in God. How could a supreme being have created such pain? But I don't believe in the capriciousness of existence, so I have to believe in something. To me, God and the universe are two different things. God is a being apart from us. The universe is a part of us and we are a part of it.
AMANDA: Still seems the same to me. When I was a kid, I was taught that God is everything. So, the universe is God, and God is the universe.
SAM: Perhaps there is more than one universe.
AMANDA: Then it wouldn't be a uni-verse, would it?
SAM: Why are we arguing about this?
AMANDA: We're not arguing. We're discussing.
SAM: Oh, so contrary!
AMANDA: I wish my life were different. I wish I were different. I don't like the way I've ended up. But I haven't "ended up" yet, have I? I haven't even begun. But begun what, I don't know. I have this overwhelming feeling that all my life up to now is prologue.
SAM: How strange; when I saw "ended up" I thought, "she hasn't ended anything yet." We think a lot alike.
AMANDA: You called me contrary. Doesn't that mean we don't think alike?
SAM: See? Contrary!
AMANDA: Even though it feels as if my life is just beginning, I still have all this sorrow. Grief doesn't seem to fit with David's idea that God wants us to be happy.

SAM: Apparently it serves the universe's purpose for us to encounter challenges throughout life that impedes pure happiness.
AMANDA: I've had enough challenges to last me a lifetime, but I haven't even started dealing with the challenges of packing up the things I want to keep, getting rid of the stuff I can't keep, and figuring out how and where to move.
SAM: You could move here.
AMANDA: Wouldn't it be hard for you if I were in the same city as your wife and kids?
SAM: No. You'd brighten the dark winter days.
AMANDA: Assuming you'd have time for me.
SAM: There is that.
AMANDA: What about a trial run?
SAM: You mean you'd come to visit me?
AMANDA: Yes. That's what I wanted to talk to you about. If I came there for a couple of days, is there any chance you could make time for me.
SAM: Spring break is next week.
AMANDA: Is that good or bad?
SAM: Good. I should be able to come up with an excuse to be away from the house for a night or two. How would you get here?
AMANDA: I thought I'd take the train. All that time to sit and watch the world go by without having to think about anything sounds lovely. When should I plan on getting there?
SAM: Monday should be good. Or any day, actually. I will make time for you.
AMANDA: I'll try to be there next Monday. That gives me a few days to get ready. I can hardly wait to see you!
SAM: I can hardly wait to see you, feel you, taste you.
AMANDA: It's like we're on speed-of-light train through the cosmos.
SAM: How difficult it is to believe our love has brought us this

close together.
AMANDA: I wonder when we meet, how long it will be before we're naked.
SAM: Depends on where we are. I imagine us in a little cafe, a quiet place where we can talk. I think we should see how long we can sit across the table from each other just talking, becoming acquainted, without touching or becoming overtly sexual in our conversation. All the while I'll know that you are wearing no underwear. No bra. No panties. Nor will I be wearing my boxers, though surely dark slacks. To hide tumescence, or the wetness of arousal.
AMANDA: Torment! No hugging? I know I'm going to want to hug you immediately to make being with you seem real.
SAM: If we're in a private place, I don't know that I can keep my hands off you although, perhaps I will be unsure; tentative.
AMANDA: I will be unsure, too, but I don't think we'll be able to part once we hug.
SAM: Hugs are reassuring; I'll give you as many as you want.
AMANDA: Lots and lots of hugging.
SAM: I'll wonder if you'll want me in real life the way you do in the virtual world.
AMANDA: Oh, god, Sam. You have no idea how much I want you.
SAM: Actually, I think I do know how much you want me; I'm pretty sure it's mutual.
AMANDA: Do you think we'll have fun together?
SAM: When my life is right, no one is more playful than I am. I think I will be playful when I'm alone with you.
AMANDA: I love that you're playful. I'll try to make sure your life is always right.
SAM: I like you, I love you, I'm crazy about you.
AMANDA: Do you realize that when we meet we will have all the firsts at once?
AMANDA: First look

AMANDA: First touch
AMANDA: First hug
AMANDA: First kiss
AMANDA: First grope
AMANDA: First smile
AMANDA: First…
SAM: Don't stop now.
AMANDA: Well, you get the picture.
SAM: No—first what else?
AMANDA: First unbuttoning.
AMANDA: First meal (actually that should come first since this is still the clean part of the litany.)
AMANDA: First night together.
SAM: Somehow you're not getting the "main attraction" here.
AMANDA: I'm sort of working up to that.
SAM: You've already got me squirming in my chair.
AMANDA: But isn't it strange? Normally lovers do these things one at a time.
SAM: Makes us abnormal, I guess.
AMANDA: I mean, we will do all these things, too, but they will all happen in such a short period of time.
AMANDA: First sleep. Sleep as in sleeping, not sleep as a euphemism for sex, but first sex, too.
SAM: Sleep; I am tired.
AMANDA: I know it's getting late, but I don't want to let you go.
SAM: I hope you know we will talk again; as soon as possible; as intimately as possible.
AMANDA: And maybe, finally, your universe will bring us together for real.
SAM: On that note, my love, I have to go. I'll talk to you soon.
AMANDA: Goodnight, Sam.
SAM: Goodnight, my love.

For three days, Amanda held grief at bay. She went shopping for clothes to take on her trip and only had a meltdown once when a clerk kept pushing her to buy a colorful sheer top to wear over a shell. Amanda couldn't make up her mind—the piece seemed too young for her and the price was more than she wanted to pay for a garment she might never wear—and she ended up running out of the store in tears, leaving her choices piled on the counter.

But mostly, Amanda felt good about moving on, even if that forward movement would come in the shape of a train ride rather than an emotional movement away from grief. At least she'd be doing something.

She especially felt good about finally getting to meet Sam. If decisions about her future would include him, she should know if being with him was feasible.

She kept the good feeling when she woke on March 7th, the one month anniversary of David's death. She prided herself at getting a handle on grief, having learned the best way to deal with the future was coping with each day as it came. She even managed not to get sick to her stomach at the thought of living in that future without David.

And then suddenly, at 1:40 in the afternoon, a grief storm rocked Amanda to the very soul of her being. This wasn't the tsunami/hurricane/tornado of those first days after David died, but it came close. Her lungs stopped working—the smallest breath took almost more effort than she could muster. Her heart felt close to bursting. And the tears didn't cease.

Tempest tossed. That's me. Tempest tossed on a sea of grief. Those were Amanda's last coherent thoughts as she huddled in bed, cradling the bundle containing David's ashes.

She noted, in a wordless place in her mind, the bright sun dimming in the afternoon shadows and finally disappearing altogether. She fell asleep, tears still wet on her cheeks and woke to a new spate of sorrow.

"I thought I was over you, David," Amanda whispered in the

light of a new dawn. "I thought I'd reached some sort of acceptance, and was moving on with my life."

Moving on without David.

The trip to Ohio and meeting Sam—that would be the first migration away from the life she shared with David. Amanda sat up and wrapped her arms around herself, holding the pieces of her shattered soul together. It felt as if David were dying again, and this time she was killing him. Killing their life.

"I can't grieve forever," Amanda murmured. Nor would David want her to. He'd preached his gospel of happiness for so many years, she knew he'd feel terrible to have brought her such sorrow.

"But grief is all I have left of you," Amanda cried.

She'd often heard aged people talking about the past being more real than the present. When she grew very old, would her years with David come alive for her once more? But that was a long way in the future, and David used to say, "Be happy today. The future will take care of itself."

David also said, "Love needs no reason for being," which seemed, in retrospect, as if he'd given his blessing to her relationship with Sam, but might also be her own rationalization for betraying her husband.

Sam seemed to be accepting of her continued grief, but Amanda wondered what he really thought of her pain. Did he think her sorrow for David a sign that she didn't really love Sam? Is that why he'd curtailed his calls and messages?

Didn't Sam know Amanda's grief for David had nothing to do with him? But maybe not. Sam's path had diverged from hers, and he couldn't share her feelings. Vivian lived, remained his wife, needed him.

But I need Sam, too.

Amanda lay down, put her arms behind her head, and tried to remember what Sam's kiss tasted like. Because surely, as quickly and as strongly as they'd connected, they'd met in some remote past.

The phone rang.

Sam!

Amanda sat up and scooted back so she could lean against the pillows. “I was just thinking about you.” Despite the tears drying on her cheeks, she could hear a lilt of happiness in her voice. No answering feeling of happiness drifted through the telephone line. “What’s wrong?” she asked.

“I have to cancel. I’m sorry.”

Dread clutched at Amanda’s chest. “You don’t want to meet me?”

“More than anything, love. I thought I’d have time for you over spring break, but my wife’s relatives are flying in. The whole passel of them. They need me to play chauffer.”

“Maybe I could come anyway, and you stop by for a few minutes when you get a chance?”

“It would only be for a minute or two now and then. They’ve got my days planned out for me.”

“I understand,” Amanda mumbled, but she didn’t. Not really. This visit meant so much to her that she’d presumed Sam felt the same way.

“There will come a time for us, my love.”

“When?”

“Maybe you could move here?” This was said in such a tentative voice that Amanda felt Sam was as unsure of her as she sometimes was of him, but why would he feel unsure of her? Sam was the one breaking their date.

“I have considered moving there. This trip was supposed to be a trial run, but if you can’t find time for me now, what makes you think you’d find time for me later? I don’t want to be one of those women always waiting and waiting for the guy to show up, and when he does, it’s slam, bam, thank you ma’am. I’m afraid you’d break my heart.”

“I’d move there to be with you, but everything is here. My

job. Vivian. My kids. My grandkids. My parents."

"Not everything is there. I'm not."

"But you could be here. What would you be leaving?"

My life with David. My memories. The connection to my past. Denver. Unable to express what she felt, Amanda sighed and said, "Thalia, but she doesn't need me anymore."

"If you were here, I could stop by whenever I got a few minutes. It would be heaven to have you so close."

It didn't sound like heaven to her. To disrupt her life for the promise of sporadic moments? To be the other woman? To always be alone on holidays? To be afraid of arguing or dressing comfortably lest he punish her by staying away?

But where else could she go?

"David would want you to come," Sam said.

Amanda made a small huffing noise. It had been so long since anything had amused her, at first she didn't recognize the sound as laughter. "David wants me to move to Ohio? You know this…how?"

"We've talked before about his worrying about you and subconsciously bringing us together so you wouldn't be alone. I think he knew I'd love you as much as he did, and would treasure you."

But not enough to leave your wife for me. Amanda tamped down the thought. She couldn't live with herself if Sam left his sick wife to be with her.

"You could be right," Amanda said. "David had a strong sense of responsibility and wouldn't want to leave any unfinished business behind. And my future is certainly unfinished."

"I'd like to finish your business."

Amanda laughed, and this time she had no trouble recognizing the sound for what it was—delight. "I don't see how you can turn any comment into a lascivious remark."

"It's a talent. Just one of several I hope to show you soon."

"Oh, Sam, it's so hard waiting for you."

"Hard is right." Sam groaned. "You should see me right now. Good thing I have my door locked."

"It's funny. I so do not see myself as the sort of woman who can get a man hard just by talking."

"You are. And you do."

During their chats before David's death, such talk had aroused Amanda so much she could feel her whole body pulsing in response, but now she didn't even feel a frisson of excitement. Panic swept through her. What if she were too old, too dried up? She couldn't even remember the last time she and David made love.

"What if I disappoint you?" Amanda asked.

"You could never disappoint me, my love. Just having you in my arms would be enough. After that, whatever happens will happen. But I know it will be beautiful."

"You always say the nicest things."

"You deserve to be showered with wonderful words. You don't know how special you are, do you? I look forward to showing you how you look through the eyes of my love."

A small thrill fluttered in Amanda's lower abdomen. Maybe she wasn't dried up after all. "It seems weird to be in love with a married man. Makes me wonder if you really love me."

There was a long silence. Had she said the wrong thing? But then Amanda heard Sam blow out a breath.

"I do love you, Amanda. We used to talk about what we would do when we are both alone, but we're not both alone. I still have obligations. Vivian and I have a past but there's not much love or tenderness between us. Just a well rehearsed cordiality. When she got the diagnosis and I moved back into our house, I promised I wouldn't leave her. She thinks that means I will stay with her even if she gets well."

"Will you?"

"I'm waiting to see what happens. We go to the doctor in a couple of days and I should know more."

"I don't know where all this leaves me."

"It's like that long poem Evangeline. Do you remember?"

"Two people are swept apart by life and find each other on his deathbed?"

"Something like that. It was a story of Canadian Arcadians who were in love but were torn apart on their wedding day when the British expelled the French-speaking inhabitants of Nova Scotia. The would-be lovers followed each other, trying to find each other for decades. Finally, just as Gabriel was dying, Evangeline found him. I hope it doesn't take us that long,"

"So that's my fate? Living alone until the end when you die in my arms?" Amanda tried to inject a teasing tone into the question but managed only to sound plaintive.

"Of course, in the 19th century when the poem was written," Sam said, "Longfellow had to leave out the great sex Evangeline and Gabriel had at the end."

"Just one night of great sex? That's all I get?"

Sam let a couple of beats go by. "We'd have more time if you lived nearby. I hope you will think about moving here."

Could I move there? Could I handle living like Mary Lynn? "I have to be out of here in less than three weeks. Maybe I'll take a trip out to Ohio. If I think I can be in the same city with your wife without my heart breaking, I'll look for an apartment near the campus."

"Amanda, darling!" The joy in Sam's voice was unmistakable. "I teach a couple of adult creative writing classes. You could take the classes. Get started writing."

Hope made Amanda's heart glow. "I don't know if I want to write, or if I can. I don't seem to be able to focus on anything anymore. But it would be nice to be with you."

"We could have lots and lots of student teacher conferences." Sam's voice grew husky. "Of course we'd have to spend a fair amount of time together going back and forth about the ins and outs of writing. As I see it, we should withhold nothing in our exchanges, making certain we deal with the naked truth. I'm not talking about merely surface issues—though those can be sensitive and require time and attention, but I mean we need to get to the depth of things and linger there, plumbing those productive recesses for what might spring forth."

Amanda laughed, surprised by how easily the sound rose in her throat. "Being your student sounds…fulfilling, but don't you think we have enough relationships going on between us? Friend, confidant—"

"Lover."

"Are we lovers? Don't we have to actually make love to be lovers?"

"We love each other. That makes us lovers."

"I wish you'd been around when I was in high school—"

"Me, too. I'd have loved to see you in your school uniform. You still have it, don't you?"

Amanda laughed at his suggestive tone. "No. I could hardly wait to throw the damn thing away."

"I interrupted you. You were saying?"

"Back in high school, I got in an argument with my mother. I wanted to see a movie. Can't remember what it was. Something about a flapper, I think. The blurb mentioned the flapper and her lover, which set my mother off on a rampage about sex in the movies. I asked why she thought there would be sex in the movie if she'd never seen it. She gave me a disbelieving look and said, 'She has a lover.' I said, 'That doesn't mean they're having sex. It only means they're in love.' Her response? 'I can't believe how naïve you are.' So bizarre. She's the one who made sure I knew nothing about sex or love or life, yet she hated my naïveté. I remember once—"

"I really am sorry, love. I could listen to you talk for hours, but I have to go now. I'm late for class. It was wonderful to hear your voice. I love you, darling."

And then he was gone.

Amanda's eyes burned. If she moved to Ohio, she'd have to get used to Sam leaving her in tears. She scrubbed her eyes with her fists. Funny, but until David's diagnosis, she hadn't cried since her last miscarriage. Now all she did was weep, and she was sick of it.

She forced herself to get out of bed and take a shower. Afterward, she felt cleansed inside and outside, so perhaps the tears were doing what they were supposed to do—relieving stress.

She thought for sure she'd shed her last tear and congratulated herself on making it through the trauma of grief. Still, she made a point to stay away from any place in the house that might evoke memories of David's death. She ate yogurt with apricot preserves and sunflower seeds for breakfast and French bread with butter and a few cubes of cheese for lunch, and didn't even feel nauseous. She spent the afternoon going through her things, discarding dingy underwear and socks that needed darning.

In the late afternoon, Amanda cleaned the drawer from her bedside table, then moved to the table on David's side of the bed. There weren't many things in the drawer: two or three pennies, a neatly folded handkerchief, a pad of paper, a pen, and a used envelope. She tossed the envelope in the wastebasket. Noticing a message written on the back of the envelope in David's handwriting, she scooped it out of the trash. A dentist appointment from a year ago. Her dentist appointment. Apparently, David had wanted to make sure he wouldn't forget to go with her, and tears sprang to her eyes.

A month before David's diagnosis, Amanda developed a gum infection that ate away part of her jawbone. Apparently, one of her forty-year old fillings had cracked the tooth. The dentist had described it as years and years of an anvil banging away at the filling, pushing it further and further into the tooth until the tooth finally cracked under the pressure. Because of the bone loss, the dentist said the tooth couldn't be repaired and it had to come out.

David commiserated with Amanda, agreeing there should be a better way of dealing with the cracked tooth than the medieval torture of yanking it out. He didn't argue with her decision to put off the extraction.

Amanda felt the tooth with her tongue, felt the cracked part wiggle. She'd kept the tooth, but David had been yanked from her life. What sort of bargain was that?

"You can have the damn tooth," Amanda screamed. "Just give David back to me."

She wiped her eyes and gently set the envelope in her box of memorabilia. Her stomach heaved. She ran to the bathroom and lost her lunch, then went to bed and huddled under the covers, shivering.

In the early morning hours, Amanda finally fell asleep.

She dreamed.

She dreamed of her grief—how lost she felt, how much she missed David, how agonizing the pain of separation—then she awoke. David lay in bed beside her. He smiled at her and joy erupted inside of her. David looked so strong, healthy, happy. She scooted over, snuggled against him, and let all the stress of grief seep from her body.

"I thought you died," Amanda said.

"I'm still here."

Amanda drifted with the joy of being with him. Gradually, she awoke for real, still feeling the wonder of having David with her. "I had the strangest dream, David," she murmured. She listened for his response, but heard nothing, not even the sound of his breathing.

The memory hit her with the power of a knockout punch. David was dead.

She sat up, gasping for breath, her heart hammering. She wanted to cry scream, do anything to relieve the horror, but the shock of losing him—yet again—paralyzed her.

When Amanda finally caught her breath, when the tears finally came to wash away the stress of her grief, she sat up and gathered the bundle with David's ashes. Hugging him, she rocked herself. And wept.

Chapter 17

TWO DAYS LATER, on the thirty-fourth day of David's death Amanda received an email from Sam.

Vivian is in remission. The doctors have been doing tests all week AND *the results are good. They say she won't officially be in remission until she's lived five cancer-free years so she has to be careful, but they all agree the cancer is gone. They have no explanation as to why she got well, though they are taking credit for it, of course. Vivian believes God punished her with cancer for falling in love with another man, and since she didn't divorce me, He forgave her and made her well. My life with her is bleak, but I can't leave her yet. She's so fragile, both emotionally and physically. Although she's cancer free, she's dealing with all the effects of the chemo and radiation. But her being better doesn't change anything between you and me. Everything is the same. You are still the love of my life. I still want to make love to you at the first opportunity. I still want to find a future for us.*

Amanda stared at the tear-blurred screen of her phone, wondering what David would think of all this. It wasn't fair that David died and Vivian got well. Not that she begrudged the woman her life, but dammit. Why couldn't David have gotten well, too?

Becoming aware of tears splashing on the keyboard, she sent a quick message—*Can everything be the same?*—and dragged herself upright. She trudged around the house, remembering pacing with David, hand in hand, for hours at a time.

And now she paced alone.

"David!" she cried. "Where are you? Can you hear me? Why don't you answer me? I need you!"

She stopped. Listened. Not hearing a response, she ran to her bedroom, threw herself across the bed, and wept until her tears soaked the frilly decorative pillow.

When the tears gave way to sobs then whimpers and finally to barely audible breaths, Amanda sat up and glared at the pillow. What a silly thing that had been, redoing their bedroom when David had decided he needed his own room. *"I don't want to disturb you,"* he'd said, and no amount of pleading had changed his mind. In rebellion, she'd turned their bedroom into a young girl's dream—white eyelet, ruffled curtains, heaps of pillows.

David had smiled benignly at her, and nodded in approval. Shortly afterward, she had met Sam online. Could their chaste affair have simply been more rebellion? Well, not so chaste. They had indulged in a few steamy chats that had aroused her painfully without orgasmic release. If David had found out, would he have given her that same indulgent smile?

"I hate this," Amanda screamed. "I hate it, hate it, hate it."

She pulled the pillow to her belly, and rocked.

I hate myself.

Amanda went from eating nothing but yogurt to eating cookies, candy, cake, crackers, chips—anything she could grab and stuff in her mouth without cooking or having to eat at the table. Sitting at the table for a meal felt lonely, standing at the sink or leaning against a counter too pathetic.

She solved the matter by reading in bed, bags of food spread around her like a modern version of a Roman feast. She dragged out all the books she'd bought over the past few months but never had time to read—thrillers, historical novels, literary tomes, and chick lit—devouring the books as she devoured her snacks. And didn't savor any of it.

She felt bloated, knew she should take better care of herself, but couldn't convince herself that it mattered. David had lived on fruits and vegetables, poultry and fish, nuts and seeds. He'd taken handfuls of supplements every day, washing them down with a protein drink.

"You'll live forever," Amanda teased him.

"That's the plan," David responded.

"What does one do with eternity?" she asked, being that rare creature—a preacher's wife who didn't believe in life after death. "You'll be fine if you spend eternity on earth, but what if you go to the next world? You will have no brain to think, no eyes to see, no hands to write, no ears to listen to music."

"No abused children to suffer over," David said softly. "No tears. No church politics. No pain."

"Still, eternity is a long time to do nothing," Amanda insisted. By then, they'd been together long enough to know that neither would change the other's mind, but it had become a running commentary to their lives, the sort of mindless talks with which one fills idle moments.

Amanda wished she would see David again, wished he waited for her in the brightness of an afterlife, but even to comfort herself, she could not believe.

And so she ate.

Thalia didn't stop by and Sam didn't contact her, so as the week passed, one lonely day after the other, Amanda sank deeper into her slothfulness.

Finally, needing to feel some sort of connection with her old world, to remember that she existed beyond her grief, Amanda went online and visited the support group for spouses of cancer patients. She didn't recognize any of the people, and the current discussion seemed unbearably sad and naïve. Those poor folks thought they were hurting now, but they didn't have a clue about the world of pain that awaited them on the other side of their spouse's death. Should she say something? Probably not. Amanda remembered herself in that situation, when she could not imagine anything worse than taking care of a dying mate. But that had been a long time ago and in another world, or so it seemed.

David's death forty-two days ago had drawn a black line ending their shared life. Amanda could see back over the line, could remember everything they'd done together, but when she looked forward, there was nothing. It was as if all hopes, all dreams, all plans, everything she had looked forward to remained on the other side of the line with David. It often felt as if she had stepped into an alternate universe, and maybe she had. Across that black line, David still lived, might even be healthy and strong. But as much as she yearned to be on his side of the line, she could only go forward from where she stood. As she journeyed further into the world in which she had been newly born, the black line would become indistinct, and the future would begin to take form again with new hopes, new dreams, new loves, new lifestyle.

Until then, all Amanda had was the pain of both David's death and her rebirth. Even thoughts of Sam, which had once brought comfort, now only brought angst. It had been nine days since Sam called. Did he even think of her? Did he really love her, or had he merely been playing games with her?

In the support group, they had been warned to be on the lookout for manipulators, those who preyed upon people at a low point in their lives. According to the moderator, a classic predator showers his victim with the attention, empathy, compliments she craves, and then, when the victim becomes used to the exhilaration of it all, the predator slowly draws away, leaving the victim confused and lonely, wondering what she had done to deserve such disregard. The predator returns, and when the prey does something the predator wants, she's rewarded with attention. She becomes more attuned to his wants, and so she gets further and further away from herself, more deeply in his clutches.

Amanda hated thinking of Sam in such a way, and yet he had showered her with attention, and he had pulled back. She didn't think he was being manipulative, and she didn't think of herself as a victim, but how could she be sure?

Unlike a manipulator, Sam did not make her feel bad about grieving, did not make her second guess her own emotional reactions. He didn't need to. Amanda second guessed herself. Maybe Mary Lynn was right, and Amanda was doing grief wrong, though intuition told her she needed to feel the emotions as they came so eventually she could be whole again.

Did others feel the way she did?

Amanda found a widows and widowers support group online. She scrolled through a few entries.

SAD SARA: My husband got in an accident while he was talking to me on his cell phone. I could hear the crash, hear him scream. Then nothing. I can't stop crying. Can't sleep. It's like I'm in a bubble where there is only me and the sound of his crash. Nothing else registers. I worry about what all this grief will do to our unborn child. Will she be haunted by that sound? Do my tears make her sad? Does she know I forget about her? Forget to eat? I want to be a good mother, but all I can think of is that her father is dead.

princess pea: my bf killed herself…we told each other everything, but i didn't know she was suicidal…i can't stop crying…it hurts so bad

Jack360: My wife died three weeks ago, and I met a woman at our hospice grief group. I'm ready to start over, but my kids are mad at me. They say it's too soon, but I don't see the point in mourning for my wife. She's dead. Life goes on.

MG: My lover died in my arms. He had an orgasm and then crashed down on top of me. Dead. He used to joke about wanting to go that way, but it sure wasn't fun for me. Good thing the hotel room was in his name. I finally got him off me, and I left. I miss him. I am so miserable, and I have to hide it. His wife doesn't seem sad at all.

Most of the entries were more conventional. The spouse died suddenly of a heart attack or slowly after a long illness. It didn't seem to matter how the loved one died—all the survivors were in shock, bewildered, lost. And all seemed to have one thing in common—a great yearning to see the deceased one more time.

Just once more, David, please? One more smile?

The memory of David's last smile had faded. If he came back and smiled at her once more, that memory would fade, too, and she would yearn for another smile. Did the yearning ever end?

"Mom? Where are you?"

Amanda hastily wiped her eyes and scrambled to her feet. Not wanting Thalia to see her in her nightgown, she looked wildly around for something to put on. She caught a glimpse of herself in the mirror and realized she still wore yesterday's clothes, a blue and red long-sleeved cotton knit top and soft navy blue slacks only slightly wrinkled from having been slept in.

Amanda grabbed a brush and ran it through her graying curls, then opened her bedroom door. "In my room." Her voice sounded hoarse, so she feigned a cough, hoping her daughter wouldn't detect the ravages of grief.

"You've been crying again," Thalia said.

Without even looking at her, Amanda knew that a line of disapproval had appeared between her daughter's brows.

Amanda hunched her shoulders. "No, I haven't. I'm getting a cold, is all."

Her daughter gave an old-ladyish tsk-tsk. "And you're letting yourself go. That's what happens when I don't come by every day to check on you."

"What does it matter to you if I'm crying? Is that why you came today? To harass me about grieving?"

"No. I came for my trekking poles. Dad borrowed them from me."

"When?"

Thalia made eye contact, then turned her face away. "About two months ago. He said he wanted to try walking with them. He wanted to get away from you."

Amanda studied her daughter. Thalia was lying, but Amanda couldn't tell which of those brief sentences contained the lie. Probably the last one. David was dead, and still his daughter seemed to be indulging in some sort of ridiculous rivalry for his affection.

"If I find your poles, I'll save them for you."

Thalia heaved a sigh. "I don't know why you aren't getting ready for your move. You haven't packed much of anything. But I understand. You're in denial."

Amanda gritted her teeth. Thalia prided herself on her therapeutic skills, and rightly so. She was a well-respected pet therapist, but she didn't have a clue how to deal with a grieving human, and especially not a widow. How could a woman who'd never had a relationship longer than three months understand this feeling of being split apart, of straddling the line between this world and the abyss?

"Do you have boxes?" Thalia asked.

"Boxes?"

"You know—boxes for packing up stuff. I want Dad's books."

"Don't you mean, 'May I have Dad's books?'"

Thalia rolled her eyes. "I'm not a child, mom."

"Whatever." Amanda turned away from her. "Take what you want."

"I want the books and the computer."

The computer? Oh, no! The journal. "You can have the computer, but not now."

"Why not? You don't ever use it."

Amanda tried to think of a lie, but as always, settled for a half-truth. "Our tax information is in there."

"Oh. Okay. Do you need help with your taxes?"

"No. I'll be fine. Do you want any of the kitchenware? I'm thinking of getting rid of everything, just keeping what will fit in my car." *Where did that idea come from? But it sounds heavenly. No storage unit. No responsibilities.*

"What? You can't!" Thalia's voice rose in panic.

Amanda slanted a curious look at her daughter. "Why can't I?"

Tight lines formed around Thalia's mouth, and for a second, she looked like Barbara Ray, her grandmother. "Well…because…you're my mother."

And Amanda would be dismantling the home where Thalia grew up and replacing it with…nothing. If Amanda, who always tried to understand her own feelings, was having such a hard time figuring out who she was in the midst of the new chaos of her life, how much harder it must be for her daughter, who never seemed to have an ounce of self-awareness.

"I'll always be your mother. It doesn't matter where I am."

"But mothers don't just take off…like…like hippies."

Amanda sat on the edge of the bed, and patted the mattress beside her. "Okay, let's figure this out."

Gingerly, Thalia sat next to her mother. "All right."

"Tell me what you want me to do."

Unexpectedly, Thalia laughed. "Stay here with Dad, of course."

Amanda curled her hands into fists and tried to will away the tears that threatened to fall. "My first choice, too, honey. But it's not an option."

"You could come stay with me."

"It's a one bedroom condo."

"Josh and I are talking about selling my condo and his house and getting a new place after we're married. You could live with us."

"Oh, honey. Marriage. Such a big step."

Thalia smiled. "I know. I told Josh I want to wait a bit and not rush into things, but we can get married now if necessary."

"You're doing the right thing by taking it easy. I don't want you to rush on my account. And anyway…"

"Yeah, Mom?"

Amanda savored the unexpected touch of tenderness she heard in daughter's voice. "You won't want me around to cramp your new love, and I don't want to be the old lady in the backseat."

"What does that mean?" Thalia asked crossly.

So much for the tenderness. "You've seen those old ladies in the back seat. Any time their daughter and son-in-law go somewhere, they pack the mother in the back seat, thinking they're doing the old woman a favor by letting her tag along. They sit in the front and chat, and there the mother is, alone, the old lady in the back seat."

"It wouldn't be like that, Mom."

"I know. You'd be more apt to lock me in the attic."

Thalia jumped up, put her hands on her hips, and glared at her mother. "I wouldn't do that!" Then a swift smile momentarily softened her fierce look. "Well, maybe I would. But only on occasion."

"Would it really be so bad if I took off for a while?"

"I could move in with Josh, and you could stay in my condo."

Amanda rose and paced around the room, adjusting the frilled curtains, fluffing the girlish pillows. *How did it get to this, David, that I'm dependent on our daughter to take care of me?* Amanda would be okay once she reached retirement age because she'd get David's social security, but meantime, there was little money.

The life insurance policy they'd counted on had become defunct when the insurance company went out of business, and until the past year, they hadn't saved anything. David poured as much money as he could into his safe house for abused children. After he got sick, he turned the project over to a foundation, and Amanda had been able to save enough to live on for a year if she were frugal. And then? A job, probably.

"What if you don't come back?" Thalia asked in a small voice.

"I don't know, Thalia. I'm sorry, but that's the truth. Dad's death—" Amanda turned her head aside to hide her tears. "It broke something in me. I don't know what I want. Don't know *how* to want. I need to learn to live again, and I can't do that by hiding out and protecting myself."

"You can't do that here in Denver?"

"One thing David felt bad about was that our life together took away my spontaneity. I want to be spontaneous again. I think he'd like that."

"What about the cyber guy?"

"He's married. His wife was in the process of divorcing him when she got sick, and he moved back home to take care of her. I met him at a support group for spouses of cancer patients nine months ago. David died, but his wife got better." Amanda blinked to try to hold back her tears, but still they overflowed. "I was supposed to go meet him last week, but he cancelled."

"Do you think you'll ever get together?"

Amanda smiled through her tears. "He says we're like that poem Evangeline. We'll probably get together on his deathbed, and he'll die in my arms. But I don't find that a romantic notion."

"Will you be upset if I get married?"

"No." Amanda sat on the edge of the bed and put her hands in her lap. "I was upset when you were sixteen and wanted to marry that twenty-five year old, but you're an adult now. If you're happy, I'll be happy."

Thalia sat next to her and put an arm around her shoulder.

"That's such a mom thing to say."

"Well, I am a mom. Or I tried to be."

"You did good. Do you think I'll be a good mother?"

Amanda rested her head on Thalia's shoulder. "I think you'll be a great mom. One thing I know, you'll let your kids keep the strays they pick up."

Thalia laughed. "You remember?"

"Of course I do. I remember every dog and cat—and skunk—you brought home."

"It took forever to get rid of the smell. I think that was the only time Dad was ever mad at me."

Amanda took Thalia's hand in hers. "Dad loved you so very much. And so do I. I hope you will be wonderfully happy." She held Thalia's hand a moment longer, marveling at how their hands looked the same yet different. Both had short fingers, but Amanda's nails were unadorned and cut short and Thalia's nails were long and wildly painted with bright swirly colors. And Thalia did not have brown spots on the back of her hand. When had those signs of age shown up? *I'm getting old.*

Thalia extricated her hand, and nodded her head toward the blanket-wrapped bundle on David's side of the bed. "When are you going to share Dad's ashes?"

Amanda felt her face grow hot. "You knew?"

"Duh." Thalia patted Amanda's knee as if she were the mother and Amanda the daughter. "You really loved Dad, didn't you?"

Amanda scrubbed away the tears with her fists. "With all my heart, all my mind, all my soul, for all eternity."

"But you don't believe in eternity," Thalia objected.

"I believe that energy cannot be destroyed, and love is energy. Long after I've been subsumed back into the energy of the whole, my love will continue. That last year, every day broke my heart. I couldn't bear to see him fighting so hard for one more clear thought, for one more minute of being himself."

"I miss Dad." Thalia put her elbows on her knees and covered her face with her hands. Her shoulders shook with silent sobs. "Who's going to walk me down the aisle when I get married?"

David, why couldn't have stayed a little longer? Can't you see how much we need you?

"I will. Or Mary Lynn. She'd be thrilled." Amanda bit her tongue to keep from mentioning her misgivings about Josh. Her daughter was old enough to make her own mistakes. And perhaps Josh wasn't a mistake. Besides, Thalia seemed to be clearheaded, thinking of keeping the condo instead of selling it when she moved in with Josh. If she moved in with him. *Clearer headed than me right now, that's for sure.*

Thalia rose from the bed. "I'm going to look at Dad's books." She scurried down the hallway. Amanda followed at a more leisurely pace. Though she entered the room a scant few seconds after her daughter, Amanda found Thalia face down on the sofa, weeping.

Amanda sat on the edge of the couch, and gently massaged Thalia's back as she'd done so often when her volatile daughter had been younger. Maybe she should stay in Denver after all? Not rob the girl of both her parents? But Thalia wasn't a girl, and she had Josh. Thalia certainly did not need a weepy old woman putting a damper on her happiness.

Ah, David. How could you leave us to muddle on without you?

"Okay." Thalia sat up, pulled a tissue out of her tee shirt pocket, and dabbed her eyes. "Enough of that. Are there any books you want for yourself?"

Amanda smiled to herself, thinking of a young Thalia who'd been heartbroken over the cruelty of a friend. Thalia had forgiven the girl her mean remarks before her tears had dried, but it had taken Amanda weeks to forgive the child for making her daughter cry.

"I've taken what I needed. You can have what you want."

"I don't see Dad's baseball bat and mitt. If you find them, can

I have them? He used to play catch with me. He never minded that I wasn't a boy."

Amanda gaped at her daughter. "Why would he have minded? He loved you. Loved that you were a girl. When I was pregnant with you, he couldn't stop talking about all the fun you'd have. He said he'd even play dolls with you if that's what you wanted."

"Dolls? Dad?" Thalia laughed. "Good thing, then, that I didn't like dolls. But we did play with my teddy bears."

"Do you remember the towns the two of you used to build out of blocks?" For the first time since David's death, the tears in Amanda's eyes came from the sweet pang of nostalgia rather than grief, and she sensed that one day she would be able to deal with life alone. But not today. Maybe not for a long while.

"I remember you tripped over the blocks once. I thought it was my fault."

"That I tripped?"

Thalia studied her fingernails. "No. That you miscarried."

Amanda's heart felt as if it were being squeezed. "Oh, honey. The miscarriage wasn't your fault. I was in a hurry to get to the bathroom because I was bleeding and scared and didn't watch where I was going. Have you been feeling guilty all these years?"

Thalia spoke so softy Amanda had to strain to hear the answer. "Yes."

Amanda put her arms around her daughter. Thalia held herself stiffly, but Amanda didn't let go. *Help her, David. Please? Keep her safe.*

"You don't understand." Thalia whimpered. "I didn't want to have to share Dad with a new baby."

"You were what? Five? You'd been daddy's girl for so long, of course you didn't want to share. I knew that. Dad knew that. We also knew that you had a good heart and would love the baby once it came. Would have been a wonderful big sister." Amanda felt her daughter relax in her arms.

"For real?" Thalia whispered.

"For real. But it wasn't to be. I couldn't sustain a pregnancy. The doctors were amazed I managed to have you. Apparently, you were so tenacious, you held on through all the bleeding and midterm contractions. You really were a special child, and to tell the truth, as much as Dad wanted more children, I think he was glad he didn't have to share you."

Thalia tore herself out of Amanda's arms and ran to the bathroom. Amanda sat on the edge of the couch, wondering what David would think about Thalia's marrying Josh. But then, if David were alive, would Thalia be planning to get married?

Amanda doubled over, thinking of all the life events she and Thalia would experience without David. Thalia's wedding. The birth of Thalia's children, David's grandchildren. Birthdays. Holidays. Christmases. Every one of those joyful events would be tinged with the sorrow of David's absence.

Life went on, people had told her, but until that moment, it hadn't occurred to her they meant life would go on without David.

It took more strength than Amanda thought possible to straighten up when she heard Thalia flush the toilet, but she managed to be standing erect when her daughter entered the room, looking beautiful and so much like David that Amanda's heart hurt.

"I have to go, Mom. I'm meeting Josh, but I'll be back to pack up Dad's books. Okay?"

"I'm glad you're taking the books. Dad would love that."

Thalia gave Amanda a quick hug, and silently moved through the house. A faint click of the door told Amanda Thalia was gone.

She'll be fine David. But what about me?

Amanda imagined disapproval radiating through the room, as if David didn't appreciate her selfish thought, but she no longer had to consider his wishes. Or Thalia's. Or even Sam's. She only had to consider her own wishes.

But what do I want? Amanda's legs gave way. She plopped on the floor, plucked a book from the shelf, and held the volume to her chest. Her whole body ached with yearning for her husband, and she felt glad the books would remain in David's room a little longer. How could she have considered for a single moment getting rid of her husband's books? All she had left of him were his things.

She clutched the book tighter. Pain shot through her arms. Realizing her muscles had cramped, she eased her grip. How long had she been sitting here? She glanced at the book in her hands as if it were a relic from an unfathomable past. A Thai Chi manual. When David noticed he was getting weak and losing weight, he refused to go to the doctor and bought the book instead. "There's nothing wrong with me except lack of exercise," he said. But he only got worse. Still, his diagnosis when he did finally go to the doctor for a physical had shocked her.

And now David was gone.

Amanda put the book back on the shelf and lumbered to her feet, battling the scream that rose in her chest. The only thing worse than David's death was packing up his life. One day soon, his things would be redistributed, and then what?

What do I want?

There was so much Amanda could no longer have. David. Sam. Security. A life untouched by grief. And yet, the world was a big place. Surely there was something for her, something she wanted.

But what, David? Tell me, please, because I am lost.

Chapter 18

QUESTIONS. THE MANY unanswerable questions of grief. Amanda lay in bed, curled against the pain. Questions rolling around and around in her mind refused to let her sleep.

Is David warm? Is he fed? Does he have plenty of cold liquids to drink? Is he sleeping well? Does he still exist somewhere as himself or has his energy been reabsorbed into the universe? Is he glad he's dead? He brought so much to my life, but what did I bring to his? Why can't I see him again? Why can't I talk with him? Will we meet again, or is death truly the end? Was it fate that we met? Fate that he died? What if he isn't at peace? What if he's feeling as split apart as I am?

Will he recognize me if we ever meet again? Will he be proud of what I become? He helped make me the woman I am today, but what's it all for? Where am I going? And why? Do I have a fate, a purpose?

Can a person drown in tears? What's the point of pain? Of loss? Of suffering? Why did David have to suffer? Why do I? Do I have the courage to grow old alone? The courage to be old alone when the time comes?

Why do we cling so much to life? In the eternal scheme of things, does it matter how long or short a life is? Does it matter that he only had fifty-nine years? Does it matter that he was alive? What is the truth of life and death? If he's in a better place, why aren't I there? If life is a gift, why was it taken from him?

Is anything universally important? Love, perhaps, but not everyone loves or is loved. Creativity? But not everyone is creative. Truth? But what is truth? Is the human mind, with its finiteness, capable of comprehending the truth? If nothing is universally important, does anything matter? Maybe it's better to let life flow, to try to accept what comes, but isn't the point of being human to try to make a difference? To try to change what is?

Any relationship I have with David, is only in my mind, in memory. What's the difference between that and a fantasy? How much of life is lived in the mind? All of it? All except the present? But even the present is lived in the mind since the brain takes the waves of nothingness and transforms them into somethingness. So what is reality? The intersection of all minds?

How do I find meaning, or at least a reason to continue living? Do I need a mate in order for my life to have meaning? But many people don't have mates and still manage to have meaningful lives. How does Sam fit into my life? Was meeting him fate? Are we supposed to be together? If not, what's the point of loving one another? Is love the point?

After a couple of hours of listening to her silent questions, Amanda sat up in bed and screamed, a long wordless cry of pain that momentarily silenced her internal voice. But she still couldn't sleep.

In the early morning hours, Amanda rose and paced the house. She forced herself to think only of the moment. To feel the rug beneath her bare feet. To listen to the sounds of the too-empty rooms—the refrigerator humming, the floors creaking, the windows rattling softly in the breeze. To breathe in the smells of the old house—the faint odor of mustiness and the fainter odors of cooking. *When did I eat last? No don't think.* She felt her heart beating, felt the pulse in her neck throb. Felt the tiredness creep up her legs and into her head. Finally, feeling as if the walls were caving in on her, she grabbed her cell phone, shrugged into a sweater, and went outside. On the sidewalk in front of the house, she found a bright penny. Smiling at the memory of how David always treasured such coins, calling them gifts from heaven, she picked up the coin, and looked skyward.

"Is this a sign you're thinking of me, David?"

Recalling all the pennies she had found when going through her husband's things, she wondered if they, too, were signs David had been thinking of her. If the coins weren't coincidence, did they mean he continued to exist, continued to remember her?

Still smiling, she trudged around the block, nodding to a couple of neighbors who nodded back. By now, everyone in the neighborhood had offered condolences, so she didn't have to steel herself against platitudes that offered no comfort. Although a pleasant interlude, the walk exhausted her, and she entered the house, glad to be back in her cocoon.

"David? I'm home!" Amanda listened for his answering voice, and as grief gripped her once again, she wondered if she'd ever remember her husband had died.

Wondered if she would ever forget he had lived.

Suddenly in a panic, Amanda ran to the bedroom where David's picture graced the dresser. It was beginning to look more like her husband, as if the David at the end of his life was retreating from memory, leaving behind a younger him.

She gazed at the photo, memorizing every beloved feature. The perfect nose. The chipped front tooth that had never been fixed. The graying, pixyish hair framing his oval face. The dark eyes sparkling with promise. The lips curved in a small smile as if he understood human foibles and forgave them all. The fierce eyebrows he didn't always remember to tame. The delicate ears that never failed to hear what people were afraid to say aloud.

Do you still hear me, David? Please don't let me forget you. Please don't forget me.

Please.

She lay down on the bed, but sat up again when the phone rang.

"Did I wake you?" Sam asked.

"I'm up.

"I have a minute and wanted to call. Tell you I love you."

"I love you back. It's so good to hear your voice. How are you doing? How is Vivian? You said she's in remission. How do you feel about that?"

"We're both doing the best we can." He sounded desolate, as if Vivian getting better ensnared him as much as her getting sick had done. He drew in an audible breath, and when he continued, his voice turned hearty. "I'm more interested in you. How are you doing?"

In the background, Amanda could hear the whirr of traffic, and knew that Sam was driving. Knowing he would be cutting her off soon, she kept her answer light, though she would have liked to settle in to talk to him, pour out her concerns, hear his.

"It's hard. I mean, it's difficult." Amanda let out a short laugh. "You've made me self-conscious about using the word 'hard' when talking to you."

Sam snickered, but he responded to her concern in his hearty tone. "You know what Nietzsche said, 'What does not destroy me makes me stronger.'"

Amanda sighed. "I'm not sure if that is strictly true. Sometimes that which doesn't destroy us makes us weaker because it makes us fearful of living, fearful of more trauma, fearful of fear itself."

"Are you afraid, darling?"

She felt herself melting at the endearment. "I keep getting panicky over the silliest things. I'm afraid I'll never get over grief, afraid that I'll forget David. Afraid of..."

"Yes?"

Amanda laughed. "You should have been a priest, not a just a

Priestly. You have the most soothing voice."

"Oh! Some guy cut across three lanes of traffic. Almost ran into a school bus." Sam paused, apparently needing to concentrate on his driving. "Okay. I'm back. You were saying?"

Amanda sniffled. "Nothing important."

"Are you sleeping?" Concern tinged his voice.

"Some. Mostly I lie in bed at night tormented by questions that have no answer. I miss the days when I thought I knew what life was about."

Sam chuckled. "Don't we all."

"If you were alone, would you be bedeviled by loneliness?"

Amanda expected another hearty reply to deflect the personal question, but to her surprise, Sam said, "You can be alone when you're with someone. You know that with the way things went with David."

"But you don't seem to get as paralyzed by loneliness as I do. Or is that something you keep to yourself?"

Amanda waited for a response that did not come. "I envy your not having to grieve for Vivian," she said to fill the awkward silence. "Grief is so bizarre. It's like a quantum nightmare where David is alive and dead at the same time. I mean, I know he's dead, but it doesn't stick in my head. I keep expecting him to be home whenever I go in the house, but he never is. I don't know if I can handle that sort of insanity much longer."

"You won't have to," Sam said, back in hearty mode.

Hope quickened Amanda's voice. "Why not?"

"You're leaving there in eleven days."

"What? No. I don't have to be out of the house until the end of April." But she did the arithmetic. It was April 19. Only eleven days until she had to leave. Amanda tightened her grasp on the phone, but the effort to get a grip did nothing to prevent a moment of dizziness. David had been gone for forty-two days and twenty-two hours. "I keep losing track of time."

"Have you decided what you're going to do at the end of the

month?" There was an odd hesitancy in Sam's voice that make Amanda think he continued to be as unsure of her as she was of him.

"I'm taking a trip to Ohio."

"To see me?"

"Yes, to see you. Is there any other reason to visit Ohio?" Amanda thought she'd made a joke, but Sam answered seriously.

"Lots of cultural activities such as art museums and botanical gardens."

"Hmm. Denver has those. What else you got?"

"Hocking Hills. Serpent Mound. Headlands Beach State Park."

"A beach? There's a beach in Ohio? If I'd have known that, I'd have been there a long time ago."

"I hate to cut this short, love, but I am at my destination. It was great talking to you. I'll try to write." And then he was gone.

Amanda threw the phone on the bed and buried her face in her hands. It happened every single damn time. As soon as she let herself be drawn into his charm, he ended the conversation. But at least he was alive. Nothing ended a lifelong conversation the way death did.

"Why are you doing this to me?" she screamed, but she had no idea to whom she was speaking. David's God? Sam's universe? Her own broken heart?

She fell back on the pillows, but after a minute, remembering that she promised Thalia to look for her trekking poles, she forced herself to get out off the bed.

"Where did you put Thalia's trekking poles, David?" Amanda searched David's room, the living room, the laundry room, behind the door in David's bathroom, and found no sign of the poles. She even went outside to look, though she had no idea what they would be doing out in the yard. But then, she had no idea why he'd wanted them.

On a final ramble through the hall, Amanda realized she

hadn't checked the coat closet. She never used the closet and was so used to passing the sliding door without seeing it that the closet might as well have been invisible. She steeled herself before opening the door so the sight of David's coat and hat wouldn't bring on a bout of tears. The coat didn't cause sorrow. But the baseball glove on the shelf with his hat and the bat leaning against the wall of the closet next to Thalia's trekking poles brought Amanda to her knees. David had loved playing ball not only with Thalia but with the kids in the youth group. During the last few months of his life, he had often talked about having one more chance to hear the crack of the bat as he hit the ball, to feel the joy of the hit all the way up his arm to his shoulder, and now he would never play ball again.

When Amanda got control of herself, she noticed David's slippers on the floor of the closet. There were so many things of his she couldn't get rid of in case he ever needed them, but she sure as heck could get rid of those ancient slippers. They were falling apart, held together with strips of duct tape.

"Duct tape and twist ties," David had often proclaimed. "The two greatest inventions of the twentieth century."

Smiling, Amanda picked up the slippers. A bit of mud flaked off onto her hand, and a frown displaced the smile. She looked at the bottom of the slippers. Mud and a seed from a Siberian elm had slipped beneath the duct tape.

Amanda remembered David repairing the slippers six weeks before he died. She'd found him sitting cross legged on his bed, picking fretfully at a hole where the upper had become ripped from the sole.

"I need my…" Confusion clouded David's eyes. "I need my…my fixer."

"Your fixer?" Amanda's heart thudded with fear at seeing her preacher husband struggling for words. Up until then, David had been weak and in pain, but his mind remained sharp. Looking back, she could see that this episode signaled the end, though he would continue to have times of clarity until the last few days of his life.

"You don't listen to me. Pay attention." David raised his voice and spoke harshly in a tone she'd never heard before. "Get me my fixer."

And then realized what he wanted, though she didn't know how she made the mental leap. She opened his desk drawer and grabbed the roll of duct tape and his scissors.

The tip of his tongue protruding from his mouth in a parody of childish concentration, he'd wrapped the tape around the front of his slipper. The sole had been clean then, and she didn't recall his going outside afterward except to sit on the porch a couple of times.

With a sickening jolt, Amanda remembered that when David had fallen in the bathroom, he'd been dressed. "I had to do my paper route," he'd said. Had he been outside? A chill ran up her spine. He could have been hurt. He could have wandered into the street and gotten hit by a car. And she'd never have known. What a terrible caregiver she'd been.

Amanda tried to tell herself she couldn't watch him all the time, that he'd wanted to be alone, that she had to snatch sleep whenever possible, but all she could think of was that while she'd been flirting with Sam, David might have been wandering around outside.

But where had he gone? There were no Siberian elms on their property.

Propelled by fury at a world that had stolen everything from her, even her belief in herself, Amanda cleaned the kitchen, took out the trash, then marched into the utility room to do the laundry that had defeated her the past two months. The piles of laundry still defeated her. She stuffed trash bags with David's bedding, including the blankets and pillows he'd used, and his clothes. At the sight of his heavy gray sweat suit, her heart seemed to leap into her throat and choke her, but she refused to give way.

When she came across the basket of her own dirty clothes, she threw those away, too, along with the memories of her wearing those pants and tops while taking care of David. "No more," she screamed. "No more."

She took the trash bags outside, and piled them on top of all the other bags of trash.

At two in the morning, she collapsed on her bed.

The chiming of the doorbell woke her. She lay huddled under the covers, a strong sense of déjà vu clouding her mind. David's ashes were due to be delivered today. No, that was weeks ago. What day was it anyway? She raised her head to look at the clock. April 20th. 11:45 am. David had been dead exactly forty-three days, twenty-two hours, and five minutes.

The doorbell chimed again.

Amanda clambered out of bed, put on her robe, and tied the sash as she plodded toward the door.

She peaked through the spyhole.

Her heart pounded. So it had been a dream after all. David was alive.

Amanda yanked open the door and clutched her chest as disappointment slammed into her. Josh stood on the porch, a stack of flat new boxes under his arm.

"Come in, Josh." Amanda moved away from the door and staggered as a wave of dizziness washed over her.

Josh dropped the boxes, stepped into the foyer and grabbed her elbow. "Steady there."

Amanda wanted to pull away from his supporting hand, but she couldn't get her balance. *Why can't I do this, David?* By now, she'd learned that much of grief was physical, but every day brought unpleasant surprises. Would it never end? But it couldn't end. David was gone, and nothing could bring him back.

"Can I fix you some tea?" Josh asked. "Or get you a glass of water?"

She gently extricated herself from his grip. "No. I'm fine. It's that…"

"I know." Josh smiled. Strangely, the crinkles around his kind eyes made him look younger. "My dad died ten years ago. My mother still grieves for him. She says she hates answering the door because it's never Dad."

A small sob escaped Amanda's lips. "No. It's never David. And you look a lot like him before he got sick. The same build. The same posture."

"I'm sorry."

"Don't be. Why don't you have a seat, and I'll fix us some tea. Or coffee if you prefer."

"Coffee. Instant is fine."

Amanda started. How would he know she didn't bother with making a pot of coffee anymore? Oh, Thalia would have told him.

She gestured toward the parlor where he could sit, but he followed into the kitchen and leaned against the counter.

"Thalia is meeting me here in a little while to pack up the books you said she could have, but I wanted to talk to you. I know you're concerned."

"About your being so much older than Thalia? Yes, I'm concerned. She had a protected childhood. Even though she's thirty and has her own business, in many ways she hasn't yet grown up."

"Which you think makes our age difference seem even greater."

Amada spooned coffee crystals into two mugs. "Yes."

"I'm not as old as I look, if that's any help."

Amanda frowned at him. Realizing he'd made a stab at lightness, she let her face relax. "If you don't mind my asking, how old are you?"

"Forty-nine. I work out. Eat lots of vegetables. Come from long-lived stock. And I know age differences can work. My dad was twenty years older than my mother."

"But aren't you afraid of setting Thalia up for heartbreak?" The thought of her only child going through the sort of pain she was forced to deal with made Amanda's stomach lurch.

"Because I might go first?" Josh said. "I prefer to think of it as giving her a life of love and happiness. And no one knows what will happen. I had a sister—Judy—who died as a teenager. Car accident."

"I'm sorry."

Josh waved away Amanda's words. "It was a long time ago."

But the pain in his eyes told her sometimes it felt like yesterday.

"I love Thalia, and to be honest, I like that she's young." Josh must have caught the look of distrust in Amanda's eyes, because he said, "I want a family. If I married someone my own age, there would be little chance of ever having children."

"Does Thalia want children?"

Josh laughed as if she'd made a joke. When Amanda didn't answer with a laugh of her own, he said, "You don't know?"

"I wondered if you knew. If you'd talked about having children. Yesterday Thalia asked if I thought she'd be a good mother, but when she was younger, the responsibility of motherhood terrified her. David's personal ministry was helping abused children, and I think she was afraid she'd hurt her children."

"So that's why she doesn't want to rush into anything. I like that she wants to be sure. Or as sure as anyone can be. But yes, she wants children. More so now that her dad is gone. She has a lot of love to give."

"Why did you wait so long to have children?"

"I wanted kids right away, but my ex-wife wanted to work a year first and somehow ended up on the fast track at Gulf Oil. I told her I'd stay home with the kids, but she said the doctor told her she couldn't have children."

Amanda reached out to hand him a mug of dry coffee crystals. Realizing her mistake, she snatched the mug back, poured water over the coffee crystals from a gallon bottle of artesian water, and stuck the cup in the microwave. She turned back to Josh and caught a glimpse of his unguarded face. Her heart went out to him.

"What happened?"

Josh took a shuddering breath. "My wife aborted our child three years ago. I found out by accident when the clinic called for a follow up appointment and I answered the phone."

"Oh, no. I am so sorry."

"We seem to be saying 'sorry' a lot today. But one thing I am not sorry about is having met Thalia. She's a special woman. You did a good job raising her."

"You think so? Often it felt as if David and I were playing good cop bad cop."

"And you were the bad cop?"

"David could deny her nothing. Someone had to add a bit of reality to the mix."

"Thalia knows that. And she appreciates it."

Tears came to Amanda's eyes. "What a kind thing to say."

"Not a thing to say. The truth."

"We so often are at odds, Thalia and I. She's definitely a daddy's girl."

"I won't be a daddy to Thalia, even though I have enough money to take care of her." Josh smiled his crinkly-eyed smile. "And her mother."

Amanda took the mugs out of the microwave. "You just want a babysitter."

"Of course."

They were sipping companionably when Thalia appeared in the kitchen doorway. "Uh, oh, this can't be good."

Josh grinned, set his mug on the counter, and went to Thalia. He kissed her, and Amanda suddenly felt good about this potential son-in-law. He seemed considerate, kissing her daughter with enough warmth to please Thalia but not so heatedly that it would embarrass her mother. Still, Amanda averted her gaze.

"Can I keep him, Mom?"

"Ah, honey. I want you to be happy."

Thalia beamed. "Josh makes me happy."

"Then you can keep him." Amanda held out her hand to Josh. "Welcome to the family."

He ignored the hand and hugged her. "Thank you."

"I'm glad you're both here," Amanda said. "I need to talk to you about something."

Thalia gave her a frightened look. "Okay."

"It's nothing bad," Amanda assured her. "I lost track of time. Didn't realize it was only ten days until I have to be out of here."

Thalia lowered her eyes. Her lashes sparkled with tears. "I know. It's like Dad is dying all over again."

Josh put an arm around Thalia's shoulders. "What can we do for you, Mrs. Ray?"

Amanda smiled. "First of all, you can call me Amanda. If you're going to be my son-in-law, we shouldn't stand on formalities. And you're too old to call me mom."

Josh nodded. "Fair enough."

"I'm keeping a few boxes of things. Not enough to merit a storage unit, and too many to cart around with me."

"Say no more." Josh smiled at Thalia, then at Amanda. "We'll be glad to keep your things."

"Also…"

"Yes, Mom?"

"Dad's ashes. I can't…I can't…" Tears ran down Amanda's cheeks. "I can't throw him away yet. Will you keep the urn for me? You can have some ashes to do with what you want, but not now. I can't…" *I can't believe you're dead, David. I can't believe you've been reduced to a container of bone fragments. I can't deal with this.*

"I know, Mom. I know." Thalia took the handkerchief Josh held out, and dabbed her eyes. "We'll keep the ashes as long as necessary."

Amanda averted her face to hide her own tears.

"Dying is a terrible way for life to end," Josh said.

Amanda jerked her head around to stare at him. How did he know?

"It's what my mom used to say when my dad was dying," Josh said, almost apologetically.

"She's right." Amanda sniffed, trying to hold back the tears, but they kept falling as if with a will of their own. "How did she ever get through this?"

Josh smiled ruefully. "She didn't."

"I'm sorry," Amanda said.

"No need to be sorry," Josh said. "What I meant is that the woman she used to be didn't get through grief. She became someone different, a woman who could survive the death of her husband. Or so she says."

Could I become someone different? Someone other than the weeping relict of David?

"It took her a long time, though," Josh said. "Years."

The hope that had blossomed in Amanda's chest cavity shrank into a hard knot. Years? She had to deal with this pain for years? *David, please. I can't do this.*

"We got you a present, Mom." Thalia ran outside and returned lugging a large box. She hefted it onto the counter and nudged it toward Amanda.

"What's this?" Amanda looked from her daughter to her future son-in-law. "I don't need anything."

"We want you to be prepared," Josh said.

Thalia stepped back to stand next to Josh. "It's to let you know I'm okay with your going on a trip alone. Josh said his mom traveled after his dad died. Camped by herself, too, and had a great time. Only problem is, she never came back to Denver. Fell in love with Pensacola and stayed there. Promise you won't move to Pensacola."

"I promise." *Ohio, maybe, but Florida? No.*

"Josh and I talked about you living with us. We'll get a place with a mother-in-law apartment. You'll have a home when you're ready, but I won't try to stop you if you still want to travel by yourself."

"I'm glad." Amanda pulled the box closer and opened the flaps. She pulled out a few mysterious bundles, and glanced enquiringly at the gift givers.

"A small tent you can put up by yourself," Josh said. "A sleeping bag. A sleeping pad. First aid kit. Emergency supplies. Food bars and other camping necessities."

Amanda struggled to breathe, feeling like a fledgling with a broken wing being forced to leave the nest. But wasn't that what she wanted? Adventure? Expanding her world?

"Is she okay?" Josh asked softly.

"Yeah. She cries at everything," Thalia responded.

"My mom was like that, too. I had to learn to let her cry."

I'm still here! Amanda wanted to say, but maybe she wasn't here. Maybe she'd become a ghost of herself, invisible even to those in her presence.

"Th-thank you," Amanda managed to say. "So thoughtful." She sorted through the various bundles and imagined herself using the products. In a campground, maybe, or under the stars. A woman, strong and fearless, embracing her wild side. *That's not me!* she cried silently. A deeper voice inside her responded, *But isn't that the point?*

She glanced up to find Thalia and Josh regarding her warily.

"I'm okay," she said. "Really. Trying to imagine myself as a woman who can camp alone."

"You can do anything, Mom."

I can't bring David back. Then a revolutionary thought struck her. *Do I really wish for his return? Wishing things were different would be negating the wisdom, courage, and determination with which he faced his life and death.*

"Mom?"

Amanda forced herself to focus. "I'm sorry. I don't seem to be able to concentrate since David died. Thank you both. Such a lovely gift!"

"Even if you don't use the gear," Josh said, "we'll feel more comfortable knowing you have it. If you get stuck in a storm on the road, at least you'll be comfortable. Oh, one other thing. Be sure to store bottles of water inside your car for emergencies."

Amanda nodded, thinking. *We? Already Thalia and Josh are a we?* Aloud, she said, "I wish you could have met David, Josh."

"I did meet him."

Amanda gaped at him. "What? When?" She glanced at her daughter, who stared defiantly at her.

"I brought Josh here one night. You were asleep."

"You didn't think to wake me?"

Josh stepped between Amanda and Thalia. "I wouldn't let her. Thalia told me you hardly ever slept, and I thought rest was more important. I figured I had plenty of time to meet you both, and then—"

"Then Dad got so much worse and there was never a good time." Tears glistened in Thalia's eyes. "I'm sorry, Mom."

"Not your fault, honey. Or Josh's. Things get complicated when someone is as sick as your dad was." *But they should have told me!*

"I talked to David one other time," Josh said. "He called me."

Amanda swayed and had to grab the counter to keep from falling. "David called you? How did he get your number?"

"When I was here with Thalia, I gave him my card."

Thalia nodded. "He did, Mom."

"I don't understand. Why did David call you?"

Josh looked from Thalia to Amanda as if wishing he were

anywhere else but in the parsonage kitchen. "He wanted me to know that Thalia would be okay. That she'd be safe."

Amanda's stomach burned not with anger, but with some emotion she couldn't identify. Fear, perhaps. But nothing could harm David now. He was safe in death's arms.

"I was worried. I tried calling right back, but I couldn't get through. I think David left the phone off the hook. I tried calling you, Thalia, but I got your voicemail. So I drove over here and saw David walking home."

Amanda and Thalia gaped at him, and spoke simultaneously.

"Dad? Walking home? From where?"

"David outside? By himself? When?"

"It was two or three months ago, I think. There were a bunch of cop cars in the neighborhood, and I thought at first they were looking for David. But they went to a house down the block a ways. I almost didn't recognize David. He was wearing slippers with slacks and a shirt. He wore an undershirt on top the dress shirt, which seemed odd, so I asked him what he was doing. He said he had to do his paper route."

Amanda closed her eyes. *Oh, David. What were you thinking?*

"He used trekking poles like canes, but he kept stumbling. I offered him a ride. He recognized me, and then all of a sudden he seemed fine. Told me Thalia would be okay now. He said he could get back to bed by himself. He asked me not to tell you he was out because he didn't want to worry either of you. Shook my hand. Thanked me. Told me to be good to his lovely daughter."

"I'm sorry," Amanda said. How many times had she spoken those words today? What difference did it make? What difference did anything make?

"Sorry for what, Mom?"

"I can't deal with this right now. Can you come back tomorrow to pack up the books? I need to be alone."

Thalia and Josh exchanged looks.

"Are you sure, Mom?" Thalia asked.

Amanda could feel a scream rising in her chest. "Please leave. Now." She stuffed her knuckles in her mouth to hold back the scream and ran to her bedroom. She fell on the bed, buried her face in the pillow, and let the scream loose.

"What did you do, David? What did you do?"

Chapter 19

DAVID KILLED SOMEONE.

The thought that had begun as a small weed in Amanda's mind after Josh's revelation grew into an infestation. *How could I possibly think David would willfully take someone's life?* He was one of those ministers who truly believed what they preached. Had the combination of the drugs and cancer crazed him? Turned him into someone else, someone he'd hate?

And what did that say about her, David's wife, that she could have been so oblivious of David that he could roam the neighborhood at night and she not know?

Amanda sat at David's computer, determined to figure out his password. If David had done what she suspected, he might have noted the episode in his journal, otherwise why password protect it?

She keyed in the obvious passwords, those she'd already tried on the off chance that she'd made a typo, and whatever else she could think of. Lucia, the name they'd chosen for the baby she'd miscarried the first time. Mike and Mikette, the names they'd chosen for the second and third baby she'd lost. She tried his favorite bible verses. But the file remained locked, taunting her.

Come on, David. Tell me. Amanda rested her fingers on the keys and emptied her mind, but no inspiration came.

She wrapped her arms around her middle to ease a sudden pang of grief, and rocked herself. Maybe it would be better not to learn the truth. But if she didn't know who David was, how would she know herself? He'd been part of her for so many years, her identity seemed entwined with his. She'd need to unentwine their lives if she had any chance of surviving her grief, but how could she separate David from her life without knowing the truth of him? If his life had been a lie, then her life would have been a lie, too.

And maybe I'm full of crap. Maybe I'm looking for a reason to hate David because if I hate him, I won't hurt so badly.

"I'm sorry, David." Amanda's voice cracked. "I don't really want to hate you, but I cannot bear feeling this way."

She continued rocking herself, disregarding the tears dripping down her face onto her folded arms. *Maybe I need a vision quest.* Bill Jensen had trekked hundreds of miles through the wilderness to honor his wife, and in doing so, found peace, but Amanda couldn't see herself doing anything so dramatic. And anyway, David didn't love places. David loved people.

Suddenly, like the moon coming out after a midnight thunderstorm, she brightened. *David loved people.* Of course he hadn't killed anyone. She did know him. She hadn't been living a lie.

Feeling as if maybe she'd be able to survive her grief after all, Amanda went to the garage for a carton and old newspapers to pack her wedding china. She dumped the newspaper and the box on the kitchen table and opened the cupboard door. Not much remained of the elegant bone china with the sterling silver rims—four dinner plates, six desert plates, three cups, four saucers, one bowl. Would she ever be able to use the china without crying for those innocent times before David got sick? Before she fell in love with another man while her husband lay dying? Before she became the wife of a murderer?

Murderer.

Amanda ran back to David's room. The password had to be written somewhere—a person who knew his memory had grown faulty wouldn't rely on that memory. She opened the center drawer and pawed through the contents so fiercely, a few pennies and paper clips flew to the floor. As Amanda stooped to pick up the objects, she recalled another time she'd recovered fallen items—when David was searching for his sesame.

Omigod! Sesame. Open sesame. Password.

Where had she put the papers, David's final "work"? She scrabbled through his inbox, checked the stack of financial files she'd set on the desk to go through when she felt more able to concentrate, frantically opened and closed the desk drawers. Finally, in the bottom drawer, she spotted the folder, pulled out the sheaf of papers with the crabbed writing, and tried to decipher the words. But all she could see, as when she first looked at the papers, was Thalia's name written over and over again.

Although Amanda already tried using Thalia's name as a password, she tried once more and up popped the same taunting message, ACCESS DENIED.

Amanda got out David's magnifying glass, a relic from his schooldays, and studied each word on the top page. Nothing but Thalia's name. Yet the password had to be here. She'd remembered David's satisfied smile when he set aside his pen. Even as sick as he'd been, his smile remained the same, the one he always wore when he finished a task.

The smile she'd never see again.

Amanda paused, waiting for the spasm of pain to pass. Did David still exist, perhaps smiling at having finished some celestial task? The thought brought her up straight. *Finished the task.* She didn't need to study all the words, just the last final word David had written, but which was the final page?

She brushed away her tears and riffled through the papers. Three of sheets had a single word that could only be "Thalia." She studied the last word on each of the other pages. Two of the words were also obviously "Thalia," but two other final words had a squiggle before the name. "A" perhaps?

Amanda typed "Athalia" into the computer. Still no entry. Perhaps the squiggle contained two letters? Something before "athalia"? No matter how much she studied the squiggle through the magnifying glass, the first letter remained a mystery. She tried one letter after another. Aathalia. Bathalia. Cathalia. By the time she reached Lathalia, she was ready to give up but kept doggedly punching keys. Mathalia. Nathalia.

Amanda was so focused on the need to continue typing other combinations that she didn't realize at first that the file had opened.

Nathalia.

Amanda jotted the name on a scratch pad she found in David's desk, then lifted her head to look at the screen. Her heart thudded so hard it shook her. Maybe it would be better not to know David's secret.

But it always came down to the same thing—if she didn't know who David had been, how could she know who she was?

She wiped away the eternal tears, and began reading.

January 15

There's so much about me you don't know, Amanda, and after all these years of our being together, you have a right to the truth. I tried telling you my dismal story several times, but my cowardice surfaced, and I found myself quailing before your clear, direct gaze. You are the best part of me. I learned to forgive in the seminary. I found atonement in my ministry. But you taught me the meaning of love.

Despite my belief that God does not enjoy our misery, that he wants us to be happy, I haven't been as happy as I should have been with you. Perhaps some of us are incapable of true happiness. Perhaps deep down I feel as if I haven't earned a life of joy.

Even now, at the end of my life, I'm stalling, not sure I want you to know the truth. Will you think less of me? Will you, as I do, focus on my cowardice, and ignore all the years I've spent atoning? There is only one way to atone, and I intend to follow. Perhaps this journal is more for me, trying to gather the courage for what I must do.

I can only write in fits and starts, and my roundaboutation has squandered what little energy I have for today.

January 18

Dying is a strange experience. I've preached an afterlife, yet I no longer know if I believe. Is this non-belief an occupational hazard? I know few preachers of long acquaintance who still believe, or rather who believe wholeheartedly. Remember all the talks we had about life after death, Amanda? Maybe you were right. I no longer know what of us survives into eternity. Not our bodies, though the lesson of resurrection is that our bodies do survive, but what use have we of those decaying carcasses when we can wear bodies of light? Yet what can one do with that light? What does one do with eternity? As you've often pointed out, there will be no books to read, no movies to watch, no games to play, no talk of the weather, no food to eat, no dreams, no place to run or walk.

Will I still be me? So much of who we are is dictated by our brains. I can feel myself change as the tumors invade more of my brain, stealing parts of me, turning other parts to mush. Little by little, I am dying. Not just my body, but *me*. So who or what will survive? I do not know. I can only try to be who I am in the days, weeks, and months (perhaps) that remain.

It's taken me hours to write this little bit. I have to pull every word from beneath a brain cloud. Will I have time to finish writing my story before I—the essential me—disappears?

January 19

Here's the truth of it: I killed my fifteen-year-old sister. I didn't mean to kill her but I couldn't pull the trigger that might have saved her life. I didn't know what was going on, and I should have. I was her big brother. I loved her, my beautiful sister Nathalia. Yet I did not see my father creep into her room every night. I did not hear her muffled cries. I could see, of course, her sadness, but I figured she was chafing, as was I, against the restrictness of our lives. Do I mean strictness or restrictions? No matter. I looked forward only to the time I could escape for good, though every day I escaped in small ways—into my studies, into my running. I made the varsity team despite weak knees and feet. Every step brought great pain, and since I forced myself to endure the agony, I prided myself on my courage.

But physical courage is not moral courage.

And moral courage is what I lack.

I did not kill my father, and so my sister died.

January 20

I'd never seen those words in writing before, so I had to stop. It took every bit of energy I had to acknowledge the truth.

And now you know the truth too, Amanda.

When I was sixteen, my mother came to my bedroom where I was studying for a physics test, and dropped a gun on my desk. It looked like one of my old toy six-shooters, but the heavy clunk when it hit my desktop told me the thing was not a toy.

I stared up at my mother. She smiled. I'll always remember that smile. When hell has devoured both of us, that sweet curve will still remain in memory.

"It's time," my mother said.

"For what?"

"To save your sister."

"From what?"

Not the sharpest response, but my stupefried brain could not come up with anything more intelligible.

My mother's smile faded and for a second she looked at me with loathing. "Don't make me spell it out."

"Spell what out?"

I don't remember what I had for breakfast this morning. Oatmeal? Toast? One of those, I think. But I remember that conversation.

My mother laughed and spoke fondly as if amused at the doings of a child. Her words were so at odds with her tone, it took a minute for them to sink in.

"You father has been making love to your sister for the past three years, and it's time you stopped it."

Your father, she said. *Your* sister. As if she were removed from the situation. I gaped at her, realizing she'd gone insane.

Me, in my naiveté, said mildly, "I know Dad loves Nathalia. She was always his favorite."

"You don't understand. She is having sex with your father."

"You mean he's molesting her?" My voice rose to a screech. "He's abusing her?"

"Abusing? No. She wants it."

"I don't believe you."

She shrugged. "You don't need to. Go see. They're making love now. In her room."

I grabbed the gun. If my father really was molesting Nathalia, I *would* kill him. My sister's bedroom was at the end of the hall. Up until three years ago, she had the bedroom next to mine. I remember the day my parents swapped rooms with her. Tears streamed down her face as we lugged handfuls of dresses and slacks and tops and shoes to her new closet. I told her I didn't know why she was crying, that I'd be jumping for joy if I got the big bedroom. She looked away from me and mumbled, "You don't understand."

And God forgive me. I didn't understand. Not until I stood in the doorway, seeing my father's naked buttocks pumping on top of Nathalia, one hand behind her neck, one over her mouth.

Tears seeped from beneath her tightly closed eyelids.

"Do it," my mother said from behind me, and I realized I'd been standing there, crucified. I mean transfixed. Is that a word? I can't think. Why can't I think? Something must be wrong with my brain.

January 21

I wanted to kill my father. Desperately wanted to kill him. I even put my finger on the trigger, but I could not complete the action.

"Do it," my mother screamed.

My father turned his head toward me, and snarled, "Go away, little boy. This is man's stuff."

Nathalia opened her eyes and looked at me without a glimmer of recognition.

I wanted to pull the trigger. God help me, I did want to, but I couldn't summon the courage, so I turned and ran back to my room. No one followed me. No one said anything.

A few minutes later, I heard my father stomp past my door and go into the kitchen. Probably for a beer—he always drank late into the night. I remember thinking that at least Nathalia would be safe for the night, which would give me a chance to figure out what to do.

I never got a chance. I went to the bathroom, and when I returned, I noticed the gun no longer lay obscenely on my desk. I assumed my mother had retrieved it. Stupid me.

A minute later, I heard the gun go off. My first thought was that my mother had killed my father. But no. Thalia had stuck the gun in her own mouth. She pulled the trigger, but I always knew the truth. I killed her with my cowardice.

January 25

Days are passing, and I still have much to tell you. In my sermon writing years, I would have written this whole thing in one evening. Now it's all I can do to sit at the computer and type. I delete as much as I write. I do not want you to know how much I have deteriorated mentally. There's not much of me left, but I hope it's enough to right both old wrongs and new ones.

My father left after Nathalia's death, and my mother always blamed me for that. She says if I'd killed him, he'd never have left. Do you want to know the horrific truth? She didn't care that her husband molested their daughter. She just wanted to move back to the master bedroom.

I stayed at the house until the end of the school year, got a job, and then found a room to rent for the last year of high school. My mother was glad I left. She only got mad when I took the gun with me. Why did the cops return the gun to her? I don't know. It never occurred to me to ask.

So that's another secret I kept from you, Amanda. I know how you feel about guns, and all these years the revolver has been under your roof. Literally under the roof. I used to keep it in a lock box in the attic. I am sorry for that betrayal, but I'm not sorry I kept it, for I have need of it.

January 26

I worried that you read those words and think I meant to kill myself. No, not that. I'll stay until the end, as much of me as is left.

I still have enough physical strength to do the necessary, and I think—I hope—I have the moral strength. But will I have the mental cuteness? Will I remember what I want to do when I get there?

I considered asking for your help, but I'd never put you in that position. I'm afraid you'd say no and look at me with horror. I'm afraid even more you'd say yes as you always did to anything I asked of you, and you'd come to look at yourself with horror. My life no longer matters. My story has been written, all except for the final chapter. You still have the rest of your life ahead of you. Well, I have the rest of my life ahead of me, too, but I only have a short time. You could have two decades, and I want them to be happy ones.

So here I am, slithering again. Will you—can you—be happy if you know the truth of me? Am I selfish wanting to tell you? Is this more cowardice, being unable to go to my end unknown by anyone?

Too much thinking. Time for doing.

Forgive me if I repeat myself. I dare not go back and reread what I've written lest I be tempted to edit, and so waste another day with fribbolities. Odd the words my mind conjures. Did I mean fribbles or frivolities?

Why am I here? I don't mean on this earth. I'm almost gone, so that no longer matters. I mean why did I log on to write? Oh, yes. My cowardice.

I killed one person because of my cowardice. Will getting the courage to kill another recompense for that spinelessness? If there is an afterlife, if there is a heaven and hell, I will not be seeing my Amanda again. I'll be burning for what I did, for what I'm about to do. Yet, if I don't commit this act, I'd only be doing it to prevent my going to hell, which seems to me a sin of an even greater magnitude than the taking of a worthless life. Are we condemned for killing a cockroach? I think not, but I don't know for sure. God must love cockroaches—He created so many of them.

Do we need an exterminator? No. Must concentrate. Keep on track. I am the exterminator. A very tired one. Will continue when I am more myself.

January 31

Now you know why I've been so obsessed with helping abused children. I saw Nathalia in every one. I saw them for themselves, too. Saw their hurt, their horrific lives. I wanted to do what I could for them, but in making their lives better, I thought in some way I was making Nathalia's better, too. Perhaps I'm as crazy as my mother. Without you, I might have become like her. You—and my work—were my salvation. And now I'm going to squander that salvation. But is it squandering? Could I be happy in heaven knowing I left a girl in hell?

She's only eight and has already endured a lifetime of abuse.

It was a mere fluke I found out. The girl, Junie, was in the churchyard playing with some bigger boys. Flirting with them. Poor girl, apparently that's all she'd ever known—inappropriate sexual behavior. I'd noticed her behavior before, but little girls learn to act like the big girls they see on television, so I wasn't sure. I tried to draw her confidence, but she never let on there was trouble at home. Perhaps she didn't know there was anything wrong. Children tend to accept as normal whatever happens to them.

That day, one of the boys let Junie ride his bike. She lost control and fell onto the bar and hurt herself. I called her parents, but couldn't get hold of them. So I took her to the emergency room.

After she examined the girl, the doctor came out to the hallway where I was waiting, and told me the little girl's vagina was huge, stretched out of shape, and the child had internal scarring, none of which had been the result of the bicycle accident.

I don't know why the doctor didn't call the police. Perhaps she thought telling me was sufficient. And it should have been. I talked to Thom. He cried. Admitted he'd been playing with her since she was a baby. He said the baby seemed to like it so he kept up with their private game.

Made me ill to talk to him. Thom Taylor. Pillar of the church. Head of the finance committee. Child molester. How had he kept it secret all these years? How could the girl's pediatrician not have noticed? How could the mother have been so blind?

I recommended a therapist, and Thom swore he'd get help. I should have followed up, but by then I was sick. I'm ashamed that I forgot about Junie until Cindy came to visit me at the beginning of January. Do you remember? She said Thom had started in with Junie again.

Cindy sent Thom to see me. He came. Cried. Promised to get help, the whole bit, but a week or so later, Junie called me, weeping. Her daddy was still playing the game, and she wanted me to make him stop.

February 5

It's hard to find words now. Not many times of clarity. But I need tell you why I won't see you in eternity. I called the father, told him I was going to report him. He laughed. Said I'd be dead soon and then there would be no one to stop him. True. I could call cops. But not be alive to testify. He'd get off. Have to save Nathalia. I will be brave.

Forgive me.

Chapter 20

THE GUN! WHAT do I do with the gun? What if the police found the weapon and connected it to David? Her husband could go prison. Even though one part of Amanda realized David was safe from prosecution, the grieving part, the part that believed him to be both alive and dead at the same time, feared for his safety. She frantically searched online for ways to get rid of the damning object, but nothing seemed appropriate. She couldn't bury the weapon because if someone found it and used it to kill a person, David would be liable for the murder. Most water bodies near Denver were too shallow to hide such an object. Dropping the gun in Cherry Creek Reservoir might have been a possibility, but with the drought, she could not be guaranteed the gun would remain forever unseen. Taking it to the police station was not an option. The cops would check and find out the gun had killed Thom Taylor, and there is no way she could let David be known as a killer. The same held true if she were to leave the weapon at a gun shop.

Finally it dawned on her there was one place she could dump the gun—with the person who had given the revolver to David all those years ago.

Amanda ran to David's closet, grabbed the old robe—the only garment left hanging—and reached up for the shoe box containing the gun oil and rags. She wiped the gun to make sure all fingerprints were removed, placed the fearsome thing in the box with the gun supplies, carefully set the box in a fancy gift bag, and stuffed the opening with festive tissue paper.

Too keyed up to go to bed, Amanda went back to David's computer, emailed the journal to herself, along with the letter he'd written her and the tax file, then deleted the originals. She went through the rest of David's files but didn't see any reason to delete his sermons, newsletters, or the notes for the book he wanted to write about abused children. Thalia might like to have those, and if not, she could delete them when she took possession of the computer.

Amanda shut down the machine, then immediately booted it up again to delete Barbara Ray from David's contacts. She kept her finger poised above the delete key for a few seconds. Would it be better for Thalia to find the name and learn she had a grandmother? Or should Amanda honor David's lie about Barbara dying before his ordination?

Amanda pressed the delete key.

As if she hadn't already checked her emails a dozen times that day to see if Sam had written her, she checked again. Still no word from Sam.

She composed a message: *Hi, Sam. I was just sitting here thinking about you. When we first met, I was flattered that you thought I was mysterious, and yet to me, you're the mysterious one. I never know what you're thinking. Never know why you call when you do, never know why you don't when you don't. Never know why you choose to divulge something personal and why you choose not to divulge other things. Never know why you like me and especially I never know why you appear to dislike me at times.*

Apparently, it's not necessary to understand someone to love him.

Amanda planned to save the email as a draft to reread the next day when she wasn't so tired, but a spurt of rebelliousness took that moment to make itself felt, and she sent the email immediately. Why should she be concerned about his feelings if he weren't concerned enough about her to write when he said he would? And anyway, everything she said was true. She did find him mysterious. Never had any idea why he alternately showered her with love and neglect.

This is not the relationship I wanted, David. What happened to truth and honesty and openness? Maybe I expected too much. After all, what do I know about Sam?

But she did know Sam. And she loved him.

Why did everything have to be so complicated?

Amanda logged out of her email account, shut off the computer, and dragged herself to bed. Her few dreams were nightmarish, but no more nightmarish than the images flooding her awake mind while she tossed and turned. David spending a lifetime atoning for a sin he hadn't committed. David spending an eternity atoning for the sin he had committed. David, barely able to crawl out of bed, laboriously making his way down the street. David shooting a gun. David killing a man. David. David. David.

When she got up in the morning, an email from Sam waited for her.

Amanda, are you aware of your incontrovertible tendency to go in the opposite direction of whatever anyone requests of you? I'm not saying this is what you do when people ask you to do something for them—though I imagine sometimes that's true. I'm saying that you always, invariably move in a contrary direction to what anyone says. Just out of curiosity, did David ever call you on that? Do you think I'll ever be right in something that I say about you or in my opinion about anything?

Amanda bit her knuckle to keep the tears at bay while she read the message a second time. Is this really how Sam saw her? Is this why he so often ignored her? Did he expect her to agree even when she didn't? Or maybe she really was disagreeable and contrary.

But I'm not contrary! Not on purpose, anyway, though it often seemed as if the world were at odds with her. Did she need to try to be more in step with the world? With Sam?

She'd felt in step with David, but now the whole world felt different, and she had no idea how to be in step. Wasn't it important to be herself, whoever that turned out to be?

She checked her messages to see what had brought on Sam's tirade, and the last thing she'd written was in response to his email about Vivian's remission and his belief that everything could remain the same. Apparently, he'd taken her cry of angst, *Can everything be the same?* as a sign of contrariness.

Didn't he know her at all? Know that she wouldn't disagree for the sake of disagreeing, that when at all possible, she'd be conciliatory?

But she and Sam were so very different. Didn't have the same view of the world, religion, the medical establishment. Amanda remembered one of their earliest discussions in the support group, long before they started messaging privately. She'd mentioned that David wasn't going for treatment, and Sam had been aghast that she'd let her husband have his way. But what could she have done? She couldn't make David do chemo if he didn't want it. Besides, it might have given her husband a couple of extra months of life, but those months would have been agonizing for him. Amanda hadn't said anything about Vivian's care, though she'd thought the Priestlys were way too aggressive. Apparently, the medical attention had paid off for Sam's wife, but that payoff seemed to put Amanda and Sam at odds.

And anyway, if Amanda were contrary, then Sam was too since he never agreed with her. Why did he care they differed? Did he think she loved him less? Did he love her less?

Could two diametrically opposed people have a chance at happiness?

I can't do this, David. Why did you leave me? We were happy, you and I.

But, unlike Sam, David had often agreed with Amanda's views. The two big differences had been concerning religion and raising their daughter, but David had never called Amanda contrary for not believing the way he did.

Amanda wrote to Sam: *Being contrary is doing something for the sake of being contrary. I do things for the sake of being myself. I need to be me. And if you think that's being contrary, then I can only take it as a compliment.* She hesitated before hitting send, afraid she'd make matters worse, but how much worse could their relationship get if she were already hesitant about responding? Could their love affair be over before it ever got started?

Sam shot a message right back to her: *What makes you think it doesn't hurt me when you constantly find fault with my ideas? I'm not saying I have to be right, but you could encourage me to see things differently if you think I'm wrong.*

Wondering if she had made a miscalculation in their relationship, Amanda responded: *I thought we were having dialogues. Give and take. I say what I think. You say what you think. I don't care that we think differently on just about every issue. Why do you?*

Amanda waited ten minutes for a response that didn't come, then closed her laptop, snatched the bag with the gun, and trudged out to her car.

Luckily, relatively few vehicles were on the usually busy highway between Denver and Colorado Springs because occasionally tears obscured her vision. Even if it weren't for the utterly incomprehensible exchange with Sam, she would still be in pain. A small voice inside her wondered if she had in some strange way fomented the disagreement with Sam so she wouldn't have to think about the concealed weapon on the seat next to her, wouldn't have to think of her devout husband as a killer.

Wouldn't have to think of the lonely years stretching in front of her.

Delivering the gun to Barbara turned out to be the easiest part of the day. Barbara opened the door. Amanda silently offered the gift bag. Just as silently Barbara accepted it.

Back in her car, Amanda noticed a red sedan with exhaust coming out of the tail pipes in a driveway a couple of doors down. She drove slowly, wary of the vehicle. Suddenly, the red car accelerated backwards into Amanda's Toyota. Amanda was going slowly enough that she was able to swerve before getting badly hurt, but still, the two vehicles clashed. Shaken, brushing tears from her eyes, Amanda got out of her car to inspect the damage. A dent in the fender was all she saw. Nothing that would prevent her from driving away.

Amanda considered getting back in her car and pretending she'd never noticed the accident, but the other driver, a young Hispanic woman with a cell phone in her hand, scrambled out of the red vehicle screaming, "Madre Dios. You could have killed me."

"Me?" Amanda gaped at the younger woman. "I didn't do anything. You're the one who rammed into me."

The woman took pictures of Amanda's license plate. "You should have paid more attention."

Although Amanda knew she had the right of way, knew she'd done what she could to avoid the accident, knew the other woman had been careless, she couldn't forget the tears that might have been a mitigating factor.

"Don't call the cops," the red car's driver said frantically. "No cops."

Amanda studied her adversary, wondering if the woman were illegal. Or maybe the woman already had too many tickets for reckless driving. Whatever the reason, Amanda nodded her agreement since she too would rather settle privately, leaving the cops and insurance companies out of the mess.

"You fix your car? I fix mine?" the woman said.

Amanda nodded. "I'll fix my car. Do you promise not to sue? To just let things go?"

"Yes. Yes. Let things go. You fix your car. I fix mine. No cops."

Since the woman had taken photos of Amanda's car, Amanda took her own photos of the scene. The pictures showed that the accident was obviously the other woman's fault, that the red car had plowed into Amanda's beige Corolla.

"You're going to keep your word?" Amanda asked.

"I swear."

"Okay."

They moved toward each other into an awkward hug. The other woman seemed to be shaking as much as Amanda, so Amanda held the younger woman a moment before breaking away.

"Thank you," the woman said. "Vaya con Dios."

"Same to you." Still shaking, Amanda climbed into her car and drove slowly down the street. A police car hurtled past her and slammed on the brakes. The uniformed cop got out and talked to the young woman.

Amanda pulled over to the curb and watched out of her rear view mirror. Should she return to the scene of the accident? Amanda could see the woman vehemently shaking her head and the cop shrugging his shoulders. After repeating the same exchange a few times, the cop got back in his car, and returned the way he came, studying Amanda as he passed. But he did not stop.

Amanda folded her arms on the steering wheel and rested her head on her arms. *I'm no good without you, David. See what happens when I'm alone?*

She gained control of herself and texted Sam. *I just got in an accident, but I'm okay. Minor damage to my car.*

Her phone rang.

"Are you okay?" Sam asked.

Her heart lifted at the sound of his voice. "I'm fine."

"What happened?"

"A woman floored the accelerator as she backed out of her driveway. Hit my car. Dented the fender."

"Did you call the cops?"

"No. Someone must have. They came but left after a minute. Didn't fill out a report."

"You need a police report," Sam said.

"Why? She and I agreed that each of us would pay for our own repairs."

"You need the report so you can sue her ass, that's why."

Amanda laughed. "We hugged. That's more my speed."

"Do you always have to be so contrary?"

Her lightheartedness faded at the disapproval in Sam's voice. "What are you talking about?"

"I bet if David had suggested you sue, you'd have done it, but because I suggested it, you won't."

"What? No. That's not true. How could you not know that I would never sue anyone for any reason whatsoever? Suing her is not going to change the fact that she did not see me. It would just make things more complicated, and my life is complicated enough right now."

"You don't see the irony in what you said?"

Amanda's heart thumped. This could not be happening. What had gotten into Sam, the man she loved, the man who professed to love her?

"I'm sorry. I don't know what you're talking about." Amanda fought the desire to cry. For once, tears would only add to the misery rather than relieve any stress. "I don't like authority, whether cops, insurance agencies, lawyers, courts, doctors, and will go out of my way not to deal with them. I'll pay the car repair bill myself. Not the smartest and most lucrative thing to do, but it's my way. It's why I haven't had a doctor's checkup in forty years. I don't want to know what's wrong with me because I am not going to let doctors cut, burn, or poison me. There's nothing else they can do except set broken bones, and that I will go to a doctor for. It's not being contrary, it's being smart. This country is too damn litigious, the medical establishment is too much in the pocket of the drug companies, and the courts are not about justice but disposing of cases. I don't want to partake. It's that simple."

"And that's not being contrary?"

Amanda wondered if Sam were joking, but no humor softened the harshness of his voice.

"What's with all this contrary business? I keep telling you, I'm not disagreeing with you to be disagreeable. We see things differently is all. From my point of view, you are the one who is contrary, but I would never call you names."

"But you're not contrary. Oh, no."

Amanda sighed, wondering how she'd become mired in such an incomprehensible discussion. "I'm sorry I disagreed with you about suing the woman. I wish I could do the typical woman thing and say 'yes, dear' and then do whatever I want anyway."

"Clearly you don't know too many typical women." Sam's voice quickened. "My next appointment is here. Glad you're okay. Talk to you later."

No words of love. No sense of connection.

Feeling utterly alone and wondering how she could get along without either David or Sam, Amanda drove dry-eyed back to Denver.

Amanda had barely walked into the house when her daughter came running in.

"You're okay?" Thalia asked, her voice rising. "What happened? There's a dent in your car."

"I was in a minor accident."

"An accident?" Thalia's voice shook. "And you didn't tell me?"

"It happened a little while ago." Amanda spoke soothingly. "A woman backed into me. We agreed to leave the cops out of it."

Thalia laughed. "Of course you did. Anything to keep from making waves."

Amanda hesitated a moment, then blurted, "Do you think

I'm contrary?"

Thalia's face screwed into a frown. "Contrary to what?"

"I don't know. Someone called me contrary today."

"A guy, right?"

Amanda nodded.

Thalia gave her a pitying look. "How are you going to navigate the dating scene if you don't know guy-speak? When a guy calls a woman contrary, he's calling her a bitch."

"No." Amanda thought of Sam, and repeated her response. "No."

"Yes."

Amanda gave her daughter a shaky smile. "When did you get so smart?" *When did I get so stupid?*

"I had smart parents."

"And we have a smart daughter." Amanda felt tears well up. *No more we.*

Thalia rolled her eyes. "Oh, Mom. Not again."

"And again and again and again." Amanda tried to swallow a sob, but it came out anyway, sounding like a hiccup. "I miss your dad. I don't know how to deal with the world without him."

"I don't know how you're going to do it, either, Mom. I worry about you." Thalia put an arm around Amanda's shoulders and gave her a quick hug. "You've lived a cloistered life. Taking care of me and Dad, working at the church. There's more to life than that."

"I guess I'll find out."

The touch of asperity in Amanda's voice seemed to amuse Thalia.

Amanda frowned at her daughter. "Well, even if I wanted to, I can't hide out in your condo forever."

"Did you find my trekking poles?"

Used to her daughter's rapid change of focus, Amanda merely shrugged. "They're in the coat closet with Dad's bat and mitt."

"Good." Thalia looked around the hallway where they had been standing. "Where are the boxes Josh brought?"

"In Dad's room."

"Thanks." Thalia trotted down the hall.

Suddenly hungry, Amanda went to the kitchen, pulled out eggs and bread and butter. She stood looking at the food for a few minutes without seeing it, then absently packed it back in the refrigerator.

Thinking about what Thalia had said about man-speak, Amanda sent a text to Sam. *I heard that when a man calls a woman contrary, he's calling her a bitch. Is that what you think of me?*

Sam responded a minute later. *You know I don't think that.*

Amanda replied: *I do know. Sometimes I think I don't know you as well as I think I do, and I wanted to make sure.* But she no longer knew what Sam thought of her, and she was afraid to push the matter any further lest he get upset and call her contrary again. If she didn't have his love, what did she have?

Nothing but the ashes of her life.

Sick of grief for David and doubts about Sam, Amanda wanted to throw herself on the bed and sleep until her final days, but she trudged to David's room to help Thalia pack books. She found her daughter sitting cross legged on the floor, open cardboard box in front of her, and her phone held to her ear.

"It's Auntie M. L.," Thalia said without lowering her voice.

Amanda nodded and started to back out of the room, but her daughter held up hand to stop her, then poked at her phone with one finger. Mary Lynn's voice came through the small speaker.

"Hello, darlin'. How are you doing?"

Amanda shrugged, though her friend could not see her. "I'm doing okay."

Thalia rolled her eyes and slowly shook her head. "No she's not. She cries all the time."

"Bless her heart. She needs to move on."

"That's what I keep telling her," Thalia said.

Amanda felt like stamping her foot, but she said, as mildly as she could, "I'm standing right here."

"Thalia tells me you're heading out on a trip at the end of the month, darlin'. Well shut my mouth!" A happy lilt. "You're coming to visit me?"

"Maybe. Eventually. I don't know. I just need to…"

Mary Lynn giggled. "Ride off into the sunset like a movie cowboy?"

"I don't do well driving at night. I'd be more apt to ride into the sunrise."

"Ain't that the berries."

Amanda forced a laugh. "I don't trust you when you go all southern on me."

"Well I am southern, darlin'. How long are you going to stay with me?"

Amanda lowered herself onto David's chair, already exhausted by Mary Lynn's exuberance and Thalia's bright-eyed expectation. "I don't know. A couple of days maybe."

"You can stay as long as you wish. The house has a mother-in-law apartment, so you can have all the privacy you want."

Thalia let out a delighted chuckle. "Josh and I are looking for a place with a mother-in-law apartment, too. Mom can travel back and forth between our two houses. That would be so cool for her."

Amanda stifled a sigh. "I'm still here."

"Well, darlin', you got to admit you're moving as slowly as molasses in January. You only have a couple days before you have to decide what to do."

"Nine days," Amanda said. "Nine days is a lifetime." She remembered when nine days sped by so fast she had to run to keep up with all the tasks she had to do as wife, mother, helpmate, but now the minutes of grief crept by so slowly, each felt like a year.

Nine days. Anything could happen in nine days. It took only a single moment for one's life to change. One moment to go from being an unwed woman to being bonded for life to one's beloved. One moment to go from being in labor to becoming a mother. One moment to go from wife to widow. One moment from quick to dead.

Nine days contained a lot of moments. Anything could happen.

But, Amanda admitted to herself, life-changing moments came seldom. Mostly life was a matter of going from one unchanging moment to the next, day after day after day. The chances of something happening to stay the inevitable during the next nine days were slim. She pictured herself locking the house for the last time, walking out to her car, sitting behind the steering wheel, and then…

She simply could not imagine driving away from the house where she'd lived with David for seventeen years, driving away from their life, driving away from everything familiar. She hadn't even left yet, and already she yearned to go back home to David. But there was no home. David had been her home from the moment she met him, and David was gone.

"Mom! Mom!"

Amanda dragged her attention back to her daughter. Thalia was looking at her with an unreadable expression in her eyes.

"What's going on?" Mary Lynn asked, curiosity more than concern coloring her sweet southern voice.

"Mom's crying again."

Amanda touched her cheeks, and felt the wetness. "I'm sorry," she whispered. And then she straightened her back. No, she was not sorry. Why did she keep apologizing to everyone for the way she felt? David deserved more than for her to blithely go into the future without a backward glance. He deserved someone to mourn for him, to care that he had lived, and to care that he had died.

"Don't cry, darlin'. Crying makes your skin blotchy and

doesn't solve anything." Mary Lynn's drawl quickened with interest. "What about the cyber guy?"

Amanda gave her daughter a disbelieving look. Thalia had the grace to avert her gaze.

"Is there anything my daughter doesn't tell you, Mary Lynn?"

Mary Lynn laughed. "I hope not. Such a delicious secret. I would never have guessed it of you. It's so out of character."

"It wasn't anything I planned," Amanda said quietly, speaking more to herself than to the other women. "I was so alone. David spent all of his time in his room, needing whatever strength he could summon to get through his days. The church people stopped coming to visit after the first couple of months."

Amanda's voice became stronger as she directed her attention to her two listeners. "Thalia, you seldom came by, and when you did, you only had time for your father, which is how it should've been. And you, Mary Lynn, didn't want to have anything to do with me and my pain. I felt as if I were disappearing. I kept my sanity by going online and connecting with people in the cancer caregiver's support group. They understood."

But Sam was the only one who truly paid attention to her. Her, Amanda. *Oh Sam, have I become all take and no give? Is that why you seem to be losing interest? In my grief, have I stopped paying attention to you?*

"I'm sorry," Amanda said. Again, the damn apology, but this time she didn't know to whom she was apologizing. To Sam, possibly, or perhaps to herself—to the woman she once was, to the woman she hoped to become. Or maybe to no one. "*I'm sorry*" could simply be a comment on the sorry state of her life.

She rose and stood over the phone in Thalia's hand. "When I leave Denver, I plan to travel slowly, so I don't know how long it will take me to get to Georgia. I will call you when I'm on the road, Mary Lynn." She gave her daughter a not very nice smile. "I'm leaving now, so the two of you can continue talking about me behind my back."

Amanda hurried to her bedroom, perched on the edge of the bed, and deliberated about calling Sam. She hated leaving matters between them the way they were, but she feared that calling him would exacerbate the earlier unpleasantness. The few times she had called him, his distracted tone had hurt almost as much as his terse, "I'm in a crowd. Can I call you back?" She sent him a text. *I love you, Sam. Please call when you get a chance.*

She sat holding the phone, waiting for him to contact her. After couple of minutes, she threw the phone on the bed, put her elbows on her knees, and rested her face in her hands.

I can't do this.

When the tears didn't come, she probed inside for the anger that never quite left her.

Anger that David had suffered. Anger that David had kept so much of himself from her. Anger that David was gone. Anger at the uncaring universe. Anger at the capriciousness of life and death. Anger at Sam, his insurmountable obligations, and his inability to make her a priority. Anger at being forced out into the world with no resources. Anger at her doubts and fears and weaknesses.

Fortified, she marched into the utility room for the vacuum cleaner, dragged the machine into the parlor, and battled the carpet.

Chapter 21

DEAR DAVID, I don't know why it never dawned on me that I can write you, maybe because I felt you were truly gone.

Irrevocably gone.

Nothing left of you but mindless energy mixed with the whole. But now I wonder. I keep finding pennies everywhere. I must have found dozens the last couple of days while I was cleaning the house, way more than simple chance could have dictated. Every time I found a penny, I told myself you were thinking of me. Were you? It doesn't matter. Even if you had nothing to do with the pennies, for the rest of my life, every time I find a coin I will think of you and pretend that you are thinking of me.

I read your journal. Didn't want to think about what you wrote or what you went through, so for the past few days I've done nothing but clean house, attacking the place with such ferocity there is not a speck of dust left, and clearing out everything I can't keep. Grief saps all my energy, so I hold on to anger to keep the grief at bay. Anger exhausts me, as does the work, so I sleep at night, but I wake every morning with tears on my face.

I keep thinking of a discussion we had during one of your lucid moments toward the end. You said I had it worse because I would be the one having to continue to live, but I said, and believed, you had it worse. You were the one in pain. You were the one dying. What I didn't tell you was my belief that I could not feel grief, and more than that, I felt sure I would be starting a new life with a new man.

I told you about the support group for cancer caregivers that I followed online, but I didn't tell you I became very close to a fellow who was in the same position that I am. Or rather, the same position that I was in. Things are different now. His wife got better.

Dammit, David! Why couldn't you have gotten better, too?

It turns out the joke is on me. You were right. I do have it worse. You're gone, gone from this earth, and I don't know where. Are you somewhere? Anywhere? I hate not knowing where you are. I hate not knowing *if* you are.

All I know is that I am alone, left with such a horrible feeling of amputation, endless tears, heartache so great I can barely breathe at times. And there is no new life with a new man. He is still married and now that his wife is better, he has so little time for me that I often feel I am mourning two men. All this emotion from a woman who always prided herself on her stoicism! The ironic thing is that I fell in love with him in part because he paid so much attention to me, and I desperately needed that. I still need someone to pay attention to me, to put me first at least some of the time, but you are off in the cosmos living your death, and he is in Ohio living with his wife. So that leaves only me.

I have to be out of here in just a couple of days, but I'm not moving anywhere. I'm just going to...go. Try to be spontaneous. See what adventure comes my way. Follow my dreams (if I ever get any). I hope you will be proud of me, David.

I miss you. (Don't mind the splotches on this page. They are just tears.)

I should not have been angry at you for keeping secrets from me because as you can see, I had a secret of my own, but oh, David, I was so hurt that during all our years together, you never told me about Nathalia and the gun and the shame you'd buried deep inside. I'm sure you didn't mean to hurt me. In fact, I'd be willing to bet you meant to protect me. And in my heart of hearts, I'm glad you did. It was hard enough carrying the pain of knowing some of the things that happened to you, such as your mother throwing away all your favorite toys to punish you for some childish slip, and your father ignoring you as if you didn't exist, but the pain you felt over your sister's death and your part in the tragedy would have scarred me.

Will scar me.

Still, you could have told me. Maybe sharing the pain would have made it easier for you to bear. And maybe you wouldn't have had to kill someone to atone for something that wasn't even your fault. (But if you weren't sick, you wouldn't have been put in a position where murder was the only answer. So not fair!) With the way you loved people, all people—you even loved the abusers while hating their abuse—it must have hurt you greatly to take a life. And yet, when the end of your own life came, the very end, after all that interminable restlessness, you were serene, as if you had no regrets. I hope your death continues to be as serene as your dying, and that you don't feel grief for me as I do for you.

If you don't mind, I'd like to write to you again. It would be nice to be able to still tell you everything I'm doing and thinking, still ask your advice, still use you as a sounding board to think things through. Writing you tonight makes me feel close to you, makes me feel as if you're still part of my life even though you are so far away.

From what I have heard, grief over the loss of a life mate/soul mate can last for years. It frightens me to think of having to continue to deal with all this angst, but I will do whatever I can to live and to be happy despite the pain. As much as I miss you and hate that you're gone, I am glad that at least one of us is beyond the sorrows of this world.

I love you, David. I will always love you. Nothing that ever happened or will ever happen can change that. Adios, compadre.

A feeling of peace stole over Amanda. She lay back on the pillows and mulled over what she had written. *I am glad that at least one of us is beyond the sorrows of this world.* A difficult aspect of her grief, besides the obvious problem of David being dead, was that after thirty-five years of being together, she and David were no longer an "us." But could she still be half of an "us"? Despite "till death do us part," could she and David still be sharing a life? If so, what did that mean to her relationship with Sam?

She had to admit that it probably didn't mean anything because no matter what Sam said about he and his wife being a signature away from divorce, he and his wife were an "us." He cared about Vivian, and he cared for her. They had children together. Which left her, Amanda, the cyber paramour, on the outskirts of his life. When Amanda felt agitation invade her peace, she whispered, "Sorry, Sam," and gently pushed him from her thoughts.

As peace settled over her once more, David stole into her room, stood at the foot of the bed, and touched her feet. Amanda smiled at him and held out her arms. David climbed onto the bed and cuddled up to Amanda. He wore white briefs, and Amanda knew he'd come from where he had been sleeping, but she had the impression he'd been with someone in a room other than his, as if he had another life.

"I miss you, Amanda," David said.

Amanda scooted closer to him and held him tightly until they fell asleep. She woke up alone.

She wept, no great emotional storm, just an acknowledgment that she missed her husband. When the tears passed, she clambered off the bed and went to stand in front of the photo residing on her dresser. *Was that really you in my dream, David? Some people would say so, but I honestly don't know. It felt real, but it could just as easily have been wishful thinking.*

She thought about future, and though her remaining life seem to stretch in front of her interminably, those years were but a wisp of time. She'd been afraid of growing old alone, being feeble alone, dying alone, but right then, feeling as if she were still connected to her husband, she chose to believe that if her end years were going to be difficult, David would not have left her. *Is that true, David?* When he did not answer, she went back to bed. Though she tried to re-create the peaceful feeling that had conjured up her husband, David did not come to visit her again.

Chapter 22

AMANDA SAT ON the edge of her bed, cradling what remained of David. She took a deep breath and let it out again and again, expelling her anger along with the breaths. The anger had done its job—she was all packed, the house was clean, and she had nothing left to do but get through this final day. Thalia and Josh were coming in a while to pick up the boxes they would be storing for her and to say goodbye.

But first, she had to be calm so she could say goodbye to David.

"This is the last day of our life, David," she whispered to the blanket-wrapped bundle. "I leave tomorrow, and I can't take you with me. You'll be safe with Thalia. She promised not to turn you into jewelry or to stuff you in a Teddy bear, at least not until I give her permission. I wonder what you think about all of this. I like to imagine you somewhere, smiling at me as I try to learn how to be spontaneous again."

She closed her eyes tightly to hold back the tears. She did not want David to remember her as a sad, weepy woman.

"I know your cremains aren't you, David, but they're all I have left of you. I still don't understand how this is possible, you dead and me alone. What happened to us? I so often want to scream how unfair this is. I mean, some people get to be together for sixty or seventy years, dying within days of each other. The thing is, I don't know where the unfairness lies. Is it unfair that you don't get to live or is it unfair that I don't get to die quite yet? People so often tell me that you're in a better place, and if this is true, why can't I be there with you? And if life is a gift, why was it stolen from you?"

Tears seeped from beneath her lids. "I promise I'll try to be happy because I know you would not like to see me so miserable, but not yet. I still have grieving to do, and not even the possibility that seeing me sad would make you sad, can take my grief from me. I need my tears. They are all that connect me to you. I love you, David. I hope you'll finally find your own happiness."

Amanda slowly unwound David's blanket from around the urn. The stark edges of the bright brass container shocked her, so different from the soft bundle she was used to. Dry-eyed, she stared at the urn. This wasn't David. This was a lifeless piece of metal, filled with bone fragments and minerals, all the parts of David that had never been alive.

"Do you want me to come back?" Thalia asked from the doorway.

Amanda looked up and smiled at her daughter. "No. I'm ready." She rose from the edge of the bed, met her daughter halfway, and handed her the urn.

Apparently not expecting the weight, Thalia almost dropped the brass container. She glanced quickly at her mother as if fearful of a reprimand, but Amanda smiled again.

"People always speak of ashes," Amanda said, "so they think cremains are light, but they aren't ashes. They are the heavy parts of the body, the inorganic parts that do not burn." Listening to herself talk Amanda marveled at her even tone. This was David they were talking about. No, not David. David, the essential David, had been gone for seven weeks, four days, two hours, sixteen minutes, and assorted seconds.

"Are you sure you're okay with this?" Thalia asked. "I thought you'd want to take Dad with you."

"I considered it. The way I had the urn bundled, it would've fit neatly into a bowling ball bag, but that seemed even more disrespectful than turning dad's ashes into jewelry or a toy. And what if someone stole the bag from my car?" Amanda gave a little laugh. "Can't you just see me at the police station trying to explain what was in the bowling bag? Or even worse, having the thief abandon the bag, and somebody else picking it up. No, Thalia. Dad is safe with you."

Thalia hugged the urn to her chest. "Thank you, Mom."

Josh entered the room. "I put all the boxes by the front door into my SUV, Amanda. Is there anything else you need us to store?"

"That's all, Josh. Thank you."

"Do you want me to load your car?" Josh asked

"Most of the stuff I'm going to take is already in the car." Amanda inclined her head to indicate the stripped bed, with her new sleeping bag, a pillow, and David's blanket heaped in the center. "Tomorrow I will only have to bundle that bedding in my car, along with a few things left in my bathroom and the refrigerator, then I'm good to go."

Josh and Thalia spoke the same time.

"Did you remember water, Amanda?"

"Did you fill your gas tank, Mom?"

Amanda smiled at her daughter and soon-to-be son-in-law. "I'm not totally inept, you know." The words echoed in her head, and she struggled against tears as she remembered saying that very thing to her dying husband.

"I know you're not, Mom. But I worry. You're the only parent I have left."

"I will be fine." But would she be fine? Things did happen to women alone. Bad things. But she couldn't think that way. The worst thing that happened to her—David's death—had happened when she was safe inside her own home.

A line of worry appeared between Thalia's brows, as if she too were thinking that bad things happen to women alone. "Are you sure you don't want me to be here to see you off, Mom? I can meet Josh in New Orleans tomorrow instead of flying out with him tonight."

"I know you're used to taking care of yourself, Thalia, but I'd rather you flew with Josh." Seeing her daughter's jaw jut out, Amanda hastily added, "That way you can take care of each other so I won't have to worry about anyone but myself."

"If I had a choice," Josh said, "we would have picked a different weekend, but I wasn't the one in charge of scheduling this convention."

"I'll be fine," Amanda said. "Truly I will."

Josh and Thalia exchanged glances and shrugged simultaneously, acting as synced as a long time couple.

"Okay, Mom," Thalia said. "We better go home and unload the car if we want to make the plane on time."

Amanda walked the couple outside. Although it was mid afternoon, the dark cloud hiding the sun made it feel like twilight.

She waited until Thalia carefully stowed the urn on the floor of the back seat, then. Amanda gave Thalia a long hug and a quicker one to Josh. The two younger people got in the car, and midst a flurry of goodbyes through the open windows, they drove away. Rubbing her forearms to warm herself, Amanda watched until they were long out of sight.

Goodbye, David.

The sun appeared from behind a cloud, and glinted off a small object where Josh had been parked. A penny. She picked up the coin.

Thank you, David. I'm thinking of you too.

Amanda trudged into the house and paced through the too-clean rooms. All signs of their presence had been eradicated. It was as if David had never existed. As if she had never been his wife. Only the feel of the penny clutched in her hand—and her memories—told her that David had existed. Did exist.

She ran to her room, scooped up the blanket that had been wrapped around the urn, held the fabric to her face like a thumb-sucking toddler, and wept.

"Hello, love. Did I wake you?"

Amanda wiped her eyes with the back of her hand. "No, I was just lying here for a bit."

"Good," Sam said. "You need your rest. You have a long drive ahead of you. When are you leaving?"

"Tomorrow. Before dawn, probably. I don't sleep much at night, and since I already said goodbye to Thalia, there's no reason to hang around here."

"Are you packed?"

"Except for the few things I'm using."

"Do you have water? Food? Emergency supplies?"

Amanda laughed. "You sound like my future son-in-law."

Sam did not respond immediately. She got the impression she'd wounded him, but did not know what had bothered him about those few words.

"Am I your future…anything?" he asked.

The question seemed so out of character, especially spoken in such a tentative voice, that Amanda's heart swelled with love. She felt deeply connected to Sam for the first time since David's death, and she could feel his love for her.

"Oh, Sam. You know you are. Just…"

Still that tentative tone. "Yes?"

"Just not yet. I need you too much."

"That's good." He sounded elated, as if he'd had doubts about her love and now those doubts had been eradicated.

"No, it's not good. Aren't you the one who thought I was too tied to David? That I lived his life, not mine? That I need to find my own dreams? If I moved to Ohio and took writing classes from you, it wouldn't be my dream I'd be fulfilling. It would be yours."

"I thought you wanted to write."

Amanda swallowed a sigh. "When I was young. Now I don't know what I want, except to be with you."

"I can't be a replacement for David."

"I don't want you to replace David. I want what you and I had in the beginning."

"So do I, love."

"But things have changed. You know that as well as I do." Suddenly afraid of saying what she needed to, afraid of hurting Sam further, Amanda took a sip from the glass of water she kept on her bedside table.

"You are coming to Ohio, aren't you?" Sam asked.

Amanda carefully set the glass back on the table.

"The only way I can have you in my life is if I don't desperately need you, don't you see, Sam? You're not going to leave your wife, and I'd never ask you to. You may not be in love with her anymore, but you still care for her and she needs you."

"Vivian is not strong. She's doing well and is cancer free, but she still has a compromised immune system from the chemo. No one knows how long she has to live."

"I can't live my life hoping someone will die so I can find happiness." The ever-ready tears filled Amanda's eyes. "And even after she's gone—"

"She might not die." Sam sounded harsh, though Amanda couldn't tell if the harshness was aimed at her or at the thought of his wife. "Knowing Vivian, once she's well, she'll probably find love in the arms of another man. And then I will be free."

"What about your children? They're all grown up with families of their own, but you are still very close to them. I don't see myself becoming part of your family."

"I wouldn't ask that of you."

"The point is, you will never have the time for me that I

want. There will always be someone who needs you. Your wife, your kids, your grandkids, your students. And I'll always be on the fringes of your life."

"You won't—" Sam interjected, but Amanda kept talking.

"I'm the opposite. No one needs or depends on me anymore. And I'm mostly alone. There's Thalia, of course, and now Josh, but they're just starting their lives and don't really want to be saddled with me. And despite our truce, Thalia has never forgiven me for loving you. Mary Lynn might be back in my life. That's it. You have hundreds of people depending on you. Including me. I've depended on you more than I should have. I need to learn how to depend on myself, to find what I need within myself."

"You can't find love within yourself," Sam objected. "Not my love."

Amanda smiled. "I know you love me. And I love you. But I can't make you my whole life. It's too lopsided, don't you see? I'd start to hate you, and I love you too much for that."

"What are you going to do?" Sam said, sounding sad.

"After I meet you? Probably visit Mary Lynn. And then? I don't know. I do know I can't move to Ohio. I'd sit by the phone waiting for you to call, waiting for you to come over for a quickie. I don't see myself as a 'quickie' sort of person. I need hours in your arms, not a few stolen moments."

"Me too," Sam murmured.

"So you do understand?" Amanda asked

"I do. I wish things could be different. I wish I could be different."

Amanda laughed shakily. "No you don't. And neither do I. The man you are is the man I love. You and David have that in common, you care about others. I just happen to fall in love with men who have no time for me. So *I* have to have time for me. Maybe someday things will work out for us—"

"I believe they will," Sam said with such conviction that for a moment Amanda believed him. "I think we'll be intimate in such a way that all our dreams seem possible, that all our yearnings will be fulfilled."

"Maybe someday we can be together," Amanda said. "But I can't believe the way you do. Or rather, I can't live my life that way, always waiting. It's too sad. I'm too sad. I miss David. I miss my life with him. Miss the me I was with him. Even though he had so little time for me toward the end, I was with him in a way I can never be with you. Which is okay. I told you, I'm not looking for replacement. I'm looking for..."

Sam sang a few bars of "Looking for Love in All the Wrong Places."

So much love welled up in Amanda that she could barely breathe. "I'm looking for love in the right place." Maybe it would work out if she moved to Ohio after all. She pictured Sam stopping by to see her after work—kissing, disrobing, thrusting inside of her, swiftly getting dressed, giving her one last kiss, and leaving her. Leaving her in tears.

No. No more tears. She had enough of crying to last forever. She wanted joy. Life. Happiness. She wanted to be her own woman, not the "other woman" in Sam's life. She hadn't a clue how to accomplish her goal, but there was no hurry. She had the rest of her life. And maybe, just maybe, one day she and Sam would be able to be intimate in the way they both wanted.

"I love you very much, Sam."

"I love you back," Sam said, but he spoke rapidly, as if he needed to get the words out before someone could overhear. "Sorry. Have to go. Call me when you're on the road."

Before Amanda could say goodbye, Sam disconnected the call.

Trying not to cry—no more tears, dammit!—Amanda reached out to set the cell phone on her bedside table and knocked over the almost empty water glass. She stared at the water dripping over the side of the table onto the carpet, and didn't make a move to mop it up.

In the dark of early morning, Amanda rolled her sleeping bag with the pillow and blanket inside, packed the few dishes remaining in the kitchen and the leftover food—a chunk of cheese, the last of a loaf of bread, an apple, and a tomato—and toted her belongings out to her car. She dropped everything on the driveway so she could open the trunk, and when she grabbed the sleeping bag to toss it on top of the camping gear already in place, she noticed that the bag had been resting on a penny. She picked up the coin, a corroded bit of metal that looked as if it had been buried for many years, and said, without a smile, "Is this the best you can do, David?"

She trudged back into the house, stuffed her toothbrush, toothpaste, washcloth, and sliver of soap into her suitcase, and rolled the case out the front door. The gleam of a shiny new penny on the driveway caught her eye. Accompanying the penny, forming a perfect equilateral triangle, were two bright dimes. She cradled the coins to her breast, and whispered "I love you too, David."

She'd packed everything, leaving nothing in the house of her life or David's, but Amanda went back inside and took one more look around the parsonage. David had always double checked to make sure he had not forgotten anything when getting ready for a church service, leaving a hotel room after a convention, preparing for a rare vacation, and by following his ritual, Amanda felt as if she were honoring her husband.

She locked the door, dropped the house key into the mailbox, and slipped behind the steering wheel. She stared blindly out the windshield, remembering the words in David's letter: *When this door closes—the door to our shared life—the whole world will open to you.*

But what if I don't want the whole world, David? What if I want what I can no longer have?

After waiting a moment for a response that didn't come, she turned the car key in the ignition, but she could not lift her leaden right foot and place it on the accelerator pedal. She sat, hands on the wheel, feet solidly on the floor, and felt the sting of tears in her eyes.

"I can't do this," she wailed. Her voice rose to a scream. "I. Can't. Do. This."

David's dying had been tougher than she could ever have imagined. Cleaning out his things had almost killed her. Finding out the truth of his life and all he had kept from her had broken her already broken heart. But this—driving away from David forever, driving away from her life, driving into the open world—this was more than she could bear.

During the year of David's dying, Amanda often thought of this moment when she would have to leave the parsonage, but in the first thrill of her love for Sam, she'd seen herself giddily driving toward happiness. But there would be no new life with Sam. No happiness. At least not for a long time. For now, all she had was herself, and it wasn't enough.

"I can't do this!" She folded her arms on the steering wheel, rested her forehead on her arms, and wept. When the last tear fell, when she could not wring one more drop of sadness from her soul, she raised her head and looked around. The darkness had given way to pearl gray skies. If she wanted to avoid rush-hour traffic, she would have to leave now.

She put the car into reverse, and whispered, "I can't do this."

Then slowly, as if the coming dawn were unveiling the truth, Amanda realized that yes, she could do this. Grief and maybe even despair would surely be her companions for years to come, but she would handle whatever life threw at her because she'd been doing so all along. While screaming "I can't do this," she had disposed of David's effects, gotten rid of his clothes, packed her things, cleaned the house, come to an easier relationship with her daughter, dealt with David's mother, solved the matter of the gun. And she'd survived the first two months of grief.

Voice tinged with wonder, Amanda said aloud, "I *can* do this."

She clutched the steering wheel until her hands ached, lifted her foot onto the accelerator pedal, and backed out of the driveway. She paused for one more look at the parsonage where she had lived for so many years. The house seemed alien, as if it had nothing to do with her, as if it had never been a place of love and laughter and tears.

Amanda steered through quiet streets toward the highway. It wasn't until she was almost out of the city that she realized she hadn't bothered to glance at the church that once loomed so large in her life. Should she go back? No, the church was the past, buried along with David.

Looking out the windshield at the world ahead of her, Amanda settled into her seat, loosened her death grip on the steering wheel, and drove into the rising sun.